"In my experience, there's always a shoe about to drop somewhere."

She raised her head as he lowered his, and their lips met in a sweet version of an age-old dance.

"What do you do," he asked slowly, "when the shoe drops?"

"Oh." Her voice sounded reedy. "It depends."

"On?"

Cass laughed, not very convincingly. "On whether it's a combat boot or a flip-flop."

"What about a nice, comfortable loafer? How do you react then?"

"To tell the truth, usually it's the combat boot, in which case I turn tail and run."

"Well, what's between you and me doesn't have to do with the orchard or the coffee shop," he whispered. "It's courtship simply for the pleasure of it. Nothing more and nothing less. No promises, no demands. No permanency." He kissed her again, treasuring her sweet response. "No shoes."

Dear Reader,

When people ask if I write about friends and family, I usually say, "Not really" (with a couple of notable exceptions). There will be characteristics and habits I borrow from time to time, but nothing identifiable. However, when Luke Rossiter, the hero of *Nice to Come Home To*, showed up with a guitar, it was my husband's fingers I saw on the strings, tugging the notes out without benefit of a pick. When Cass, the heroine, sat at the corner table in a coffee shop with her laptop, she was every writer I know. It was a reminder of how deeply personal our Heartwarming stories are and how beloved the people that we write about are. I hope you love them, too.

Liz Flaherty

HEARTWARMING

Nice to Come Home To

———

USA TODAY Bestselling Author

Liz Flaherty

HHARLEQUIN® HEARTWARMING™

Recycling programs
for this product may
not exist in your area.

ISBN-13: 978-1-335-63376-7

Nice to Come Home To

Copyright © 2018 by Liz Flaherty

Printed in U.S.A.

Liz Flaherty retired from the post office and promised to spend at least fifteen minutes a day on housework. Not wanting to overdo things, she's since pared that down to ten. She spends nonwriting time sewing, quilting and doing whatever else she wants to. She and Duane, her husband of...oh, quite a while...are the parents of three and grandparents of the Magnificent Seven. They live in the old farmhouse in Indiana they moved to in 1977. They've talked about moving, but really...over forty years' worth of stuff? It's not happening!

She'd love to hear from you at lizkflaherty@gmail.com.

Books by Liz Flaherty

Harlequin Heartwarming

Back to McGuffey's
Every Time We Say Goodbye
The Happiness Pact
Nice to Come Home To

Harlequin Special Edition

The Debutante's Second Chance

Visit the Author Profile page
at Harlequin.com for more titles.

Although their help was unwitting, I am grateful to McClure's and Doud's, the local orchards I visited to give Keep Cold Orchard its sense of place. I'm grateful to every barista in every coffee shop I've written in over the years—I hope the book does you justice. Thanks to Cheryl Reavis for giving the orchard its name and introducing me to the Robert Frost poem from whence it came. And thanks, Charles Griemsman, for everything.

To Nan Reinhardt, friend and writer extraordinaire—this one's for you.

CHAPTER ONE

"WHY DIDN'T YOU ever come back here?"

They were the first voluntary words Royce had spoken since they'd left the Missouri hotel early that morning. She'd read for a long time with her earbuds in, eaten a drive-through lunch in sullen silence or monosyllabic responses to questions, then stared out at Illinois until she fell back to sleep.

Cass Gentry looked over at the half sister she sometimes felt she barely knew. "The orchard is where my mother and aunt grew up, not me. Mother and Aunt Zoey inherited it from my grandparents and when Mother died, she left her half to me." How many times did she have to say this? Royce was sixteen, not six.

"Why didn't you sell it and stay in California?" Royce looked out the passenger window again, at the seemingly endless fields of corn, soybeans and hay that filled this part of central Indiana. Barns and silos and old windmills, some of them in disrepair, sat spare and silent sentinel over farmhouses.

There weren't as many fences as Cass remembered. Not nearly as many cows, either, which could explain the reduction in fences. A few miles from the highway they traveled, she could see the eerie moving silhouettes of a wind farm. She didn't remember that being here before.

"There's nothing here." At the back of Royce's disgruntled voice was a thread of fear. Cass recognized it. Remembered it. She wanted to say something sympathetic, but sensed it wouldn't be welcome.

"I know." People had been saying that eighteen years ago, too, when Cass had spent that utopian year in the little community that surrounded Lake Miniagua.

"This isn't a place people move to," her stepcousin Sandy had said as they'd kayaked around the lake's six hundred acres. "It's one they leave."

That had been true then and probably still was. When the summer people left the lake, its population was sparse, its activities on the slim side. The bed-and-breakfasts and Hoosier Hills Cabins and Campground shut down between October and April. The closest supermarket, movie theater and department store were in Sawyer, five miles away from the lake.

But. "It's the only place I was ever happy." A sad truth speaking from the downhill slope of thirty-five, but a truth nonetheless. Memories of the childhood visits to the orchard and the year in the lake house had saved her sanity on more sleepless nights than she wanted to contemplate.

Royce's expression was both disbelieving and disdainful. "Come on, Sister Smart One. You were married. You didn't have to follow Dad all over the world with the army and make new friends every couple of years. There had to be some happiness in there somewhere. You had a life. You had choices."

"I did my share of Dad-following, too, but I did have a life. You're right. Let me change what I said. The year on the lake was the happiest I've ever been." She'd had choices, too, and she'd too often made the wrong ones. She hoped this move wasn't one of those.

"You chose to divorce Tony and let him keep most of everything you guys had."

"It's called a prenup." And she'd given up more than she had to, just because she thought it had somehow all been her fault, but Royce probably wouldn't understand that. Cass wasn't sure she understood it, either.

"My mother told Dad he should come and help you, but he wouldn't. He said you'd made your bed and you could lie in it."

"She has always been very kind to me." This couldn't be said about all of Cass's stepmothers. The one after her own mother had been determined to marry an army officer, regardless of the cost to anyone else. She'd had a handsy son who had made life difficult for the pubescent Cass. The next one had borne shocking similarities to all the stereotypes ascribed to a Barbie doll, a fact made worse by the fact that her given name was Barbara Ann and Cass's father's name was Kenneth.

Royce's mother, Damaris, came into the picture when Cass was eighteen and married to Tony Moretti, and had been a friend from the very beginning—even more so after she divorced Cass's father. That Damaris and Cass's mother had become friends as well had made them into a quirky but workable family.

Royce snorted. "Until she foisted me off on you, right?"

"She's deployed to Afghanistan. Not exactly her choice. Would you rather have stayed with Dad?" Cass heard the exasperation that laced her voice. Royce's smirk said her sister heard it, too.

She supposed this was the good side to why she and Tony hadn't had children. If they had, their progeny would be about the age of Royce, give or take a few years. Divorce had been bad enough as it was, when there hadn't even been pets to decide the custody of. How would Cass have handled Tony's defection and a harrowing battle with breast cancer at the same time if grumpy teenagers had been added to the mix?

She rubbed her arm absently. It didn't hurt much anymore, but less than a year past chemo and radiation, she still expected it to.

"Are you all right?"

The solicitude in Royce's question surprised her. It was nice to hear. "Yeah. Thanks."

"Where will we live?"

"I've told you that already, several times." Cass kept her voice even with an effort. Had she been like this at sixteen when her parents, in a rare mutual decision, had sent her to stay with her grandparents? Probably. "We have a cottage on the lake called Little Dream for two weeks. Many businesses and a lot of houses in Miniagua use Cole Porter titles— or parts of them—as their names." She raised a quelling hand. "If you ask me one more time who Cole Porter is, I'm going to stop the car and make you walk."

"I know, I know. He's a really famous songwriter who grew up close to this lake of yours. You sang 'Don't Fence Me In' halfway across Kansas to punish me for asking the last time."

Cass laughed and, to her profound pleasure, so did her sister.

"What about after the two weeks? Will we go home?" Royce sounded wistful, and Cass stared into the eastern sky as she drove toward the lake. Her heart ached.

Home. To Royce, that was California because that's where her friends were. It's where the duplex was that she shared with her mother. Their father, retired somewhere in Idaho, paid her no more attention than he had Cass, but Damaris had given her daughter all the security she could within the bounds of what the US Army decreed. They'd been in California for five years. Royce had a California driver's permit, which to a sixteen-year-old meant permanence.

"I don't know," Cass admitted. *But I hope not. I don't want to go back. I was happy here once. I want to try to find it again.*

"I don't want to start school at your lake if we're not staying." That she didn't want to stay there at all was patently obvious, but she was enough of a military brat not to bother saying so.

Cass nodded. There was still another few weeks before school started in either place and the sky wouldn't fall if she started late— she was a good student. However, she didn't blame Royce for wanting to know if she was going to have to start all over again. Get another learner's permit if that was what Indiana required.

Was she doing to her little sister all the things that had been done to her when she was sixteen that she'd never truly forgiven her parents for? Moving her all over the place with no regard for her emotional needs. Making uncertainty a major part of every day.

"We'll know soon," she said, and then made a promise she hoped she could keep. "I won't force you to do anything you don't want to."

"So, who's the other owner?" Royce grinned, hiking her pretty young knees up onto the seat and twirling a lock of her shiny dark brown hair. "And I *haven't* asked you that because it wasn't my business. It's still not, I guess, but I'm curious. Maybe he'll be some hunk, and you and he will fight over apples until you meet up over the Golden Delicious and the Honeycrisp and fall in love forever."

"I'm impressed. You can tell apples apart."

"Only those two. They're the ones Mom buys when she's on a health kick and the ones your mother always had in that green glass bowl in the middle of the dining room table. I never saw her eat them, but they were always there."

"I understand the health kick thing. I've always thought apple dumplings with ice cream should qualify as fruit and dairy in the daily food pyramid." Cass smiled with the memory her sister's words had called forth—part of it, anyway. "Even when I was your age, Mother had that bowl in the middle of the table. I still have it somewhere."

Cass took the exit that put them on the first two-lane road they'd been on since they left California. "Oh, to answer your question, his name is Lucas Rossiter. Apparently he bought Aunt Zoey's portion a few years ago and would like to buy mine, too. I imagine that's how it will work out, but I wanted to see it first." She sighed. Sometimes life was heavy. "I wanted to come back to the lake."

"I DON'T GET IT. This is your orchard." Seth Rossiter looked down from the ladder propped against a tree in the back field of Keep Cold Orchard.

"Half of it is," Luke corrected, hefting a box of Earligolds onto the back of the flatbed and handing an empty bag up to his younger brother. "Half of it belongs to the woman who's coming today, Cass Gentry."

"Why's she coming? What does she want?"

"I don't know for sure." Luke was as confused as Seth was by the sudden correspondence from the woman who'd inherited half the orchard. Her mother and Zoey Durand's sister, Marynell Bessignano, had been a silent partner, a woman he'd only met twice. Once at Zoey's sixtieth birthday party two years ago and once when they'd met in the lawyer's office to sign the agreement. He did all the work, so he got a larger percentage. Zoey had maintained ownership of the farmhouse on the property and still lived in it. Zoey's sister had been good with that—he hoped Zoey's niece would be, too. Actually, he hoped she'd just want to sell out.

"You've never met her?"

"Yeah, I did. Well, saw her, anyway." She'd sat with Zoey at Marynell's funeral in California six months before. Cass Gentry was tall and nearly too slim—her black dress had been too big on her, but her posture was military straight.

She'd also been wearing a wig, which he'd wondered about but hadn't mentioned to Zoey even on the long plane trip home. Zoey was a close friend, but she was as private as they came. All she'd ever said about family was, "You know that word *dysfunction*? Well, we invented it."

Cass hadn't looked either right or left during the funeral, and when he'd gone to see if Zoey was ready to return to the hotel, her niece had disappeared.

"So, she's coming today?" asked Seth. "Here or to Zoey's?"

"I don't know. She's staying at the lake for a while, I guess. She might just go there. I don't think she and Zoey are close."

"So." Seth handed down the bag of apples from his shoulder, his muscles bulging with the effort. "Have you decided?"

"Decided what?" Luke knew what the kid was talking about. He'd been asking every other day for two weeks already.

"You know."

Seth had been hassling him for an answer ever since their parents had followed their dad's auto industry job to Detroit in June. It had been fine this summer. Seth stayed with Luke and spent the occasional "parental unit" weekend in Michigan; sometimes the folks drove down instead. It would be different during the school year. High school senioring was busy stuff, plus their father and mother still worked—they'd used up most of their time off this summer. "Have they said anything more?"

"Mom doesn't want me to stay here in case you get another job somewhere else. Dad's waffling back and forth. But they're going to let me if you say it's okay." Seth came down the ladder. "I know it's asking a lot, letting me stay with you the whole school year. I cramp your style and all. But geez, Luke, I don't want to change schools now. I want to spend my senior year as a Miniagua Lakers running back, not a benchwarmer at some school around Detroit where I don't know anybody." He grinned hopefully. "Don't forget, me being here keeps you off the ladders."

There was that. Luke wasn't precisely afraid of heights, but he wasn't crazy about them, either. Zoey had nearly laughed her head off when she'd found that out. "Son," she said, "you do realize you just bought half of sixty acres of fruit trees, right?"

He'd realized it, all right, but when he bought into Keep Cold Orchard, he'd planned on it being an investment, his house on the lake a weekend getaway. However, when the company where he had been an engineer closed its doors three years before, he put his severance pay into his retirement account and went to work for himself at the orchard. He didn't intend it to be his life's work, but it was satisfying for now.

"You are good for something." He grinned at his brother and looked at his watch. "You need to call it a day and get something to eat before practice." The football team was doing two-a-day practices and Seth was working several hours at the orchard between them. It was a brutal schedule.

They unloaded at the apple barn and Luke tossed Seth his car keys. "I'll take the orchard pickup home. Be careful."

"All right if I go out after? Just swimming over at the public beach. Playing some music."

"Just swimming and music," Luke reiterated. "No booze or anything else that will get us both in trouble with either our parents or the law."

"Gotcha."

Luke was the last one to leave the orchard. That was a promise he'd made to himself and the employees when he became a hands-on boss. Most of the time it worked out well, but there were occasional middays that found him asleep on the couch in the office.

"That's why it's there," Zoey had said. "Anything happens, they'll wake you up."

"Anything" usually meant something had broken down. Luke had gotten good at keeping the sorting machine and the tractor running. The cider press, an antique by any standard, presented more of a challenge. He'd taken to calling it Rachel's Revenge because his two-years-younger sister had been threatening retribution for years for brotherly sins both real and imagined.

"Mr. Rossiter?"

The voice came as he was locking the door of the apple barn behind him. He turned, squinting into the setting sun. "Yes? We're closed, but can I get you something quick?"

"I'm Cass Gentry."

"Oh." The sun moved enough that she became less of a silhouette and more of the tall, slender person he remembered from Marynell's funeral. She wasn't as slim now, and the cap of light brown hair was almost certainly her own, but he'd have recognized her anywhere. He extended his hand. "Nice to meet you. I expected you earlier today."

"My apologies. I underestimated the time it took to drive from the western edge of Missouri with an unfriendly teenager."

He smiled at her. "I've done that. Well, to Detroit, anyway. Two hundred miles of loud silence." He was inexplicably disappointed that she had a child. Did that mean there was a husband, too? He gestured toward the door. "Would you like to look around?"

"No, it's all right. I'll come back tomorrow. I didn't even think about what time it was when I came by. I just dropped Royce off at the house we're renting and came here. I thought a little time apart might be a good thing."

"Probably," he agreed. "A little breathing space never hurts. How old is your daughter?"

She smiled at him this time, the expression hesitant enough he thought maybe she didn't use it much. "My sister is sixteen. Going on thirty. Your son?"

Luke nodded in acknowledgment of her remark. "My brother is seventeen going on twelve. My father was transferred to Detroit with his job and Seth's a senior in high school. It looks like he's going to spend the school year with me." He wasn't sure what they'd do if an ideal engineering job presented itself, but he wasn't going to worry about it—there were worse things than long commutes.

"Ah. Royce's mother, a couple of my dad's wives removed from my mother, was deployed to Afghanistan. It's probably her last deployment—she's ready to retire—but she had to go. Royce preferred my company to our father's. At least she did before driving across country with me. I think now her choice might be up for grabs."

"Have you seen Zoey yet?"

"No." She looked uncomfortable. "I don't really know her very well anymore. Royce knows her even less. She met her when my mother died, but only briefly." She hesitated, looking up at him in the darkness that followed the sun's drop into the horizon. "You were there, weren't you? You came all the way to California for a woman you didn't even know."

"I came for Zoey, whom I know very well. She's hale and hearty, but I didn't like the idea of her traveling cross-country by herself when she was grieving." He gentled his voice. Cass Gentry wasn't as slim as she'd been, and warm color washed the cheeks that had been ashen the last time he saw her, but he sensed fragility in the woman beside him. "I'm sorry for your loss."

"Thank you." She started toward her SUV, which was parked beside the pickup. "When can we talk about the business?"

"Whenever you like. When would you like the fifty-cent tour?"

"As soon as possible."

"Tomorrow? There will be a hayride through the orchard at ten. It gives you a good view of the place."

"A hayride? Seriously?"

He wasn't quite sure if she'd meant to

sound derisive or if that was just how it came out, so he pushed back impatience. "Yes. We have them for groups by appointment or spur of the moment if someone wants to go and there's an available driver. In October, we have evening ones."

"All right, Mr. Rossiter. I'll see you at ten."

"It's just Luke. Mr. Rossiter's my dad, who would tell you, no, Mr. Rossiter's my grandpa."

She nodded, looking uncertain. "Can you tell me where the nearest supermarket is?"

"Sawyer." He pointed. "Three miles that way."

"I remember." She sighed. "I think that can wait until tomorrow. I'm sure Royce won't mind going out for dinner. What's available at the lake?"

"Anything Goes Grill and Silver Moon Café. There's also a pizza place that does carryout. The bulk foods store is great for groceries and has an excellent deli section. Are you staying at the lake?" Why would she do that with Zoey rattling around alone in that twelve-room farmhouse behind the hill of the orchard?

"Yes. For two weeks. That's how long I'm giving myself to decide what to do."

"What to do?"

"Yes." She turned in a tight circle on the gravel drive, lifting her chin and gazing outward.

He followed her gaze with his own, wondering what she saw. The apple barn was there, its retail store convenient for customers. The cold storage barn, newer and bigger, had been built farther up the rise. The replica round barn, smaller than an original but true in shape and scale to the ones built in the area during the early twentieth century, held pride of place across the parking lot from the apple barn. The grapevines were behind it. The pumpkin patch filled the area between the driveway and the apple barn.

Trees were everywhere. Close to a hundred varieties of apples grew in neatly rowed sections all the way back to where Cottonwood Creek created the farm's boundary. The way the orchard's land rolled made keeping up with everything a challenge sometimes, but it was always rewarding.

The drives and parking lot were still gravel. Something always needed fixing.

There was evidence of too many ideas conceived of but never hatched—the round barn being the greatest of those, the grapevines behind it another. Luke thought it was the most beautiful place in the world.

He wondered what she saw. With more urgency than he liked, he also wondered what she thought.

CHAPTER TWO

"WHEN ARE WE going to go see your aunt?" Royce stood at the bar that separated the lake cottage's minute kitchen from its living area.

Cass slid the take-and-bake pizza out of the oven. "Come and get it. Ouch!" She licked the thumb she'd accidentally dipped into pizza sauce. "I don't know. It's complicated with Aunt Zoey. You know that."

"Not to be rude—" which meant that was probably exactly what the teenager was going to be "—but everything in your family is complicated. Once we move back to the real world and I go back to school, I'm going to write a paper on it. You and your aunt and your past and present stepparents and Dad can be my expert witnesses. Do you want some milk?"

Cass shuddered. "No, thank you. And don't forget, you're related to some of that family, too."

Royce bit into her pizza, chewed and swallowed before saying, "Just you and Dad. Mom's not weird like you guys."

"No, she's not." Cass poured coffee, glad whoever had been in the cottage last had left an opened bag of breakfast blend in the pantry. "Your mother has been a port of calm for me ever since I met her." She eyed her sister's plate when Royce took two more slices of pizza. "At least until now. Can you really eat that much pizza?"

"In a heartbeat."

A half hour and an entertaining conversation later, Cass was surprised to realize that she, too, could eat four pieces of pizza without so much as blinking an eye. "What do you say?" She got up from the table with a groan and put their plates into the dishwasher. "Want to take a walk along the lake? As I remember it, there's a nice path. Or we can walk on the road."

Royce looked scandalized. "I don't know if you've realized it, Sister Authority Figure, but it's dark out there."

"I know." Cass put on one of the hooded sweatshirts they'd hung inside the entry closet and tossed the other one to Royce—the evening air was cool. "That's why I'm taking you along. I might need protection."

Royce was right about it being dark, but it seemed to be social hour on the lake's narrow graveled roads. Not only were people walking and running, the bicycle and golf cart traffic rivaled that of the retirement community where Marynell had lived.

Cass had thought she might recognize people and had dreaded it. She'd also looked forward to it. She'd love to explain to them why she'd left without saying goodbye. Why letters forwarded by her grandmother had gone unanswered. Why, when people had looked for her, she hadn't responded. Why, in an electronic world that fascinated her, she remained anonymous.

But she couldn't even explain it to herself.

"Where was the house where you lived with your grandparents that year you were here?" Royce interrupted her admittedly maudlin thoughts.

"On the other side where the condos are. They sold it to a development company within a few years after I left. The lake has gotten a little more upscale than it was when I was in high school. We'll drive around there tomorrow and see." She pointed toward a large Craftsman house. "That's Christensen's Cove. Two of my friends lived there. Arlie's dad, Dave, and Holly's mom, Gianna, were married. They were some of the best people I've ever known."

When they reached the south end of the lake, Royce stared at the two estates that took up most of the frontage. "They look really out of place here," she said finally. "It's like a what's-wrong-with-this-picture thing."

"It is. The one over there is where the Grangers lived. Chris and Gavin were always away at school, although they were here in the summer. I think their family owns the winery we drove past. What was it called?"

"Sycamore Hill. We liked its sign, remember?"

"That's right. The other house is Llewellyn Hall. Everyone just called it the Hall or the Albatross. Jack Llewellyn was a senior when I lived here. He dated Arlie. His brother Tucker was in my class and he dated *every-*one, but he was such a nice guy you didn't even mind it. Libby Worth—" she turned in a thoughtful half circle trying to get her bearings "—she was in my class, too. Her brother, Jesse, was a senior. They lived on the farm out by the winery. As a matter of fact, I think the winery used to be part of that farm." She turned the rest of the way, heading back toward their cottage.

Royce stayed in step with her. "Who else do you remember?"

"Sam. We dated for a while." The prom had been the last time they'd gone out. "His dad worked at Llewellyn Lures and his grandfather owned the hardware store. It was called Come On In. Sam had a bass voice you could lose yourself in. Gianna used to say he was Sam Elliott in training."

"The hardware store's still there," said Royce. "I saw it when we drove through tonight. It was just down the street from the bulk food store where we got the pie from the Amish bakery."

"We should probably get another one of those, since all that's left of that is the pan," said Cass drily. "Between that and the pizza, I'm still feeling fairly miserable, and we've been walking for at least a half hour."

"I'm walking. You keep starting and stopping. There's a difference." Royce gave her a sisterly elbow that felt better than Cass could have begun to explain. "Come on. Who else?"

"Let me think. Nate Benteen. He was one of the best high school golfers in the country. He was so much fun! He and Holly kept us laughing all the time."

"Which one was your BFF, the one you'd have stayed in contact with forever and ever if you had any normal social skills?"

"That was cold. And we didn't say 'BFF' then," Cass retorted. She walked a little farther, separating herself a few steps from Royce. Maybe her sister wouldn't notice that her breathing had somehow gone awry or that the color had left her face—she'd felt the blood drain from her cheeks as soon as Royce asked the question.

She would say she didn't remember if her sister pushed her for an answer. Chemo brain hadn't entirely left her, after all. Getting lost in the middle of a conversation was nothing new. Rather, it was exhaustingly old. So was being pale and washed-out and a mere tracing of who she'd once thought she was.

"Cass, wait up."

She realized her pace had taken her away from Royce as if her intent was to leave her behind. "Hey." She stopped. "Can't keep up with the old lady?"

"Y'know what?" Her sister caught up with her and tilted her head, waiting. Cass couldn't look away from the blue-green eyes she knew were replicas of her own, a gift from their father.

"No," she said lightly. "What?"

"You don't have to answer me. I get that you're the grown-up and I'm the kid. But don't make things up or fluff things like those 'alternative facts' they talk about on television. If you don't want to talk to me, just say so. I've been on my own most of my life, just like you. I can deal with it fine. I'll see you back at the house."

Royce took off at a run Cass couldn't have kept up with on her best day, so she didn't try. She went down to the path that followed the curves of the lake and sat on a park bench. She thought of those friends she'd told Royce about. They'd been closer than anyone she'd met in all the years both before and since. Although there'd been much to grieve for in that time, she mourned nothing more than the empty space she'd created in herself when she left the lake without looking back.

Cass closed her eyes, leaning her head back because suddenly it felt too heavy to hold up. With the scent and sound of the lake filling her senses, she remembered that year and gave herself permission to wallow in it.

Her father had been in Iraq, her mother in

a new state, job and marriage that didn't allot room for a recalcitrant daughter. Her grandparents had been willing to keep her for the school year, but not one minute longer. She was sixteen when she arrived at the lake, five feet eight inches of long brown hair and attitude. Especially attitude.

By the time she'd been there a week, improved posture had given her an additional inch and her hair had been streaked by the sun in a way she'd maintained until chemotherapy robbed her of it fifteen or so years later. She'd made more friends than she'd ever had at one time. She'd even been recruited for the high school volleyball team. "We suck," Arlic had said complacently, "but we have so much fun."

And they had. She'd spent as many nights at her friends' houses as she had in her grandparents' cramped cottage. She'd never missed attending a football or basketball game and the volleyball team had managed—for the first time in a history the length of which they exaggerated when they talked about it—to garner a winning season. She'd asked Mr. Harrison, the high school principal, if there was a writers' club in the school, expecting to be either ignored or forgotten. Instead, he'd said there wasn't such an organization at the present time and suggested she form one.

She wondered if the Write Now group still existed. Holly had thrown in with her to start monthly meetings. It had been a thrill, but not really a surprise, ten years before when she'd been in an airport bookstore and found a Holly Gallagher romance on the shelves. Cass had bought that book and at least one copy of the dozen the author had released since then. Sometimes in reading them, she thought Holly had written subliminal messages directly to her; however, life had taught her not to be fanciful, so she always set the notion aside. Mostly.

Sometimes, hidden in the chapters of her own *Mysteries on the Wabash* stories, Cass left messages to the friends she'd left behind. Of course, those friends didn't know who Cassandra G. Porter was—they'd never understand the messages.

The sound of footsteps on the paved lake path brought her out of the pleasant reverie of memory, and she straightened in her seat on the bench.

"Hello." The voice was cheerful, welcoming. A blast from the past that made Cass's heart feel as if it blossomed in her chest, one whose name had been in her mind only seconds before. "Beautiful night, isn't it?"

"Yes." She cleared her throat to make her voice audible, but her breath still hitched and hesitated on its way in and out. "It is."

Not only did she know the musical voice of Holly Gallagher, she recognized the tall profile of the man who walked beside her. Jesse Worth. Always quiet, always a loner, and one of the good guys she'd known in her life. He'd been a gifted artist, but he had gone into the navy after high school and eventually become a veterinarian, opening his practice on the farm where he'd grown up.

Panic rose in her throat.

Cass hadn't thought it through long enough before she came back. She hadn't considered that she'd come face-to-face with the one person who would never want to see her under any circumstances. The one who'd loved Linda Saylors—the BFF Royce had wondered about—as much as Cass had. The one who would remember more than anyone else that Cass should have been sitting in the van seat Linda had occupied. The one who would know that on that prom night so long ago, it should have been Cass who died, not Linda.

LUKE STOPPED BY Zoey's the next morning as he often did. It gave him a chance to keep her up on business concerns and to see if she needed anything done. She would never ask, but he was nosy enough that he could usually find out on his own.

"She's here, then?" Zoey handed Luke a cup of coffee and set a piece of coffee cake in front of him. "How does she look? Healthy?"

He hated the anxiety in the voice of the woman who'd slipped effortlessly into the place of the favorite aunt he'd never had. "Still thin, I think," he said, "but not like she was at your sister's funeral. She's not wearing a wig and her color's good. Her hair—it's about the color of maple syrup with gold stuff in it—is pretty. About this long." He shelfed his hand just below his ear and squinted at the woman who'd sat across her kitchen table from him. "I thought she had your eyes, but they're more green than blue."

"They're like her father's. Marynell's were darker, like mine."

Luke thought of Seth, of Rachel and their sister, Leah. They'd been fighting each other all their lives. Their parents made a practice of professing amazement that they could have four so completely different children. Yet the siblings had never stopped speaking to each other, even when most verbal communication was done in shouts.

"What happened?" He didn't want to pry, but the sadness in her expression prodded him.

Zoey shrugged, staring past him out the floor-to-ceiling windows in the dining area of the farmhouse kitchen. "Just one of those family stories they make TV movies about." She lifted her cup, then set it down without drinking. "I was engaged to Ken when he discovered he preferred my younger, prettier sister. While I was covering the afternoon shift for her one day at the orchard, he picked her up in his snazzy convertible and they eloped."

"Ouch." Luke remembered when Rachel and Leah had argued over a friend of his they'd both liked. It hadn't gone well for the guy. Afterward, the girls had sneaked cheap wine into their room and played the "Sisters" song from *White Christmas* until they'd emptied the bottle and nearly wore out the videotape.

He needed to call his siblings.

"Marynell came back here with Cass when they divorced two years later. She left her with me and married a navy pilot. It was a pattern. She was married several times, lived in different places. If Cass couldn't spend her summers with Ken or if he or Marynell just needed time with a new spouse, they shipped Cass back here." She stopped, as if gathering her thoughts, and regret deepened the lines in her face. "The last time, when Cass came for her junior year, I had said no, she couldn't come. The folks had retired and weren't well, and I was working half the time at the orchard and half of it as a phlebotomist in Indianapolis. Marynell brought her anyway and left her with our parents, even though dementia and rheumatoid arthritis were severely limiting their ability to take care of themselves, much less a teenage girl. My sister told Cass I didn't want anything to do with either of them and I was too exhausted to argue the point."

"And that was it? Seriously? A whole family split asunder over *that*?"

She sighed. "Pretty much. Marynell and I made up, of course. She came and visited and helped when our parents' illnesses progressed and later when they died. She created no difficulty with the management of the orchard after we inherited, although she chose to remain uninvolved." Zoey chuckled almost soundlessly. "Oddly enough, the thing she never quite forgave me for was introducing her to Ken. He's one of those men who is ethically and maybe even morally good, but is an emotional empty shell."

"What about Cass?"

"She and I always exchange birthday and Christmas cards. I sent a gift when she got married right out of high school, but I never really connected with her again until her mother died. I know she was ill, that she had chemo, but that's *all* I know. I thought I should go and help then, but she said she was all right, that it would be better if I helped with her mother. It probably was—Cass could take care of herself, but taking care of her mother at the same time was too much. We would see each other in passing, but that was all."

Luke heard all that she said, but his focus stayed on one point. "She's married?"

"Not anymore." She raised her hands, palms up. "I sent money when she got the divorce, just in case she needed it. She sent it back with a very nice thank-you."

"Children?"

"Not that I know of. Her little sister's a sweet one, though. I think I know her better than I do Cass, and I only met her when Marynell died." Zoey looked away from him again. A tear crept unchecked down her cheek. "There's this part of me that says Cass should have been my child and that failing her is like failing as a mother."

"That's crazy, Zoey."

She smiled at him, just a little curve of lips that had thinned and paled over the years. "You have a problem with crazy?"

"No." He tilted his head, looking at Zoey's long neck and the shiny white sweep of her short hair. "It wouldn't be much of a stretch. I think Cass favors you more than she did her mother."

"You'll let me know if she needs anything?"

"I will. Or you could let her know yourself. You come to the orchard nearly every day. Are you going to stop because your niece might be there?"

Zoey frowned. "I don't know." She filled his go-cup and gave him a push. "But you have given me something to think about."

CHAPTER THREE

"WHERE ARE ALL the fall colors we're always hearing about?" Royce peered out the windows as they drove along Lake Road toward the turnoff onto Country Club Road, where the orchard was.

"It's only the first week of August. The fall colors start up next month and peak in October." Unless something stilled the restlessness in Cass's mind, they wouldn't be here. They'd be back in California with Royce in her old high school and Cass going to the coffee shop every day to sit in a corner booth and work.

"You can do what you do anywhere," Royce had remonstrated when Cass had informed her they were making the trip to Indiana.

It was true. She could. Being the author of a bestselling mystery series gave her a lot of residential latitude; however, if they stayed at the lake, someone would eventually find out that Cass Gentry and Cassandra G. Porter were one and the same. While it was true that neither of her personas had anything to hide, keeping them separate had worked for a long time, both personally and profession-ally. "We'll see," she murmured, braking for the turn.

"See what?"

Cass started. She hadn't realized she'd spoken until her sister replied. "Oh, nothing. Well, yeah, we'll see how you feel about hay-rides. I went on a few when I was here. They were fun." They'd been at night, though, under starry skies and the harvest moon, and she'd had a boyfriend—that had made all the difference. Not that she and Sam had ever been serious, but they'd had a good time.

"He owns the hardware store," Holly had said last night, holding onto Cass's hands as if she'd been afraid she'd disappear again. "He's married to Penny and they have three little Sams—all that's missing is the eye patch."

They'd sat together on the park bench while Holly had filled Cass's mind and an empty place in her heart with reports of the friends from that year of her contentment. Arlie and Jack had married in June. Libby and Tucker were engaged and so were Holly and Jesse. Gianna had been dating Max Harrison, the high school principal, for years. Nate owned the golf course and spent half his time in Indiana and half of it in North Carolina. His wife's name was Mandy. Linda's family lived in Fort Wayne.

"It's like there are no scars." Cass had known even as she'd said it that it wasn't accurate—all of the survivors of the prom night accident had scars whether you could see them or not.

"Oh, they're there." Holly had pointed at her prosthetic foot. "We miss Daddy. We miss Linda. Tuck and Jack have had to get past knowing their dad caused the accident. But we've all reached the point of not letting the scars define us. We had to give up some dreams, but we've found new ones." Her dark eyes had searched Cass's face. "How about you?"

Cass had shrugged. "When I was here that year, I thought I'd found perfection. I even wrote a paper one time about how the lake should have been called Lake Utopia. I've been looking for that same thing ever since, so in a way I guess I do let it define me." Something needed to because she didn't really have a clue as to who she was.

Holly hadn't asked why she'd left, although Cass could read the question in the other woman's dark eyes. Jesse had spoken little, greeting her and then stepping aside.

"Will you see all of us?" Holly had asked. "We've all wondered. We've all looked for you at one time or another. We wanted to respect your privacy, but we wanted to know you were all right, too."

"I want to see you all." That decision had been instant and much easier than Cass had anticipated.

"Are you lost?" Royce's voice interrupted her reverie. "I think we drove past the orchard back there."

"Oh, good grief." Cass looked in her rearview mirror and braked. The wreck had happened somewhere near the country club that sat at the top of the hill on her left. She didn't want to be reminded, but no sooner had the thought crossed her mind than she saw the beautifully carved crosses at the side of the road. One for Dave Gallagher and one for Linda Saylors—she knew without looking. Jack and Tucker's father had died instantly when he'd hit the van carrying one set of parents and ten prom-goers, but no one would have included him in the roadside memorial.

"Sorry, Roycie," she said. "I didn't realize coming back here would be so overwhelming."

Royce's hand brushed her shoulder in a pat. "Bad overwhelming or good overwhelming?"

Cass laughed, surprised at the sound. And a little pleased with herself. Her life was okay in a lot of ways. She was successful in her field. She'd survived breast cancer and divorce. But she didn't usually laugh much. It felt good.

When they pulled into the orchard driveway after turning around near the crosses, the wagon was all set for the hayride. Two pretty horses were anxious to get going. A young Amish man, his clean-shaven face announcing his bachelorhood, was on the driver's seat. Another young man, bearing a marked resemblance to Luke Rossiter, sat beside him.

"Sorry we're late," said Cass, joining Luke at the back of the wagon. "I was daydreaming and missed the turn. This is my sister, Royce."

"Royce." Luke shook hands with her. "That's Isaac Hershberger and my brother, Seth. The wagon's going to be almost full of a 4-H group from near Kokomo. There's room for you, Royce, if you want to go, but your sister and I are going to take the motorized tour."

"I don't know." Royce wasn't normally shy, but she looked uncomfortable. "Maybe I should just wait here. I won't be in the way."

Seth jumped down from the driver's seat and came around. "If you'll come along, I'll ride in the back with you. Mary Detwiler will sit up front with Isaac and they'll pretend they're not going out."

Isaac turned in his seat, smiled a greeting at Cass and Royce and tossed his flat-brimmed hat at Seth.

"Come on." Luke urged Cass in front of him. "They'll settle down once the passengers are on board." He waved at his brother. "'Settle down' might be the wrong way to say it—they'll entertain them. How's that?"

He led the way to the utility vehicle on the other side of the orchard truck. "Do you want some coffee to take along? It's always fresh inside the store."

"That would be good."

A few minutes later, they were back on the four-wheeler. "There are sixty acres here, as you probably know," he began, starting down one of the wide paths between the rows of trees. "We have nearly a hundred different varieties of apples, plus a few acres of pears, cherries and plums. We also have some grapevines. Chris Granger, from Sycamore Hill Vineyard and Winery, is helping with those and eventually we hope to serve and sell wine. We already sell all kinds of jams, jellies and honeys on consignment."

"I'm surprised," Cass admitted. "I thought it was more or less a hobby farm. I know the income was more substantial than I expected when I inherited, but I had nothing to compare it to." Nor had she paid much attention. She'd put the monthly checks in the bank, uncomfortable with receiving money she hadn't earned. The cumulative amount had made her accountant raise her eyebrows.

"We've expanded quite a bit. The apple barn closes in January, but we're hoping to keep the store open this year with the consigned items."

Something in his voice jarred a distant and sweet memory. "Dumplings. Do you have apple dumplings? I remember Aunt Zoey making them when I'd visit during the summer when I was little. They were like bowls filled with heaven."

"We do have them, although Mrs. Detwiler and a few other Amish women make them for us now. Zoey had a class and taught them all how she does it."

Cass peered at the structures. The climate-controlled storage barn stood apart. She was almost certain it had been built since the last time she was here. The retail store was in the apple barn. The round barn seemed to be waiting to be used. "Have you thought of putting a restaurant here?"

He nodded. "Zoey's always wanted to, but Miniagua's not big enough to support another one. There's already a café, a bar and grill, a pizza place and a tearoom on the lake, plus we're a few miles from there so it would be out of the way for nearly everyone. The tea-room doubles as an event center. So does the lake clubhouse and even the country club if you're in the mood for some exclusivity."

"What about a coffee shop?" Cass didn't know anything about restaurants or demand for them, but she did know coffee shops. Most of Cassandra G. Porter's *Mysteries on the Wabash* series had been written in them.

Luke looked thoughtful. "There used to be one in Sawyer, but the owners weren't big on either cleanliness or quality—or paying their utilities, for that matter—so it didn't last long."

Cass gestured with her empty cup. "You have a good start with this. It's good coffee." She was almost sure it was the same kind she'd found in the house.

"The bulk foods store sells it."

"You could serve those apple dumplings. Maybe have a limited breakfast and lunch menu."

"It's worth some thought. Summer people might like it. I'm not sure lakers would care one way or another, but it could be worth its while with summer traffic, I imagine—although the location might still be a problem." He didn't sound especially encouraging, but he didn't give an unequivocal no, either.

They pulled up at the barn the same time as the hay wagon did. The group of 4-H club members climbed out the back and went into the store, waving at the young people on the driver's seat. Seth and Royce were the last ones off the wagon. Royce ran to where Cass and Luke were getting out of the utility vehicle.

"Seth says I can help pick apples. Can I? Isaac and Mary are going to help, too. He says they're picking the Earligolds now. I promise I won't get in the way."

Cass looked at Luke. He shrugged. "A dollar an hour over minimum wage. Keep track of your hours and do what Seth says. Fill out your paperwork in the office after work today. Be careful. If you fall out of a tree, Zoey will have my head and it would increase the possibility I might have to climb one."

"What are you going to do for lunch?" Cass protested. "You can't go two hours without eating, much less the rest of the day."

"I will bring enough for Royce if it's all right." Mary's English was lightly accented, and Cass remembered the musical sound of the Pennsylvania Dutch the Amish often spoke. "She can bring lunch for me tomorrow."

"Well then, sure, if you want to, Royce. Thank you, Mary." Damaris had been concerned about the influence of some of Royce's friends in California. Cass had a feeling she'd be pleased with Mary, Isaac and Seth. At least on the face of things.

"If you'll come to Zoey's with me," said Luke, when the teenagers had gone to work, "we'll get a good lunch plus she and I can explain how the business is run. She still knows more about the orchard than I do. It's up to you how active you want to be, but you need to make an educated decision."

"I don't think Aunt Zoey wants to see me."

His gaze went to the round barn, then flicked back to her. He took off his baseball cap, pushed back his thick brown hair and put the cap back on. "Based on what?"

"What?" She frowned. What was he talking about?

"Yes, what? What makes you believe that?"

"My mother told me, although what she said turned out to be not exactly true. But the year in high school when I lived here, Zoey didn't want me to come even though I didn't have anywhere else to go. And I hardly ever saw her when I was here." That still stung. Her aunt had been her favorite person in all the world. Finding out the feeling wasn't mutual had hurt.

"Even if that's true—and I know Zoey well enough to think there's more to the story than you've been told—would you seriously hold that kind of grudge for, what, twenty years?"

"It's not a grudge," she protested. "I love Aunt Zoey. Having her come out to California when Mother was ill and again when she died was what got me through those days." She hesitated. Talking about her personal life wasn't something she did, especially with stomach-clenchingly handsome men she hardly knew. "I had divorced parents and numerous stepparents whose revolving-door comings and goings made me relationship shy. My father and some of those stepparents were military—not that there's anything wrong with that, but it makes for a complicated lifestyle. Add my own shockingly bad choices to the mix and you have someone who stays inside a shell because it's comfortable there."

"I'm sure it is." He touched her arm, leading her away from customer traffic. "Did you like it here? In high school, I mean."

"Like it?" She shook her head. "I loved every minute, I think." She frowned. "Did you live here then? I don't remember you, but I wasn't here that long."

"No. My folks transferred here from Pennsylvania long after I got out of high school. Dad worked in Kokomo, but they lived in Sawyer. I liked it so well that when life dictated a change, I got a job as close as I could and bought a fixer-upper on the lake. About the time I got the kitchen paid for, the company I worked for closed. I'll go back to real work one of these days, but for the time being, I'm enjoying the orchard and the lake." He stopped. "I just told you my entire life story in what I'm sure was less than a hundred words. Are you impressed so far?"

She laughed, the sound coming easily. "You know, I am."

"Impressed enough to come to Zoey's with me? If it doesn't work out and you have to spend an hour making polite noises, will it really hurt anything?"

Images of her last conversation with her father, facing Tony in court the day their divorce was final and watching cancer claim her mother made a painful collage in her mind. So many things that couldn't be unsaid or undone. Maybe, just maybe, the fissure with Aunt Zoey could be healed. "No. It won't hurt a thing. I'll be glad to go with you."

"You up for a walk?"

She was. She fell into step beside him to go down a grass-divided lane to the big house that sat watch over the orchard. "I'd forgotten that everyone walks at the lake. Or rides bikes or golf carts."

"Or all three. Where did you live in California? Not where, exactly, but how? Were you in a house or an apartment?"

"When I was married, we lived in a house in Chula Vista, but when I got divorced, I moved up to an apartment in Sacramento. My mother and Royce and her mother all lived there." She swallowed, pushing her hair out of her face when a gust of wind tunneled down the lane. "I was sick, and even though I could take care of myself most of the time, I didn't want to be alone. Then Mother got pancreatic cancer, and I helped take care of her." She took a deep breath and then another, trying to remember the things she'd learned in yoga class. "I sound pathetic," she said apologetically, "and I'm not at all."

"I didn't think you were."

The house came into full view when the lane meandered around a wooded curve, and Cass stopped, unable to keep in the soft "Oh" that passed her lips. The big Queen Anne farmhouse, still painted dark blue and trimmed in cream, hadn't changed so much as a board since her summer visits here. White picket fence still surrounded the lawn. Lacy iron furniture, painted the same cream as the house's trim, sat under the maple trees.

Although the garage doors were new, they were still carriage-house style.

It was the safest place she'd ever known.

"It's still beautiful," she whispered.

"It is."

"There used to be a swing on one of the trees in the backyard. I spent hours out there, watching the apple trees and catching a glimpse of the creek that was the property line."

"It's still there. Well, not the same swing, but one on the same tree, with the rope wrapped around the same limb."

"Aunt Zoey spent so much time with me then. She was the best aunt ever. I must have driven her nuts."

"That's not the way she tells it."

He had to be wrong. Surely he was wrong. Her mother would have told her, wouldn't she, if Aunt Zoey had wanted to see her again? Marynell had been...difficult, but not possessive. She'd been relieved when Cass spent more time at friends' homes than she did theirs. Even when Cass's father hadn't wanted to take advantage of his court-ordered visitation, Marynell had forced the issue. That alone had accounted for most of her summertime visits to Miniagua.

Luke didn't wait for her to say more, just

led the way up the front porch steps and around the side of the house to the kitchen door. "Zoey?" he called through the screen. "I brought you company for lunch."

The sound of quick footsteps preceded Zoey to the door, and there she was, unchanged from how she'd looked when Marynell died. Almost unchanged from those long-ago summers. Her hair was white now instead of the light brown it had been, but she still wore it short and parted on the side so that it lay in a sleek curve over her ear. Makeup brought out the deep blue of her eyes. She was as tall as Cass and nearly as slender. She wore jeans and a floaty top, and her smile of welcome was wide and tremulous.

Cass's heart thumped so hard she thought it was probably visible from where her aunt stood on the other side of the old-fashioned screen door. "Aunt Zoey."

Zoey drew in an unsteady breath. "Cassiopeia."

"Really?" said Luke. "You don't look like a Cassiopeia."

Cass spared him a glance. "No, but it's who I always wished I was." Her name was simply Cass. No Cassiopeia. No Cassandra. No middle name. She didn't mind it now—

she'd given herself Cassandra as a present when she'd chosen her writing name—but she'd hated it as a child, feeling that her parents hadn't even cared enough to give her a whole name.

"It's who you are to me." Zoey pushed open the door. "Welcome home."

CHAPTER FOUR

"SHE IS SO PRETTY." Seth stared out over the windshield of Luke's boat as they cruised Lake Miniagua after helping Father Doherty and Chris Granger trim the hedges at St. Paul's.

"She sure is," Luke murmured, lifting his arm to wave at Tucker Llewellyn as the big pontoon boat he and Jack owned glided past.

"That's just sick." Seth sounded disgusted.

"What's sick?"

"What are you doing looking at a sixteen-year-old girl? You could be her dad."

"Who's talking about a sixteen-year-old girl?"

"We are."

"Well, I wasn't," said Luke mildly. "Who are *you* talking about?"

"Royce Gentry."

"Oh." She *was* a beautiful girl. Prettier than her older sister, but not as striking. She worked hard, too, laughing at herself as the new kid, and falling into easy camaraderie with the others. She'd arrived her second day at work with enough lunch for Mary and herself and doughnuts from the Amish bakery that she shared with everyone.

"So, who were *you* talking about?" Seth passed him a sly look. "Someone Mom would get all excited about? She thinks there's something wrong with a guy being thirty-eight and single. Dad says—"

"—leave the boy alone," Luke finished in unison with him.

"Don't you *want* to get married again?" Seth steered the boat carefully as they approached Luke's dock. "I mean, I hope I don't get married real young, either, but you're kind of pushing the envelope on that, aren't you?" He hesitated. "Jill has been gone a long time."

"It's Mom's envelope I'm pushing. And her grandma buttons, too—that's for sure." Luke stepped out of the boat to tie off. "Jill died ten years ago, and she'd be in line behind you and Mom telling me it's time to get married again. But, you know—" He stopped, staring toward where the evening sun was dipping into the water. "I wouldn't give up a minute of the time we had together, but the truth is, I don't want to feel that way about somebody again. Losing her was a kind of hell I'm not willing to chance going through twice."

"She was so great." Seth had only been seven when Jill's faulty heart had failed for the last time. Luke thought his little brother's grief had been nearly as intense as his own. The young woman who knew she'd never be a mother had been a sister-in-law extraordinaire to the little brother no one ever had enough time for. She'd been his first babysitter, had seen him take his first steps and heard his first words.

"She was." He smiled at Seth and gave his shoulder a squeeze when he stepped onto the dock a lot more lithely than Luke had.

"So, she'd want to know, too. Who's pretty besides Royce? And don't give me the whole none-of-your-business thing. It's my night to cook and I have no problem with build-your-own bologna sandwiches."

Luke's stomach growled as if on cue. "Her sister, Cass. She's pretty."

"Oh." Seth thought over that for the length of time it took them to reach the back porch of the house. "She is, I guess. For someone nearly as old as you, I mean."

"Keep it up and I'll send you to Rachel for the school year."

"Oh, no, say it isn't so!" Seth threw himself up against the back door, his arms raised in supplication, and Luke pushed him aside, laughing.

"You should be in drama instead of football."

He showered while Seth prepared dinner. Sometimes he felt guilty because the kid worked so hard, but he was also proud that Seth thrived on it.

"I want you to take this weekend off," he said when they were seated at the bar in the kitchen eating spaghetti with meat sauce. "It'll be the last one for a while, between football and apples coming on."

"Can I use your car?"

"As long as I'm not in it, you can."

"No curfew?"

"None at all."

It was a safe concession to make because no matter how often Seth intended to stay up late, he was invariably asleep by eleven. Luke had even bought a TV for the cottage's second bedroom that had a timer on it, because his brother was usually out for the night within ten minutes of lying down.

"I'm going to meet Cass for a drink at the Grill." Luke loaded the dishwasher. "If you have friends come over, stay out of the liquor."

"Nah." Seth already looked sleepy. "I'm tired. Two-a-days are deadly."

They were. Luke remembered that. Plus the kid had done more than his share of work at the church. "Get some sleep, then," he suggested.

"I will." But Seth was already reaching for his guitar, and Luke hesitated. They usually played music together for an hour or so—it was a habit he didn't want to break.

"Go." Seth waved him off. "The more I practice and you don't, the better I get…and you don't."

"In your dreams, little brother." But he left, a little puzzled by how eager he was to see Cass again. Admittedly, there was some sort of connection between them, but he thought that was probably because they both cared for Zoey. He was anxious to hear how both women felt about the lunch of the day before. They'd been affectionate with each other but also uncomfortable. He'd left them alone after lunch and hadn't seen either of them since.

Cass was at the bar in Anything Goes, talking to Mollie, the bartender, and sipping from a tall mug of hot chocolate.

"You do know that chocolate comes loaded, right?" He took the stool beside hers, waving at Mollie.

Cass flashed him a smile that had his heartbeat moving around the way his parents did when they danced the jitterbug. "I do, but I'm on foot. I can take it."

"If you two kids want to sit at a table, the lake view ones are emptying out," said Mollie. "I'll bring your drinks over."

"Good idea." Luke got up. "Thanks for the 'kids' thing. Having Seth in the house has added considerably to my age."

Mollie flipped him with the business end of a bar towel. "Shame on you. That's a good kid there and you know it."

"He is." Luke held up a hand to protect himself. "Mom and Dad were already over the having-babies thing by the time he came along, so Rachel, Leah and I take full credit for how he's come out." He smiled. "We all admit Jill got him off to a good start."

Mollie's face softened. "She sure did. What a mom she would have been."

The bartender was one of the few who didn't avoid talking about Jill, something Luke appreciated.

"Royce thinks he's a good kid, too. The

word *hot* entered the conversation about ten times." Cass followed him to a booth beside the window-lined wall. "She hasn't been nearly as bored as she anticipated when we drove in. Of course, it's only been two days. Things could change."

When they'd sat down and Mollie had brought their drinks and a bowl of popcorn, Cass asked, "Who's Jill, or shouldn't I ask?"

"My wife. She died of heart disease ten years ago."

"Oh." Cass withdrew the hand that had been reaching for popcorn. "I'm sorry. How awful."

"It was."

"How long were you married?"

"Nine years and change." He waited for the pain to strike, even knowing it wouldn't anymore. He'd loved his wife and he missed her, but time had faded the memories to where they were a gentle kind of pleasure.

"I hope you had a great time every minute."

He nodded, a smile breaking loose. "We did that. We knew there wasn't much time, so we were able to make the absolute best of it." It had been hard when they'd argued, because he hadn't wanted to waste that time, but Jill had argued anyway. She was unwilling to miss out on any of life's experiences just because she didn't have enough time for all of them.

"Children?"

"No. She couldn't, but she and Seth worshiped each other from the day he was born, so he was as much like our kid as my little brother." He met Cass's eyes and held her gaze, thinking how strange it was that despite their acknowledged connection, he had no clue what she was thinking. "You were married, too?"

"Yes." She looked almost embarrassed, and reached for the popcorn again, taking a handful and dropping it onto a napkin. She ate a few bites. "He had the ideal family. They stayed in one spot, stayed married to each other and had enough money to buy anything they wanted. Not rich, but more comfortable than I was used to. Tony always said I married him to get his family, and he was probably right." She shrugged. "It only took us fourteen years or so to figure out it wasn't working. Eventually he settled in on someone younger and prettier and we got a divorce ten years after we should have. I got sick while it was going on, so it was an eventful few years there."

Luke could think of absolutely nothing to say. "Wow." It was weak, but it was accurate.

She looked appalled. "I am so sorry. I can't believe I just did that. People have been asking me how I'm doing ever since I got sick and I have managed to say 'doing fine' a gazillion times, even when I was bald and the color of cigarette ashes. I just blew that record for nobility in one short conversation and you didn't even ask how I was."

"You have hair and your skin's a nice golden color, too." Luke was laughing. He couldn't help it. "You know, nobility's overrated anyway. I tried that with Seth the last time he used my car. He said the only reason I let him use it was that it always came back cleaner than it left. He was pretty much right."

She laughed, too. "I'll remember that the next time the martyr cross gets too heavy to carry."

"Seriously." He caught her gaze again. And held it. He thought he might very well get lost in those ocean-colored depths. "How *are* you doing?"

"Seriously, doing fine. I had my two-years-after-diagnosis testing done this spring and am still clear. At least until November, when

I go back into full-scale panic when they test again."

Relief cleared the air between them. "I am so glad for that." He reached for her hand and squeezed it, wanting to touch her and hoping it didn't come across as creepy. She squeezed back, so it must not have. "So we can talk about important stuff then, right? Like what you think of everything we've done at the orchard." He rested his forearms on the edge of the table and did his best to look macho—an automatic fail. "I am a guy, you know. My sisters say I am the master of making things all about me. I don't want to disappoint them."

Cass beamed, her eyes lighting. The expression opened a place in him he'd thought was permanently closed. *Oh, boy.* "I love the orchard, and I love everything you've done to it."

Encouraged, he asked the question that had lingered uppermost in his mind since they'd toured the orchard earlier in the day. "Do you know what you'd like to do? Stay a silent partner like your mother was? Sell out? I don't have the money, but having a financially savvy brother-in-law has ensured I have good credit."

It was as if he'd slapped her. The light left

her eyes and her beam faded to a polite smile. She started to speak, then stopped, turning her head to gaze out at the lake. Spangled with moonlight, starshine and colored lights on boats cruising the calm water, it was a good thing to look at. Calming and exhilarating at the same time.

What had he said? Whatever it was, she was neither acknowledging nor answering.

"Cass?"

"I'd like to try the coffee-shop thing. I talked to Neely at the tearoom this morning, because that would be the most direct competition, and she thought it was a good idea." She turned back to meet his eyes again, and he thought she looked defeated. He hoped he hadn't caused that.

"In the round barn," she specified. "It wouldn't need to be a big shop. Maybe ten or twelve tables. Wi-Fi. Coffee and pastries in the morning. Soup and sandwiches at lunch. Just coffee and packaged things in the evening, unless it works out really well, in which case we could continue the lunch offerings."

He hadn't wanted her to be defeated, to feel like a stranger in a strange land. He also hadn't expected—or wanted, his snarky inner voice muttered—her to want to *change* things. She was being naïve. It wasn't as if he hadn't considered having a café on the premises, but it hadn't seemed to be a viable use of resources. He'd been running the orchard for three years. She'd been at the lake for two days and had taken exactly one tour of the premises.

She also owned half the orchard. Exactly. There was no 51 percent or anything like that to give him a louder voice in negotiations. He wasn't a proponent of loud voices anyway, but…well, he'd expected her to pick up where her mother left off. That amounted to cashing the checks, signing things that required both their names and exchanging Christmas cards.

"We could think about that," he said slowly. "Maybe you could come up with some numbers."

"I can do that. I've spent hours of many hundreds of days in coffee shops for the past fifteen years. I already know a lot and I know where to find out the rest. As far as numbers go—" she scrambled in her purse for a pen, wrote on a napkin and pushed it across the table "—I can invest that."

"She's your aunt. Why are you so nervous?" Royce scowled at the table Cass had set in the dining area of the cottage. "I thought we were the beer-and-brats segment of the family. This looks like the way Dad used to want the table set when officers came to dinner. There are too many forks and glasses."

Cass laughed. "You're right. Okay, let's back it off."

They started from scratch, using the jewel-toned placemats that had come with the house instead of the embroidered tablecloth Cass had bought at an antiques store on Main Street. They left water glasses on the table, but set wineglasses and cups and saucers out of the way on the counter. They replaced elegant tapers with squatty candles and set the autumn centerpiece back on the end table in the living room where Royce had put it when they brought it home.

Dinner was a combination of their talents. Cass had cooked a pot roast with vegetables and Royce had made a salad and deviled a pretty little platter of eggs. They'd bought dessert and dinner rolls at the Amish bakery and wine at Sycamore Hill. Cass had promised her sister she could have a glass if she wasn't going out afterward, but a phone call from Seth Rossiter asking her to go to the late movie in Sawyer put an end to that.

Zoey was right on time. One shoe on and one shoe off, Royce opened the door. "Aunt Zoey! I'm so glad to see you!"

Cass watched the two tall, slim women she loved as they hugged each other, drew back to take a good look and hugged each other again. She was happy for Royce, she told herself, that Aunt Zoey's love for a girl who wasn't actually her niece was so unrestricted. She was jealous, too.

"Come here." Zoey stretched her arm toward her. Her eyes were awash with tears, something Cass didn't remember seeing before. Even when Marynell had died, grief had made new lines in Zoey's face, but Cass hadn't seen her cry. "I know we have issues, but right this minute, we don't."

Zoey smelled like pink Dove soap and the same kind of shampoo Cass and Royce used. Her hug, complete with strong, thin arms and a soft, wrinkled cheek against her own, made Cass know more than anything else that, at least for now, she was home.

By the time they reached the table, Zoey had handed Royce a handful of photographs. "A record of your sister's life you can use for blackmail if the need arises."

Cass laughed, although it took all she had

not to snatch the pictures away. They were a record of a childhood she didn't want altered by someone else's perception. "Did Mother do that with you?"

She could have cut her tongue out as soon as the words left her mouth. She'd forgotten that Zoey had been engaged to her father first, before he'd met her younger sister. Marynell had been the first of the young, beautiful women he'd pursued and caught. "I'm sorry," she said. "I shouldn't have—"

Zoey shook her head. "No, it's all right. I wouldn't say she blackmailed. She never had to. Marynell was so beautiful we all enabled her." She met Cass's eyes and grasped her hand. "It didn't make any of us bad people." She grinned wickedly. "Even your father."

Royce laughed, delighted, and Cass joined her. In his own way, Ken Gentry loved his daughters, but they'd both always known where they stood in his line of priorities. Even Royce, gorgeous as she was, was a testimony to his aging. He'd been fifty-two when she was born, and inevitable queries about his "grandchild" were still hard for him to take. He was generally happier just being able to show off her pictures.

"Everyone has weaknesses," Zoey concluded, "and mine combined with your parents' created quite a cluster of pain and sorrow."

Seth came as they were finishing dessert, and Cass excused her sister from cleanup duty. Before the cottage's front door closed behind the young couple, awkwardness slipped inside.

"I should go." Zoey pushed back from the table. "Let me help with the dishes."

Cass almost let her leave. That was how she'd spent most of her life, wasn't it, walking the long way around to avoid being hurt more than necessary? She'd learned to live without her beloved aunt's emotional support. Why take a chance of regaining it only to lose it once more?

Because she was thirty-five, not sixteen, that was why. Because she had a little sister she needed to set an example for. Because there were steps out of loneliness and she was ready to take a big one.

"No," she said. "Please." She stood up. "Will you make coffee while I clear the table? Or would you rather have more wine?"

"Coffee would be good."

"Yours always was, even when it was half

cream and two-thirds refined sugar. Did Nana know you gave it to me like that?"

Zoey chuckled. "I doubt it. It didn't seem to have taken, though—you've been thin as a rail your whole life."

When the coffee was done and they were once more sitting across from each other at the table, Cass revealed, "I got chunky in high school, when we were in Korea. Dad found a doctor who put me on a program that un-chunked me in a matter of months. I took pills that were illegal here, but that was during the Barbie-stepmother time and she used them all the time. We both survived and I stayed thin until after I was married."

"You gained weight then? It's hard to imagine."

"Some. Enough to make Tony panic. So I became an exercise and fasting addict. I couldn't stop losing weight when I was ready to and it scared me to death. My metabolism was *so* messed up, and it pretty much stayed that way until I got the breast cancer diagnosis." Cass smiled, although the gesture cost her—there was nothing funny in the memories. "So now I'm your basic slug. I walk for exercise, but I do it better if there's ice cream at the end of it."

Zoey laughed, a big sound that filled Cass's heart and gave buoyancy to her own chuckle. "I'm with you, sweetheart." The older woman sipped from the coffee in front of her, then leaned her forearms on the table and met Cass's eyes. "Where did you go, Cassandra? Did you really believe I didn't want you here? That I ever didn't want you at all? That the people at the lake didn't want you? Gianna Gallagher used to ask me, but I never said where you were, just that you were all right even though I was never really sure you really were."

"Mother could be pretty convincing. You know that. It wasn't until she got sick that she admitted she'd made most of it up, that you'd only been concerned about me staying with Nana and Grandpa because they weren't all that well. I should have talked to you then." Marynell had made other confessions, too, all in one long, pain-ridden night. She'd asked her daughter's forgiveness and Cass had given it.

She hadn't meant the words of forgiveness, but she'd said what a dying woman needed to hear. Six months and change later, she thought she'd done the right thing, but a pardoning heart had come harder than the words had.

"Will you forgive me?" she asked. "For believing her and for not making it right even when I knew better?"

"Oh, honey." Zoey got up, came around the table and drew Cass out of the chair and into her arms. "Marynell was who she was and she couldn't help that. We all fell prey to her at one time or another. Let's just concentrate on not losing each other again. What do you say?"

"I'd like that a lot."

When they were seated again, their cups refilled and second servings of dessert on plates in front of them, Zoey said, "What do you think of Luke?"

"He must be a good businessman. The orchard looks great."

She thought more than that, of course. Noticed more. Thought about him before she fell asleep in one of the cottage's two little bedrooms. She knew he had beautiful, sun-streaked dark brown hair and thickly lashed eyes the color of milk chocolate. That he would probably be a little taller than she was even if she was wearing heels. That he was built really nicely but not as if it was on purpose—it was more like the muscles were a by-product of pruning and picking apples. That his voice warmed places in her that hadn't known warmth in a long time. Maybe ever.

She took a deep breath. "I suggested a coffee shop on the premises, in the round barn. I don't think he likes the idea."

Zoey shrugged. "Convince him, if it's something you'd like to do that you think would be successful, but remember that he's run the place by himself for several years. As long as your mother got her checks, she never offered any input. I'm sure Luke expected the same thing from you." She smiled, her eyes twinkling. "I'll be so delighted to see him be wrong."

CHAPTER FIVE

HE WASN'T READY to give in on the coffee shop idea, but Luke had to admit he liked having an active partner in the orchard. For one thing, she didn't mind climbing trees and she was—for someone he thought was on the skinny side of slim—strong enough to fill the bag over her shoulder as full as her sister did. It was the busiest time of year at the orchard and she pitched in wherever help was needed. She was great in the retail store and on the sorting machine—not so good when it came to making the orchard's signature dumplings.

"It skipped a generation. That's all I can figure," Cass said, laughing, when Zoey and Luke looked at her first attempt with something like horror.

She often joined him and Zoey at the farmhouse for coffee in the morning. This became an increasingly pleasurable point during the day, since Zoey seemed to be on a one-woman crusade to fatten up her niece.

Not wanting to make anyone feel uncomfortable about eating in front of him, Luke filled his plate and joined them at the table. They brainstormed about the orchard, about the Miniagua Lakers football team, about the coffee shop.

The daggone coffee shop.

She was serious about it. She'd even hauled him over to Peru on Monday morning to a place there called Aroma, where he drank two cups and got one to go of something really strong and good. She'd had something girly. Then, just when he'd built up a good argument, she'd taken him to a chain coffee place in Kokomo and another local one that sat just off campus at a nearby university. He'd eaten pastries at that one, and they hadn't been as good as the ones from the Amish bakery, but Cass had shown him how popular they were and gotten off-the-top-of-her-head numbers from the barista about what their revenue was on a fairly slow weekday.

He was running out of arguments.

On Friday, Cass texted and said she couldn't make breakfast and Royce called Seth and said she'd be late at the orchard. Neither of them offered an explanation. Zoey came to the apple barn, looking fretful, and stood at the sorter for a while. Sort of helping.

"What are you doing here?" Luke asked bluntly, dumping a box of Galas onto the conveyor. "Not that you're not welcome—you most certainly are—but you don't generally hang out in the barn. You go up to the store and the apple dumpling assembly."

"Luke, what if they're getting ready to go home? Royce needs to start school, so even though they planned to stay two weeks, they might not. It's a long, hard drive."

She literally wrung her hands, and Luke wanted to wring Cass's neck. She'd had no business getting her aunt's hopes up that she might stay at Miniagua if her intent all the time was to hightail it back to the West Coast. While he was relieved in a way not to have to come up with more reasons not to open a coffee shop in the round barn, he was seriously ticked that she would get everyone all excited and then just take off, even though from everything he'd heard that seemed to be her modus operandi.

Her friends from the wreck had stood by her since she'd come back. All the ones who were local had met at Gianna Gallagher's on

Tuesday night. "Not to ask questions," Gianna had said, "but to welcome you home."

Cass had cried when she'd talked about it at breakfast. Not the boo-hoo kind that Rachel had made into an art form when she was in high school, but silent, heartfelt weeping that she apologized for.

He knew all the other survivors of the wreck, what they'd been through and how they'd come out on the other side. Having her come back only to leave again would be like a slap in the face to them as much as it was to Zoey.

And to him. Daggone it. He didn't want to take her likely desertion personally, but he did. They were getting to be friends, weren't they? And he liked her. He thought she was pretty hot, too, but that was incidental and not to be acted on—she had way too much baggage going on and he just wasn't going there. Not with her. Not with anyone.

"There's nothing we can do either way," he told Zoey. "You're reestablishing a relationship with her and she's not going to let that slide any more than you are." *I hope.* "She has to consider Royce, too. Don't forget, I've got that running back out there with me for the whole freakin' school year because of a consideration like that." He didn't feel like defending her, not at all, but he owed her that one as one custodial sibling to another.

"I know, but it would be so nice for Royce to go here this year while her mother's gone. It was great for Cass regardless of how things ended up. I believe that with all my heart."

It was Zoey's heart he was worried about. As far as he knew, she was healthy, but that heart was big and pretty wide open—he hated to see it get broken.

"Well, come on into the store. I'll buy you some coffee and a dumpling." He stepped away from the sorter and waited for her to join him.

They were at the open doors of the barn when Cass's red SUV pulled into the parking lot, spitting some gravel when she stopped a little more suddenly than she maybe should have. That was explained when Royce got out of the driver's side and took off running toward the trees where Seth and the others were picking. She had papers flapping in her hand, and she didn't bother closing the door.

Cass got out of the other side, moving more slowly but with a certain buoyancy in her step that made Luke's heartbeat go skippy for a couple of beats. She walked around to close the other door, then approached where Luke and Zoey waited. "Sorry to miss this morning." She hugged Zoey and smiled at Luke. He couldn't see her eyes behind the sunglasses she wore, but he'd have bet they were smiling, too.

They didn't ask her the circumstances of her absence. She was a grown-up and he knew Zoey didn't want to push her away. Luke didn't, either, but he was still in the stage of maybe they'd be friends and maybe not; trying to bring her closer might scare her off completely.

She spoke before he could. "I have had no coffee. Can we get some?"

They went into the store, waving at the woman behind the counter, and back to the self-serve coffee station. Cass had replaced the foam cups with promotional cups from all over Miniagua and Sawyer. He didn't know how she'd found time to collect them, but they were nice for customers and the environment, and the coffee sure tasted better out of them.

"Royce and I talked a lot last night," she said when they'd gone back outside and taken seats at one of the patio tables on the wide porch. "I said we needed to leave by

Wednesday of next week in order to get her into school for the second week. Not being there the first week is fine, not so much another one. She misses her friends, misses the shopping and looks forward to the advanced placement curriculum and getting into Berkeley. She has mentioned a minimum of seven hundred times that there's nothing to do here. I thought, other than her no longer seeing your 'seriously hot' younger brother and my 'seriously cool' aunt every day, that Royce was ready to go home." She cleared her throat and took a long drink of coffee. "I was wrong."

"Oh." Zoey clasped her hands in anticipation, and Luke almost did. What was wrong with him anyway? Any minute now, he'd be telling her he thought the coffee shop was a fine idea. And it wasn't. For heaven's sake, it just so was not.

"Yes." Cass sounded gleeful, and Luke caught a glimpse and a sound-bite of the girl she must have been when she'd spent her junior year here. "Even though she wants to return to California when her mother comes home, she'd really like to try school here and she'd like to spend quality time—yes, she actually used that term—with Aunt Zoey and…

yeah, she wouldn't mind seeing Seth occasionally, too." Cass bounced—literally—in her seat. "Where is that boy? I need to find him and kiss his face."

"So, you're staying." He couldn't be wrong if he stated the obvious, could he? And he wasn't going to think about her kissing Seth's face. Or anyone else's.

"Yes. At least until Royce's mother gets home, and longer if I can find a place to live and settle in. We enrolled Royce in school this morning and have spent the last thirty minutes discussing the fact that she doesn't have a single thing to wear, which means spending a whole day and a bunch of money in Kokomo." Her brows knit into a slight frown. "It shouldn't be a problem finding a house to rent, with the lake season ending, should it?"

"No." Zoey sounded frantic. "No." She pointed in the vague direction of the farmhouse. "Twelve rooms, Cass, and four of them are upstairs bedrooms. You and Royce wouldn't even have to share a bath because there are two of them up there. It'll be yours someday anyway, so move in now. Make it your home."

"Aunt Zoey." Cass pinned her gaze to her

aunt. "How long has it been since you've lived with a sixteen-year-old? It's not for the faint of heart."

Zoey laughed, that big, full sound that delighted everyone within hearing. "I shared a room and a bathroom with your mother and lived to tell the story. Any more questions?"

"Are you sure?"

"More than sure."

It was already a sunny day, but Luke thought it had gotten brighter within the last few minutes. "I've been thinking," he said. "Maybe a coffee shop would be a good idea."

IT HAD BEEN a busy, busy day. When they'd gotten home from the orchard, accompanied by a pizza and two milkshakes, Cass had to convince Royce they couldn't move into the farmhouse that very minute. After supper, she spent an hour trying to decide what to do with her apartment in Sacramento.

When Royce Skyped with her mother that evening, Lieutenant Colonel Gentry asked to talk to Cass.

"Is it okay," asked Cass, "that we're staying here?"

"More than okay." Damaris bit her lip, and Cass thought she looked tired. "Your dad probably won't come there. I think that's a good thing for both of you."

"I think so, too." Cass hesitated, frowning at her favorite stepmother's flickering image. "Damaris? You doing all right?"

"Yeah." The other woman's face cleared. "Not a good place or a good time. I'm so grateful to you for keeping Royce. It's still okay…you know, if anything happens— you'll still keep her?"

Alarm shivered up Cass's spine. "I'll always keep her," she said, her tone as level as she could make it, "but nothing's going to happen to you. You survived life with Major Gentry, *sir*, remember?"

They all joked about it, even the two stepmothers Cass hadn't bonded with, that they'd escaped unscathed from life with her father. They used to say that when he'd read Pat Conroy's *The Great Santini*, he'd thought it was an instruction manual.

"You're right. Nothing's going to happen. Except we both know something might. I've always heard about the lake. From you. From your mother. Even from your aunt Zoey when Marynell was ill. I like the idea of Royce being there and of her being with you." She smiled. "Are you giving up your apartment?"

"I'm trying to decide."

"Let me help with that." Damaris leaned closer, and it was as if she was reaching through the screen of Cass's laptop computer. "Let it go. Hire someone to pack it up and ship it to you. You're home now. Plan on staying there."

Where shivers had been, Cass thought maybe some steel was working its way up her spine. *Home.* "I think you're right."

"I need to go. Give my girl a hug for me. I love you, stepgirl."

Cass went still. Damaris called her that sometimes and, occasionally, she added a casual "love ya" at the end of their conversations, but not like this. Never like this.

"Damaris?"

"Got to go."

"Okay." She shook off the wave of foreboding. "Love you, too, Colonel."

After Royce went to bed, Cass poured herself a glass of wine and sat at the table in front of her computer. She hadn't been very productive since they'd gotten to the lake, something nearly unheard of—one of the things Cassandra G. Porter's readers counted on was that she would have a new mystery on the shelves every June and every December.

That meant writing a certain amount every day. She still wrote every day, but the word count had taken a serious road trip to the wayside.

She'd finished a book while she was taking chemo. "It's not my best," she qualified when she sent its file to her editor, "but it was my best at the time." Lucy Garten, the sleuth who was the protagonist in the series, had developed breast cancer and gone through treatment as Cass did, solving *The Case of Daisy's Ashes* while she was bald, grouchy and nauseated.

Damaris had been her beta reader, proofreading as she went. It had cemented a bond born from the tenuous threads of their step-relationship.

To date, it was her bestselling book. Clutching that success close was what had given her the courage to come back to the lake, but now she needed to stay successful.

The thought made her grin at herself. It also led to getting several pages done by the time the wine bottle was empty and her eyelids were drooping. Before she went to bed, she walked down to the lake, looking out over its surface. The moon was waning, but still lent its light to the ruffly little waves that slapped the shore. She thought of the look on Damaris's face, of Royce's almost palpable excitement when it was decided they would stay in Miniagua, of the warmth of Zoey's jubilant hug.

She thought of Luke Rossiter and of what tables and chairs she'd find for the coffee shop and wondered if she was insane for wanting to be a barista. *You're a writer, for heaven's sake, and you can finally almost make a living at it.* But the round barn at the orchard had called out to a part of her she'd been holding back since she left the lake, the part that didn't want to be alone. As much as she loved writing and the solitude that went along with it, she needed something that would force her away from that aloneness.

And she loved coffee shops. What more reason did she need?

Back in the cottage, she went to bed, thinking again of Damaris's tired face. And then, before sleep overtook her, of Luke Rossiter's smiling one.

"TELL ME AGAIN why we can't just have the coffee shop in the center corridor of the barn. It's plenty big enough and access is right there from both entrances. That leaves the side areas for offices or even other little shops if this thing takes off." Luke looked both tired and impatient. And on the edge of angry.

Cass wasn't good at standing her ground— it wasn't something that had ever worked particularly well for her. But... "Because the coziness factor would be gone. It would never be quiet or intimate or conducive to working." She had said all this. She knew she had. Who knew that under that straight, silky hair of his, Luke Rossiter had such a thick head?

"Working? I thought it was for coffee. If people want to work, they should rent their own office space—maybe in the side rooms of the round barn."

"How did you get through college without studying in coffee shops?" she demanded.

"Easy. I studied in the student union or even occasionally—call me crazy—in the library. I thought a coffee shop was for drinking coffee." He grinned, but it wasn't his usual funny, endearing expression. It was more like a smirk.

"It is. And for visiting, studying and working. It's a great place for parents to recharge after a day with kids. For artists to sketch and writers to write. Even for music. Open mic nights or karaoke."

"Cass."

"Do not speak to me in that tone of voice."

His eyebrows shot up. He took off his cap, pushed his hair back and put it on again. "Exactly what tone of voice is that?"

"The one that says I'm too stupid to waste your time talking to. I'm not."

"Of course you're not, and I never for one minute thought you were. I do think you lose sight of the fact that we're in North Central Indiana, not California or the East Coast. Things are different here. People go to coffee shops to drink coffee or get a cup for the road."

"Oh, good grief. Were you even there when we went to those coffee shops in Peru and North Manchester and Kokomo? Have you seen the liars table at Silver Moon? Those people aren't there just to drink coffee and eat eggs over easy with bacon—they're there to talk." She lifted her hands in supplication, conscious that she was raising her voice as well. It felt kind of good. "Did all those people we saw sit there in silence and drink their coffee or wait for carryout, or did some of them have laptops or notebooks or books?

Were some of them actually sitting and talking to other people? Wasn't there a guy sitting in the corner with a guitar?"

"There was, and I admit I got a little itchy to sit and pick with him a little because I'm pretty sure he was better than me. But we have the Silver Moon for that. Or—what's the name of the tearoom now that Seven Pillars was destroyed in the tornado? Oh, right, Just One of Those Things. I'm not saying it's not a nice thing, but Miniagua's a small farming and resort community and I think the kind of venue you're suggesting won't fly here. The orchard's doing fairly well, as you know, so is it really the time to take chances with that? We're a down-home kind of place and we're proud of it. We don't need the same kind of trappings they require in larger places."

"How many people drink coffee in the orchard store every day?"

He looked bewildered. "What?"

"How many people drink coffee in there? Besides staff, I mean."

"I don't know. A couple of dozen, I guess. More on nice days, fewer when it's cold and rainy. But they're not going to come over here to a fancy coffee shop where people are sitting with laptops and sketchpads, especially if it's in a confined space instead of an open one."

She walked over to look at the room she wanted to use—it had great light, great windows, the perfect amount of space—then came back to where he stood in the center of the empty barn. She counted to ten. Twice. "So what you're actually saying is, fine, we can have a coffee shop, but only if we do everything on your terms."

He hesitated. "I have business experience," he said finally. "I've been part owner of the orchard for three years and I clocked some part-time hours here a couple of years before that. So, yeah, I think you should listen to me."

She hadn't expected him to admit it, and wasn't sure how to feel about it when he did. She hated what he'd said, *hated* it, but she thought she probably would have hated it even more if he'd been less than honest.

"Well." The problem with standing her ground was that it always gave way beneath her, and this time was no different. While it was true they were equal partners, she agreed that his seniority and his knowledge gave him a leg up on her when it came to business decisions. "Okay, then." She looked at her watch. "I said I'd work in the store this afternoon so Lovena Beiler could be with her daughter. I need to get over there. Sarah's near delivery and anxious—apparently she's miscarried a few times."

"She has." He nodded short agreement. "All right. We'll talk more later?"

"Sure." Maybe. And maybe the whole idea of a coffee shop was just a pipe dream that she should put away behind her heart and forget about.

He watched her walk away. She could feel it, but didn't turn around, just stiffened her back and went on. She had enough failures on her résumé—she wasn't going to let this partnership be another one because she hadn't gotten her own way.

CHAPTER SIX

"HE's A GUY. His thought processes are skewed. Don't tell me you were surprised by that. Remember when Sam and Nate suggested skipping the prom in favor of a senior class golf tournament?" Holly nodded affirmation of her own point. "In retrospect, of course, we all wish we'd skipped prom—there's no getting around that, no matter how we try—but a golf tournament was a non-starter as a replacement."

Her sister, Arlie, laughed from Cass's other side as the three rode their bicycles along the gravelly Lake Road. They were on their way to the lake's small library, where Holly was going to give a talk and sign copies of her latest book. "They wanted our wedding reception to be a golf outing, too, but had to make do with playing golf as a bachelor party instead."

"It was suggested that the bridesmaids and

the bride might want to caddy for them," said Holly.

Arlie snickered. "Yeah. Like that was gonna happen."

Cass laughed. It was so much fun being with them again. How was it that friends she'd known for less than a year more than half her lifetime ago could still hold such a big and warm place in her heart?

"I wish you'd been here for the wedding." Arlie reached with one hand to pat her shoulder, her bicycle's front wheel swerving dangerously close to Cass's. "You'd have been one of the bridesmaids."

"You can be one of mine," said Holly cheerfully. "I'm writing regency era romance these days, so we might have a costume wedding. Jess is really scared about wearing breeches and a velvet coat with tails, not to mention the powdered wig. I showed him a picture that might have been a little exaggerated, but so far all the bridesmaids are in."

Arlie's throaty laughter surprised Cass every time she heard it. She hadn't gotten used to the change in the other woman's voice brought about by the accident. Arlie had been a singer, planning to major in musical theatre in college. Instead, she'd become a nurse-midwife whose clinic, A Woman's Place on the Lake, had been the recipient of Cass's plethora of medical records when she'd made the decision to stay in Miniagua. "Thank goodness they're all electronic," she'd said with a nervous laugh the morning she visited the clinic. "If it was all on paper, I'd have to rent a room to keep them in."

"Come on back," Arlie had said easily. "Let's see what we have here."

So it was that a friend she hadn't seen since she was seventeen now knew more about her than any living soul. If Cass chose to keep her life a secret, she still could—she had no fears about Arlie's professional integrity. Secrecy had worked well for her. In a manner of speaking.

"Well, I think you should stick to your guns. It will be good for Luke to learn to bend," said Holly.

"So says the woman whose fiancé doesn't even know the definition of 'bend.' I'm anxious to see how sticking to your guns goes with Jess." Arlie laughed again, the sound softened by affection.

"You and Jess both seem so happy," said Cass.

"We are." Holly grinned at her. "At least I

am, and unless Mr. Strong-and-Silent-Type says otherwise, we're going to assume he is, too."

"Has he read your books?" One of Cass's regrets with deciding to use a pseudonym and keep her identity secret from anyone outside of family was that she was unable to discuss her books or the writing thereof with anyone she knew other than an online writers' group.

"He says he hasn't, but every now and then he'll let slip a reference that makes me think he has. Something he wouldn't have known unless he'd been between the pages." Holly steered her bicycle into the rack at the library and dismounted more quickly than either of her companions.

"Like that you made the hero in one of your contemporary romances a veterinarian?" It was Cass's favorite of Holly's early books, the story in which she'd found herself as a character and wondered if her old friend was trying to tell her something.

Holly stopped for a moment, meeting Cass's eyes. "Did you see it? The message for you?"

Cass nodded. "But I never intended to come back here. I didn't think I'd ever see anyone from the lake again. I did write you a letter," she admitted, "but I never mailed it."

She thought that sometime soon they would ask why she'd left the lake and never come back. They'd want to know why she'd never responded to the messages sent through her grandparents for the first year or so after she'd gone. Early the past spring, Sandy had emailed her.

They want to see you. I feel terrible saying I don't know where you are when I do.

Cass had demurred. But the orchard, Aunt Zoey and custody of her little sister had made her realize coming back had progressed from an unconfessed longing to a need.

Especially for Royce, who in a growing-up time much like Cass's own, had never had a year at the lake.

She could see the questions in her friends' eyes, in the looks they exchanged, but neither of them spoke until they were at the door of the library.

"Jack left me at the end of that summer, once he knew for sure I was going to live and would be all right even if I was different," said Arlie calmly, her hand on the library door's old-fashioned handle. "Guilt drove his life and his absence left a big, gaping hole in mine for sixteen years. We're good now and we're happy. We know we can never get back people or time we lost, but what we learned and what we gained during that time we were apart—like his son, Charlie, who I tell everyone was my real motive for marrying Jack—they're the reasons for the good and the happy."

"Mama, who still bosses us around even though we're in our thirties, was pretty insistent on us letting things go when Jack came back to the lake." Holly smiled. "As usual, she was right."

Cass smiled back at her and Arlie, and they went inside.

She'd never had a book signing, although some of the authors she knew online had taken part in some. Except for a few who were far more extroverted than most of the group, they hadn't enjoyed them.

Holly did. Her talk lasted a half hour, with ten minutes of prepared remarks and the other twenty spent on questions and answers and her request from the audience to help her brainstorm a story. Cass found herself laughing and tossing out ideas with the dozen or so women who were there.

When the talk was over, Holly sat behind the table full of books and signed and dedicated copies for everyone who asked.

"Let's ride while she's doing that," Arlie suggested. "It's her hour with readers and I never like to get in her way. She always ends up introducing me and talking more about me than about her book."

"Great idea." Cass mouthed, "Break a leg," to Holly and followed Arlie out of the old building. "That was fun."

"It always is," Arlie agreed, pushing off. "You want to ride around the lake?"

"Sure."

If they'd been walking instead of riding, they would have been sauntering. It was a beautiful day to take their time. Birds serenaded them from overhead and a few brilliantly colored leaves floated down around them as they rode. "I wonder how they know it's time to change and go," said Cass, "when most of the leaves are still summer green."

Arlie laughed. "You sound like Holly. Are you sure you're not a writer?" She braked suddenly, stopping to stare at Cass. "You were, weren't you? You and Holly started the writers' club in school."

"Write Now. Yes, we did." Cass kept riding. Remembering those perfect days was almost painful in the pleasure of it, but for the warm, wonderful moment under the sycamore trees on Lake Road, she allowed herself to do just that, with no thought of all that happened later. "There were, what, ten of us?"

Arlie pedaled hard to catch up. "I think so, although I wasn't one. Jed Whitcomb was one, and he owns and edits the newspaper now—the twice-a-week one here on the lake. Dorothy Shepherd is a reporter for the *Indianapolis Star*. I don't remember who else was in it, do you?"

"Sam was, but only because we were dating and we thought it was romantic. Linda Saylors was." The name caught in Cass's throat and she had to take a couple of deep breaths. *Oh, Lin, I'm so sorry.*

"Oh, she was. She was the editor of the yearbook, too—the first junior at the time to ever hold that position."

"She was good." And beautiful. And so very nice. All the things Cass hadn't been. Yet she was the one who'd died.

"What a loss it was." Arlie's voice, always

husky, thickened. "Do you think about the wreck a lot, Cass?" It was the closest anyone had come to asking why she'd left the way she had. "Do you wish you'd stayed here?"

She didn't even consider lying or avoiding the questions. "Every day. Every single day."

"OKAY, I THINK maybe I was—" Luke looked out over the grapevines behind Zoey's house because it was the easiest way to avoid Cass's eyes, and went on "—wrong."

"Yowzer!" Seth's voice came from behind him. "Hey, Roycie, my big brother just admitted he was wrong. Somebody needs to call the radio station and—oomph." He doubled over when Luke smacked him flat-handed across his hard-earned washboard abs.

Cass tried not to laugh, but failed miserably. "Did you seriously think he wouldn't grab that and run with it?"

"No, I seriously thought there was no one around to hear me except you. What was I thinking? This is Grand Central Station Orchard, is it not?" Luke was laughing, too, although the color in his cheeks revealed his embarrassment. He gestured at where his brother and her sister were strolling toward the apple barn. "Truly, I thought they were on the wagon headed back to unload."

"Well, do go on," she invited, joining him to walk toward the store and turning halfway around to wave at Zoey where she was planting chrysanthemums around the back porch. "I'm always interested in hearing when a man is wrong. It so seldom happens, you know."

"Well, yeah, I do know, because I'm not sure it's *ever* happened to me before." He grinned at her and flipped the bill of the visor she wore at the orchard.

"Well, that sounds more like it." It was so much fun talking to him like this, feeling comfortable and easy despite their disagreement on—so far—virtually everything. She wasn't sure she'd felt this level of camaraderie with Tony in nearly fifteen years of marriage.

He sighed heavily. "As I was saying before my brother interrupted and I'm sure your sister encouraged him, I'm still not sure a coffee shop is going to be a successful venture. But if we're going to try it, I have no business steamrolling you to do things my way in the process. We'll put it where you think it should go, furnish it how you like. I will undoubtedly give my opinion, whether you want to hear it or not, but you should feel free to ignore me or even tell me to go do something terrible to myself if you feel pushed. I tend to micromanage and often such intervention is neither wanted nor needed."

"Are you sure?" If he was going to be gracious, she could be, too. "I know the orchard was running just fine before I came along." She hadn't seen or heard any evidence of him micromanaging it, either, but she wasn't going to tell him that right now.

"I'm sure."

"Then, would you like to go shopping with me?"

"Shopping? I have sisters. And a mother. So, no, I never want to go shopping."

"This means then that whatever Zoey and I come back with, you're not going to complain?"

"I didn't say that exactly."

"Okay. Planning session, then. Do you want to do that?"

"That I'm good with." He looked at his watch. "Seth and Royce are going somewhere tonight, so we have no custodial responsibilities between six and ten. If you'll come over,

I'll cook steaks on the grill and we can make some plans. What do you say?"

"What should I bring?"

"Salad from the deli at the bulk foods store?"

"I can do that."

They arrived at the door to the store. Luke left her to go to the barn and she went inside to replace the woman behind the counter, drawing in a deep breath to enjoy the scents of apples and spices that filled the room.

She loved the orchard. And Aunt Zoey.

And she was liking Luke Rossiter a little more than she thought was probably good for her.

"IT'S NOT AS if you've never dated. What is your problem?" Seth moved over to share the bathroom mirror, looking pained.

"I don't do relationships, and that's what dinner at the house feels like." Luke frowned, pushing Seth. "My biggest problem is sharing a bathroom that's only big enough for one really skinny person."

"That's your fault. You need to finish the one in the hallway."

That was true, and as soon as he had time, he would. For now, Luke and Seth were sharing the master suite's bathroom. While it did boast two sinks, the room wasn't big enough for two oversized men.

He concentrated on combing his hair, reminding himself of his little brother with that very concentration. Usually, he brushed it back and put on a cap. Speaking of Seth, he needed to make something clear. Perfectly so. "It's not a date. It's a business meeting. And if you tell Mom I'm dating someone and get her hopes up, you're going back to Detroit forever."

His brother snorted derisively. "You don't do business meetings outside of business hours, and you have them at the orchard back in the coffee corner or in your office if you can find a clean spot for someone to sit."

"Usually. This is…different." So different he'd stopped by It's De-Lovely after work and gotten his hair cut. He'd put on clean jeans and a blue button-up shirt he wore with the tails out.

He'd even left the orchard early, putting Lovena in charge until closing time. She'd smiled and agreed, her eyes twinkling, and he'd felt the color rise in his face. He'd always read in books that blushing was a girl thing. It didn't seem especially fair that he did it all the time and Rachel wouldn't know a blush if someone poured it down her cheeks. One more thing to hold against her.

When Cass arrived, waving Seth off when she got out of her SUV, Luke thought he wasn't the only one who'd dressed up a little. She was wearing a sundress—not unusual on the lake, but uncommon for her. She always wore capris or, on cool days, what his sisters called yoga pants. They just looked like close-fitting sweats to him and they looked sleek on Cass.

The dress, though, accessorized with strappy red sandals and some sparkly jewelry he'd have bet the farm Royce had forced on her, looked even better than sleek. Her hair had grown in the two weeks she'd been here, and she'd added some blond streaks—or the sun had—that gave her an added glow. She was still slim, but she looked strong. He thought she was.

They talked while they ate, filling in blanks about each other. She was surprised he'd not only played football in high school and college, he'd also been in drama and had played the guitar most of his life.

"That's amazing." Her eyes were wide. "I wanted to be in drama, but when I couldn't even memorize Bible verses in Sunday school, I kind of knew there was no hope. I did help with makeup, though."

"I was Atticus Finch in *To Kill a Mockingbird*," he said. "I wore the glasses and the suit, but we didn't color my hair. Even though it was a great part and the play went well, I kept thinking about Gregory Peck the whole time and knowing I was profaning perfection."

She laughed. "I loved that movie. And the book, too. Our class read it the year I was here."

"What were you in? Besides volleyball, where I heard you set a record for kills that still stands. Seth said your picture was in the athletic hall at school."

"Besides doing makeup for drama and playing the clarinet—really badly—in the marching band, I was in a writers' group."

"Write Now?"

"Yes. Is it still there?" She looked surprised, but pleased.

"Yeah. Seth is in it. Holly helps with it sometimes."

"How many kids are involved?"

"You'd have to ask Seth. Quite a few, I think, for as small a high school as Miniagua is."

"I helped start it."

"Really?" He raised his eyebrows. "Do you still write?"

It was her turn to blush. "Sometimes," she said briefly, and turned her attention back to her food. "So, do you want to help look for tables and chairs? Oh, and kitchen equipment. An espresso machine is a huge part of the investment."

He blinked, not sure how or why the subject change had happened so abruptly. "No, actually, that's a place you probably don't need my opinion. Won't you just get stuff from a supply house?"

"Nope. Auctions and attics. And antiques stores."

"Lots of them around."

"I'll go to Indy to get the coffee machines. Everything other than that can be either bought or constructed locally. I think Aunt Zoey will like helping to put it together, don't you?"

"I think she'll love it."

They ate in silence for a few minutes, more comfortable than he would have expected, then she asked, "When did you and Jill get married?"

"While we were in our first year of college. We were going to wait, but when we found out it was pretty much a sure thing we weren't going to have a long life together, we went ahead. We were lucky that our parents supported the decision because we were so broke meals and gas for the car were sometimes out of reach. Jill quit school so she could spend what time she had doing what she wanted, but I kept going." He stopped, remembering, and smiled. "I saw a movie once—I think it was about Lou Gehrig— where his wife said she wouldn't give up a minute of either the bad or the good, although that's not how she said it. I wouldn't, either."

"Is that why you're still single?"

"I'm still single because I haven't met anyone else I want to spend my life with." *And I don't intend to, ever again.*

Sitting across the table from Cass, feeling that same connection he'd felt from the moment they'd met, it didn't seem impossible anymore that it would happen again. She was nothing like Jill, but he was pretty sure his wife would have liked her.

He knew he did.

CHAPTER SEVEN

"I THOUGHT YOU didn't want them to match." Zoey looked at the tables and chairs in the back room of the antiques store in downtown Peru. "You have eight tables and twenty-four chairs here, and they're all exactly the same style and color. I'll bet they even have matching wads of gum stuck to their undersides."

"I know." Cass leaned in to whisper the price in her aunt's ear.

"Oh." Zoey straightened. "Well, then, exactly alike is good, isn't it?"

"Certainly is." Cass counted in her head. "The cabinetry is being put in today and tomorrow, the electricity and plumbing are already done. I am so excited!"

"How many names are entered?"

Cass and Luke had hung a poster in the orchard store, offering a prize to the person who named the coffee shop. They were having an employee luncheon the next day at Just One of Those Things and choosing the winner from the top three names picked by Zoey, Luke and Cass.

"Thirtysome. There were over fifty entries, but there were a bunch of repeats."

Zoey leaned in to whisper again. "What's your favorite? I won't tell."

"You won't tell because you won't know." Cass bumped shoulders with her. "What's yours?"

"Hmph. None of your business."

They laughed together and went into the front room of the store to arrange delivery.

Cass was amazed by how quickly the coffee shop had come together. The carpenters they'd hired had worked long hours on sanding and finishing the plank floor and making countertops to fit the random cabinetry she'd found in shops offering scratch-and-dent cupboards. Electricians had gotten them up to code and gained them plenty of outlets and switches in a single day. A one-day painting party complete with pizza had gotten the walls painted in the purple-and-sage color scheme that had horrified Luke into silence until he saw the final result. After that, he'd told everyone it was all his idea.

"You're having fun, aren't you?" asked Zoey, when they were heading back to the lake.

Cass didn't hesitate. "I am, the most fun I've had since I was here in high school. And Royce is ecstatic." She dipped her head, keeping her eyes on the road. "When I think about it, though, I keep waiting for something to come along and stop the whole project in its tracks."

"I know the feeling." Zoey sipped from her coffee from the shop they'd just gone to. "When it does, honey, just start up again and keep on going." She frowned. "I hope you ordered better go-cups than this."

"I did."

It was hard to think about the shoe dropping. Cass and Royce had both settled into the farmhouse as if they'd always lived there. Zoey was delighted with the company and they were just as happy to help maintain the big house. Royce had even mastered the riding lawnmower and the Weedwacker. Cass, being mechanically challenged in all avenues of her life, had avoided them both.

In the two weeks since they'd moved, Zoey, Cass and Luke had met nearly every morning after Seth and Royce left for school. They made business plans and parceled out the labor.

There were, of course, a few things that

worried Cass. She was happy, but she'd learned never to trust fate to hands other than her own.

Royce and Seth had become troublingly close, and even though Cass reiterated the necessary talks Royce had already had with Damaris, she still worried about her little sister. She had married Tony when she was eighteen—it wasn't something she wanted Royce to consider, no matter how nice a kid Seth was. Tony had been a nice kid, too.

Luke was wonderful. He was handsome and fun and Cass had never in her life enjoyed talking to someone as much as she liked spending conversation time with him. But they'd gone from just conversation to real dating. Sort of. Or as close to it as two people who weren't interested in dating could become.

Then there was the Damaris thing. "Don't worry," she'd told both Cass and Royce, "if you don't always hear from me. Things are weird here."

The sisters were both military brats—they knew about weird things. They both worried.

It had been nearly a week since they'd heard from her.

Cass also worried because it was becoming increasingly hard to keep her alter ego a secret. She wasn't even sure, if she were pinned down to telling the absolute truth, why it *was* still a secret, but it was. She guessed she needed for Cassandra G. Porter to be safe at all costs, because she was the only thing in Cass's life she'd never lost.

Then again, she knew that Zoey hadn't gone anywhere. She'd never lost Royce, either, because she'd never really had her. Now that her little sister had appropriated such a huge chunk of her heart, she couldn't bear the idea of not having her in her life.

Sometimes at night, when she'd stopped thinking about Luke, she'd have pipe dreams about Damaris joining them at the lake. There were still two empty bedrooms upstairs at the farmhouse. That way, Cass wouldn't have to give Royce up when the girl's mother came home.

Not only was secrecy becoming difficult, but the two thousand words Cass-as-Cassandra demanded from herself every day had become less than half that. She'd never missed a deadline in her life, but the one looming was…well, looming.

"What is it with me?" she muttered to herself that night, when the house was silent save for the clicking of her computer keys. "Can I only write when I'm miserable? Come back to me, Lucy. There's a perfectly good murder just waiting for you to jump in and solve it."

But her trusted protagonist was silent, sitting thoughtfully in the vintage MG convertible she'd driven from the first page of the series. Thinking about cancer recurrences and harm coming to loved ones and being alone. And about a handsome man with thick brown hair and chocolate brown eyes.

Where had *that* come from?

But she knew where it had come from, and with a sigh and a soft whiff of laughter, Lucy Garten's creator gave in to the inevitable and provided her heroine with a hero.

"ZOEY'S CHOICE, POUR Barn Brewing Company. Name entered by Arlie Llewellyn and Charlie Llewellyn," Luke read from the paper in front of him. "I think it was a family thing, although Jack suggested Coffee Shop. Needless to say, that didn't make the final cut."

The suggestion—or maybe it was Jack's—was met with both cheers and boos. Luke grinned around at the twentysome orchard employees attending the luncheon at Just One of Those Things. "I know. I don't like it, either."

"Well, some of us like it," said Zoey with a sniff.

"So, what's your choice, Luke?" asked Isaac.

"Keep Hot Coffee Room, suggested by Mollie Bender. I thought this was perfect. However, before you cast your vote for this inspired choice, I have to admit that Cass reminded me we're not trying to compete with the tearoom and the 'room' part of that name does sound a little confrontational in that regard."

Neely, the owner of the tearoom, made a sweeping bow as she walked around the long table refilling cups. "We appreciate that. Thanks for keeping him in line, Cass."

Cass waved at her. "It's a hard job—"

"—but somebody's gotta do it," the occupants of the table finished.

Luke tried to look offended. "Okay, final choice, the one Cass picked out. Ground in the Round, in reference to the round barn that houses the shop. This one was entered by Bill Shafer. Neely's going to pass the ballots around. Check your choice and toss them in the basket. She'll count, since Seth suggested

I might cheat." He glowered at his brother. "Which explains why you didn't have a vote in choosing the finalists."

Papers rustled and employees talked among themselves. One asked if he would be fired if he voted against Luke's choice.

"Not fired," said Luke. "Laid off, maybe."

"And brought back with a raise in pay," Cass offered from the other end of the table.

Her comment was met with laughter, Luke's included. His gaze held hers, and it nearly took his breath away. Everyone else kept talking, eating, laughing, but it all went past him without notice—all of his attention was focused on the blue-green eyes smiling into his. He remembered, with a bone-deep ache, being alone with Jill in a room filled with people.

Never again.

He grinned at Cass, but he could tell by the change in her expression that she'd absorbed the momentary change in his mood. *Are you all right?* He could see the silent question in her eyes.

He nodded slightly, his grin softening into a smile meant just for her. *I'm fine.*

For now.

"Votes all in?" He watched as Neely passed a basket.

While they waited for the count, he gave a so-far-this-season report on how things were going at the orchard. Sales were better than anticipated. All the apples were yielding nicely—some better than others—although there was a row of trees near the back that would be cut this year. Their replacements had gone into the ground in spring and were doing well. He still hoped to keep the orchard store open through the winter. The coffee shop would open the next morning, although the sign with its name obviously wouldn't be done yet.

"That's not a problem," Cass assured everyone. "People will just call it the coffee shop anyway."

"Then why did we go through all this naming thing?" asked Royce. "Not that it hasn't been fun, even if my suggestion was ignored. I'm sixteen. People always ignore me."

Everyone either groaned or jeered. Seth patted her back and looked sad.

"A lesson in marketing," Luke said over the sound of laughter. "Like you said, it was fun. It increased awareness that the coffee shop was coming. People who entered suggestions stayed at the orchard longer, which translated into purchasing more things or eating another apple dumpling."

"Got a winner," Neely announced, bringing Luke a sheet of paper with numbers on it. "It was by a landslide, I might add."

He took the paper, put on Zoey's green plaid reading glasses—which he didn't need—and made a show of trying to read the results.

"From this day forth," he said sadly, "the coffee shop will be known as Ground in the Round. Congratulations, Cass."

"Why, thank you." She got to her feet and sketched a curtsy, beaming at the occupants of the table. "I appreciate your votes."

"And you'll pay us later, right?" said Seth.

"Yes." She met Luke's eyes again, and he put on a look of outrage. "When they told me how much you offered, I just upped the ante a little."

Zoey nodded wisely. "Sound business practice."

Everyone dispersed after dessert. Isaac, Mary, Seth and Royce rode back to the orchard in Isaac's parents' buggy. Zoey drove her car. She offered Luke and Cass a ride, but didn't argue when they demurred, choosing to walk the two miles.

"That was nice." Cass waved at Neely as they left the building. "Do you do that often? Have meals with the employees?"

"Not often, no. We start the season with a picnic and end it with a harvest supper that's basically a pitch-in. We give bonuses then and say goodbye to our seasonal employees. Most of them return for the next season, but not all of them and not every year. We have a Christmas party for the skeleton crew that works year-round."

"Do you ever have to fire anyone?"

He flinched. "I have before, but I admit they almost have to cause bodily harm to someone else before I can make myself do it."

Cass chuckled, the sound coming soft from her throat. "An orchard manager who's afraid of heights and doesn't like firing people. What a combination."

"Oh, there's more." He leaned in close to her and admitted in a stage whisper, "Unless they're wrapped up in pie or dumplings or pressed into hard cider or a few other manifestations, I don't much like apples, either."

Her laugh rang out then, bouncing off the lake. They walked on toward the orchard, their hands swinging between them and touching often enough that Luke finally caught and held hers.

"Keep Cold Orchard," she said, looking up at a sign that assured them they were going in the right direction. "It was Country Club Orchard when I was a kid. Where did the new name come from? I've meant to ask you that a dozen times, but always forget."

"Zoey came up with it. It was before I came to the lake to live, and that's been eight years. It came from a Robert Frost poem." Finding that out had given him a new appreciation for Frost. "Are you excited about the opening?"

She nodded. "Probably more than I should be. My husband was an entrepreneur and I was there for more business openings than I can remember, but it wasn't the same. I was never invested, and I don't mean financially—my heart was never involved and now I'm afraid it is. I knew I'd never get to know the people who worked in the places we started, never even get attached to the product. Ground in the Round is different. Everything else was already here, but this particular part of Keep Cold Orchard is my baby."

Her eyes were shining and he thought

maybe her heart was in them. If he didn't watch himself, his heart was going to get involved, too.

"So, yes," she said, "I am excited. Are you going to be there for the first pot in the morning?"

"I wouldn't miss it. Half caff. One cream and two sugars, light on the cream. You'll have that, right?"

"Even worse." And now she sounded a little breathless. "I have it memorized."

SOMETIMES YOU JUST know things.

When the reporter from the lake's biweekly tabloid-size newspaper interviewed her at the end of her first week as Ground in the Round's chief barista, he'd asked her what made her want to serve coffee in a barn in a small community in Indiana.

She'd said, "It's a new venture and a new *ad*venture. What's not to like?" But in her heart, she'd just known.

Before adopting Cassandra G. Porter as her alter ego, she'd always worked from home and liked it—there was something to be said for not getting dressed until noon—but writing in coffee shops had given her a longing to be the Cass Gentry she'd never been. To be Cassandra.

After a week in Ground in the Round, with her feet sore and virtually every top she owned coffee stained, she was both jubilant and exhausted. Her only concern was that she hadn't gotten very many new words written and she knew she needed to cut back her hours in the shop. This would be easy— the other baristas were willing and eager to work more.

But it was so much fun. Learning the combinations and remembering who drank what. Writing names on cups.

"You know," Zoey worried, as they ate dinner together on the last Thursday in September, "you might be compromising your health. Should you be running at full tilt the way you are?"

Arlie's friend Kari Ross, who had become Cass's gynecologist, had voiced the same concern a few days earlier. "I know you feel good and that your scans were good, but there are still fragile places there. It won't hurt at all to nurse them along for a little bit."

But what if a little bit is all I have? It was something else she never said aloud, although it was sometimes difficult to quiet the inner voice that spoke the words into the dark silence of night.

"Aunt Zoey, is there a room I can use as an office?" she asked abruptly. Although everyone in her family knew about Cassandra and the *Mysteries on the Wabash* books, they never asked her questions. "I'm going to fall too far behind if I don't get busy."

Her aunt looked ready to object, but she didn't. "There is," she said. "The bedroom beside yours or the sunroom back here—either one would work and we can do anything to them you like or need. There's the maid's apartment off the other side of the kitchen, too, but I'd rather keep that as the guest room. But why don't you just take your laptop to the coffee shop with you and write there?"

"Because then they'll know." Cass sipped from her wine, willing the beverage to keep panic at bay.

"They won't know anything you don't tell them, and who is 'they,' anyway? Do you go up to every customer who's using a computer and ask them what they're doing?"

"Well, no, but…" She stopped. Why wouldn't it work? She'd written at least half her books at corner tables. What would be different about it being a table in her own shop?

And if someone found out, so what? She didn't have to worry about embarrassing Tony or her father anymore with what they'd called her "little stories"—they'd both removed themselves almost completely from her life. She was back at the lake, not hiding from that happy year in her past anymore.

"You have a very good point." She nodded, keeping her voice brisk. "I'll take my laptop to work with me."

"*Does* anyone know?" Zoey asked.

"I don't think so, unless it would be Holly. I picked myself out in one of her books immediately. It wouldn't surprise me if she latched onto the cheerleader with a prosthetic foot in one of mine."

"Is your cheerleader a romance writer of Italian descent?"

"No. I didn't want to be *too* obvious."

"Of course not." Zoey laughed. "You can still have an office here in the house. There's plenty of room. It will be yours one day anyway."

"Let's not even go there." Cass frowned at her and got up from the table, gathering her dishes.

"Leave it." Zoey fussed at her. "You cooked. I'll clean up. Besides, unless I miss my guess, our business partner will be here any minute asking you if you want to go get ice cream."

Luke's distinctive rap came on the door at that moment, and the women laughed as Cass went to open it. He called, "Evening, Zoey," and pulled Cass onto the porch, wrapping his arms around her. "This is probably wrong on so many different levels, but I can't care right now. It's a kissing kind of day." The last words were murmured against her lips, and all she could do was swallow a sigh.

They'd avoided physical contact beyond the occasional one-armed hug, even though they'd talked all around the subject. The conversation always ended with the assertion that neither of them was interested in dating anyone, much less someone they were in business with. If they got a little hormonal, well, that was just the way it was. They were adults, after all—they could handle themselves. Besides everything else, they were in charge of two teenagers whose hormones made their own look like rank amateurs.

But all those sensible conclusions were before Cass stood on the back porch in Luke's arms. She thought she could still feel the day's sun in his skin, taste the sweetness of the cherry lollipops that were his guilty pleasure and see an expression in his eyes she hadn't seen...ever. He was taller than she was, but not that much; meeting his gaze meant only the slightest upward tilt of her head. When her arms went up over his shoulders, she didn't feel as if she was clutching him for balance. She just liked touching him.

It had been such a long time since she'd wanted to touch someone or had wanted someone to touch her. His hands were firm at her waist, his body solid against hers, but it was his lips, warm and welcoming on hers, that made an ordinary evening into something star-spangled and joyful.

She came to believe, in the space of a few minutes, that the kissing kind of day was the best kind of all.

CHAPTER EIGHT

"WHAT DO YOU THINK?" Luke held his double-dip chocolate cone in one hand, Cass's slender fingers in the other. "Business is wicked good at the orchard, and you're proving me more wrong about the coffee shop on a daily basis." In certain ways his life had started anew the day her red Equinox pulled into the orchard's parking lot.

He frowned, trying to sort out how he felt about that. He didn't want a new life.

"Think about what?" She swirled her tongue around her scoop of butter pecan. Swallowed as if it were ambrosia in her mouth. She licked a drop off her bottom lip slowly, delicately, then slurped the ice cream into a point she promptly bit off with even, white teeth.

He watched her, unable to look away. Only when she looked questioningly at him did he realize she'd asked him something. What was it?

Oh. "How do you like the way things are going?" A chill rippled up his spine with the words and he wished he could take them back. Nothing like tempting fate. Thinking about a new life was more than enough of that. "At the orchard, I mean." Not about the interlude on the porch. That was still too new. Too fresh.

Too exciting.

"I like it." She smiled at him, but the expression wore caution around its edges. "But I…" She stopped.

From a boat on the lake came the sound of the Eagles singing "Peaceful Easy Feeling," and Luke chuckled. "Did I just interrupt that 'Peaceful Easy Feeling' they're singing about? You don't roll that way, do you?"

She didn't answer, and they walked on. Eating their ice cream. Their fingers still linked. But with a distance between them that he'd have described as a chasm if he'd been trying to use his junior high vocabulary words.

What had happened since the interlude on Zoey's back porch, when they'd found what Rachel would have called "kindred spiritedness"? When they'd been so close that Cass's heartbeat had kept time with his.

They reached the park bench beside the dock outside Anything Goes and sat down. Only then did Cass speak. "I guess I don't. In my experience, there's always a shoe about to drop somewhere."

It was a feeling he didn't understand. Even losing Jill hadn't been a surprise. It had been horrible in every way and they'd fought against its inevitability with the persistence of the very young. But they'd known it was coming. Only when Jill had said, "Let it go, Luke, and let's just have a good time," had they given up.

And what a good time they'd had. Even after ten years, he could relish that last year of equal parts pleasure and pain. Just like in that movie, he wouldn't have given up either.

He'd become a partner in the orchard before his other job had ended. The former manager had been ready to retire so that Luke had never missed a day's work. He'd had to do some financial scrambling, but more than three years after losing his job, he was better off than he'd been. He'd never be rich, which was fine with him, but he was comfortable, and he liked that.

Having the second bathroom finished would be nice, too, but even with a few thousand dollars and some travertine tile still to go, he knew it would be done one day and that the quality of the finished product wouldn't be a surprise.

But how he'd felt on the porch and how he felt a few minutes ago when the gulf had spread between them—those were both unexpected. And maybe dangerous, at least to his peace of mind.

"What do you do," he asked slowly, "when the shoe drops?"

"Oh." Her voice sounded reedy. "It depends."

"On?" He could tell she didn't want to talk about it. Zoey's voice thinned when she was finished with a subject, too, and her chin did the same upward tilt as Cass's.

Cass laughed, not very convincingly. "On whether it's a combat boot or a flip-flop."

He nodded, finding sense in that. "What about a nice, comfortable loafer? How do you react then?" He kept his voice slow, with a smile in it. Just because he was feeling a little nervous himself, he didn't want to scare her away from the conversation.

She was silent again, for a long moment. When she spoke, her voice was quiet. "I haven't had many loafer drops, to tell the truth. Usually it's the combat boots, in which case I turn tail and run."

"So." He stared out at the lake's glassy surface and crossed his ankle over his knee. "I hope there's no shoe this time."

"Me, too." But her voice told him she knew better.

He put his arm around her, drawing her into his side. She raised her head as he lowered his, and their lips met in a sweet version of an age-old dance.

"What's between you and me doesn't have to do with the orchard or the coffee shop," he whispered. "It's courtship simply for the pleasure of it. Nothing more and nothing less. No promises, no demands. No permanency." He kissed her again, treasuring her sweet response. "No shoes."

HOT CHOCOLATE BEFORE bed became a habit for Cass and Royce with the cooling evenings of late September. They sliced and shared different varieties of apples and talked until sleep beckoned. Sometimes Zoey joined them, but more often it was just the two of them. It was one of Cass's favorite times of day.

"I love school here," said Royce, filling her backpack while Cass made the cocoa. "It's so friendly. There are cliques, I guess, but no one cares all that much."

"That's nice." Cass thought back to the terror of changing schools—even with eight moves in twelve years, it had never gone away. "You've been okay with making friends, right?"

Royce spent more time with the kids who worked at the orchard than with anyone else, although she had attended a couple of parties. Cass was happy with her sister's social life, but she wasn't sure how the girl's mother would feel about it—it wasn't anything they'd discussed at length. When she came home, Damaris would take Royce back to California and to the life they shared there. It was a good life, but it was different from being at the lake and going to one of the smallest high schools in the state.

"Oh, sure." Royce sipped her chocolate and licked away the resultant mustache in a gesture so innocent, Cass knew the unreasonable yearning to protect her little sister from all pain forever. "But Seth and Mary and Isaac are my best friends, even though Mary and Isaac don't go to school anymore." The Amish didn't usually finish high school, a concept that had shocked Royce.

"What's your favorite thing at school?" Cass remembered going to the Gallagher house after school. Holly's mother and Arlie's stepmother, Gianna, always had snacks ready, and then she'd sit at the table with the girls and everyone would talk about their day. No story was too slight, no hurt feelings too unimportant, no victory too small to share. Cass's grandmother had been too ill and her own mother mostly uninterested, so Cass had kept both her victories and her losses to herself. She had known, if she ever had kids, that she would sit with them at the kitchen table and listen to them talk.

This chance with her sister, complete with hot chocolate and sliced apples, wasn't one she was giving up.

"A few years ago the senior class project was that they developed this everybody-needs-a-friend program where if someone was sitting alone in the cafeteria, one of the seniors would sit with them and make sure they were okay and, you know, just be their friend," said Royce. "It's not a formal thing anymore, but now people just do it on their own. It's not just seniors and it's not required, but it is so cool how many people do it."

"That *is* cool."

"Yeah. Today, I got the chance to do it. To be a friend, I mean. I just said, 'Hey, how you doing? Can you believe it's raining again?' and before I knew it, this girl was crying really hard. I took her outside with a whole wad of napkins from the table and we just sat there on one of those benches in front of the school until she was okay again. I didn't say hardly anything at all. When we went back in, the guidance counselor was waiting—I don't know how she knew." Royce shrugged, but her eyes were shining. "I still don't have any idea what she was upset about, but I do know I did the right thing. That can happen anywhere, not just little schools in the middle of nowhere, but it was one of the best feelings I ever had. I saw her later…the girl, I mean, and she thanked me for listening. I asked her if she wanted to go to the movies Sunday afternoon." She paused, reaching up to stroke away the tear that slid down her cheek. "It's a gift, isn't it, when you know you've done something good for someone else?"

"It is." Cass set down her cup and leaned to hug Royce close. "You're a gift, too, Sister With-Good-Hair. I'm way proud of you." She tousled the good hair that rested against her shoulder. "Your mom will be, too."

Royce sniffed. "Do you think she's okay, Cass?"

"Yes." Cass hugged her again. "We're military brats, remember? We know weird." It wasn't the first time she'd said it over the past week, when they'd heard nothing from Damaris except a short, cryptic I'm okay email. "If there was anything wrong, Dad would know and he would call." She was certain of that, at least.

"I know." Royce blew her nose and reached for her cup. "I'm glad to be with you, but don't tell anyone I said that. Okay?"

"Okay. And I won't tell them I'm glad to have you with me, either."

Later, lying in the middle of the queen-size bed in her room, Cass thought back over dinner with Zoey, ice cream and kisses with Luke and the chocolate-and-apples time with Royce. She'd never really considered the quality of her days having anything to do with food and drink, but this had definitely been a delicious day.

SHE DIDN'T RECOGNIZE the ringtone, which meant it was probably a robocall from somewhere on the other side of the world. Why else would anyone call at—Cass opened one eye and peered at the screen of her phone—3:17 a.m.? Surely even robocallers knew people slept, didn't they? It wasn't that she begrudged them making a living, but she wished they'd do it during daytime hours.

She connected, muttered something and disconnected, shoving the telephone under her pillow.

It rang again.

"Cass!" The voice, strident and familiar, reached her ears before she could hang up again. She sat up in bed, reaching for the lamp switch and getting it first time.

"Sir?" Even at 3:18 a.m. she addressed Major Ken Gentry as sir. If she were wider awake, she'd probably think there was something inherently sick about that. He was her father, for heaven's sake. "Is something wrong, sir?"

"It's Damaris."

"Oh, no." Not Damaris. While it was true enough that things were weird with the military, female officers didn't die, did they? Especially ones who sat at desks even when they were in the desert. "Is she all right?" Cass had to push the words out, knowing how stupid they were. Of course her stepmother wasn't all right—Ken wouldn't be calling if she was.

"She will be. I'm not entertaining any other possibility."

Cass wasn't in the mood to massage her father's god complex. Her words came quick and sharp. "She's hurt? Where is she?"

"The vehicle she was in made contact with an IED. Pure carelessness on someone's part."

"Sir, how badly is she hurt?" She made no effort to contain her impatience. The man was an unfeeling jackass. On his good days.

"Broken bones. A few burns. She'll be fine. It'll just take some time."

"Were there other casualties?"

"What?" He sounded startled by the question.

"Were others hurt?"

"I suppose so."

Cass sighed. "Where is Damaris?"

"At Walter Reed. She just flew in today. I'm here, too. I'll stay until she can be released for rehab. I have friends here to stay with, ones I served with in the old days."

"When did it happen?"

"Four days ago."

"Four days? You're calling at 3:17 in the

morning after *four days?*" Her voice raised so that she thought it might have rattled the windowpanes a little bit. She was good with that. "Sir, she's Royce's mother—don't you think you might have let her know?"

Her bedroom door flew open. Royce stood there in her pajamas, her eyes wide. "Mom?"

Cass beckoned her sister to join her on the bed and turned the phone on speaker.

"I didn't want to let either of you know until I was sure Damaris would survive. I'm sure of that now. She's on the mend."

"Do we need to come there?"

"What for?"

"Once again, sir, this is Royce's mother you're talking about. She might want to see her daughter." Or maybe not. Marynell wouldn't have wanted Cass—she'd scarcely wanted her around even when she was dying.

"Well, she does, but…here, she wants to talk to you."

A second later, Damaris's voice was there. "Are you girls all right?"

"We're fine," said Cass. "What about you? Why are you awake? Do you want us to come there?"

"No. Your father's right on that one." Damaris sounded grudgingly enough that Cass and Royce grinned at each other. Anyone who knew Ken Gentry very well didn't like for him to be right—he enjoyed it far too much. "I'm awake because no one sleeps in hospitals. Royce, are you there?"

"Hi, Mom." Royce's voice squeaked. Cass saw her chin tremble and firm. When she spoke again, her voice was stern and not at all adolescent. "You do know you're grounded after this, right?"

Muffled laughter came from the other end of the connection.

"The nurse who's in here agrees with you," said Damaris dryly. "But listen to me, girls. I have some heavy-duty rehab ahead of me. Royce, are you all right staying with Cass until I'm on my feet again? Cass, I should have asked you first—is it okay if Royce stays with you until then?"

"Actually—" Cass had to clear her throat. She ran a hand through her sister's messy hair where it had come to rest in her lap and picked up the phone, tapping the button that took it off speaker. "Actually, I'd like her to stay the whole school year. And maybe instead of going to Sacramento to rehab, you could come here. Aunt Zoey has plenty of room, and she'd be glad to have you stay with us."

Royce sat up, staring at her. "Shouldn't we ask first?" she whispered.

"I'll ask tomorrow," Cass mouthed, then spoke aloud. "It would be good for all of us, Damaris. Before we know it, we'll have you selling apples and pouring cappuccino with the best of them."

"I'll think about it," Damaris promised. She sounded tired. "I'll try to talk to you tomorrow, okay? Your dad will call or you can call him."

They exchanged goodbyes and hung up. Cass and Royce exchanged a silent gaze. "We won't sleep now, right?" said Cass. She knew she wouldn't, but she had hopes for Royce.

"Maybe after some more of that chocolate."

They made their way to the kitchen as quietly as they could; nevertheless, Zoey was there before them. "He called me first," she said flatly. "Honestly, your father's had four wives and the woman he calls when he doesn't know what to do is the one he jilted before he married the first one—what's wrong with that picture?"

She set a mug of cocoa in front of Royce, cupping her cheek. "Are you okay, baby?"

"I am, but I'm scared, too. What if Mom's hiding something?"

"Even if she'd wanted to, Dad wouldn't." Cass accepted a cup of tea from her aunt, breathing in the comforting scent of bergamot before taking a sip. "Compassionate falsehoods aren't in his wheelhouse."

"That's sure true. Mom said he used to call you Olive Oyl." Royce looked stricken. "I'm so sorry. I think I must take after him."

"It's okay." And it was. Being forced in front of the mirror by Damaris and Tony had convinced Cass that her only resemblance to Popeye's girlfriend was that she was tall and slim. "He was wrong, and we both know we love it when that happens. What did he call you?"

"He didn't. Sometimes when I'd come home from school, he'd give me this curious look as if he'd forgotten who I was. I think he really did. After he and Mom got divorced, he bent over backward to avoid visitation." Royce grinned, and some color came back into her face. "I think that may have something to do with how you ended up with me."

The way her insides turned to mush almost made Cass roll her own eyes. "Well, then," she said, "I guess I've got something to thank him for, haven't I?"

"Me, too," said Zoey. She sat at the table with them. "I was thinking."

Royce beamed at her. "The last time you said that, we drove all the way to Peru to have ice cream at the East End. Whatever you're thinking, I'm in."

"I'm thinking maybe your mother could come and stay with us. There are very good rehab places close by, and enough of us around to get her there. Rent-a-Wife provides transportation, too. What do you girls think?"

Cass laughed. "I think you're a genius."

"I think you're clairvoyant," said Royce sleepily. "Cass already asked her."

Zoey didn't look surprised. "I'm glad to see the family grow."

Royce took her cup to the sink and rinsed it, kissing the tops of Zoey's and Cass's heads on the way. She left the room, and after a few minutes, Cass found her asleep on the couch. She covered her with a quilt, stroking her silky hair back from her face, and returned to the kitchen. "She's out."

"Which is exactly what I'm going to be." Zoey looked speculatively in her direction. "Going to write?"

Cass nodded. "I'm behind. A couple of

quiet hours will get some words. Whether I like it or not, emotional stress is good for my productivity. I wrote most of one book and did revisions on another during the sixty days Tony's and my divorce took. I wrote another one during chemo."

She set her laptop on the kitchen table, glad she wasn't opening the coffee shop today. There might be time for a nap before she went in later. When the teapot was empty, she made a pot of coffee and wrote without stopping.

Sometimes when she wrote, she thought how odd it was that she was so much more at ease in the persona of her pseudonym than when she was being herself. There was something inherently wrong with that, but she wasn't sure what.

This morning, though, with thoughts of Damaris, Royce and Luke crowding her mind, calm and collected Cassandra was able to take over, clearing a hurdle that would make the next few chapters easier to write.

She didn't hear Luke until he opened the kitchen door and whistled softly. "Everybody asleep?"

When she jumped and turned to look at him, her heartbeat thumping, he raised a hand in greeting. "I knocked," he said, "but you were really concentrating. What's going on?"

She closed her laptop, not ready to share her other identity, and got up to make more coffee. "Nothing, really."

He stopped her as she passed him, holding her in place with a hand on her stomach. Its warmth spread from her center to the ends of her fingers and toes, and she stood still to absorb the comfort—and something else she wasn't ready to identify. He kissed her, and she leaned into it. This would help get through the day.

He released her before she was ready, and held her gaze. "What's going on?" he said again.

Thoughts of the story were going from her mind as if they'd been written in disappearing ink, replaced by visions of Damaris, Royce and her father. She relaxed, her forehead against Luke's shoulder. "The shoe dropped."

CHAPTER NINE

LUKE ENJOYED THE busyness of the orchard in autumn. He never had to worry about where his brother was because he was either at school, playing football or working—there was no time for other options. Luke didn't have time for alternatives, either. He had to admit, as he locked the doors of the apple barn on the second Saturday in October, that this was the first year since Jill's death that he'd been in the market for a social life. Business craziness had always been his friend, but this year he'd enjoyed some respite. Not a lot, but some.

"Remind me one of these days," he'd told Cass that morning, when they'd left Zoey's farmhouse after breakfast, "that I'd like to ask you on a real date."

"Now, that's romantic," she said, veering off toward Ground in the Round. She looked back over her shoulder, her expression flirtatious enough his heart did a strange little bump against his ribs. "But I might say yes."

He watched her go, liking the easy swing of her gait. He thought she might have gained a few much-needed pounds since she'd come to the lake.

She seldom mentioned her illness and had never given it a name, but Zoey had told him it was breast cancer, asking him not to let her work too hard. "She's healthy now, the way I understand it, so I'm trying not to baby her. I just thought you should know," she'd said.

He was glad she'd told him. Not so happy with himself at his gut reaction, his immediate need to pull away before the attachment grew too deep. He'd lost one woman he'd loved—the idea of getting involved with someone else who had a threatening illness made his blood run cold.

They could be friends and partners. That would be enough. The pleasure they'd both found in kissing made him think, before he fell asleep at night, that it probably *wasn't* enough, but it needed to be.

They went to football games together, picked up and dropped off each other's siblings when the other couldn't and ate breakfast together at Zoey's many mornings. They had occasional last-minute business meetings and shared breaks at Ground in the Round.

Usually when the coffee shop wasn't busy, though, she sat with her laptop at a table along the wall near the counter. If he came in, she closed the computer and poured coffee just the way he liked it before coming to meet him.

It bothered him that she felt compelled to hide what she was doing, as if she was afraid he was going to snoop, but he never said anything. It was her business.

After closing the orchard for the night and running a few errands, he went to the coffee shop—open for another hour, at least. They hadn't really solidified its hours yet, but it seldom closed before nine. Cass was behind the counter. "You look tired," he said bluntly.

She fluttered her eyelashes at him. "I'll bet you say that to all the girls."

He noticed that the mascara she started every day with had worn off, but had the sense not to mention it. "I do say that," he admitted heavily, "and it never gets me anywhere. What do you suppose the problem is?"

She handed him the mug with his name on it filled with the half caff he favored. "I can't imagine."

"Got time to sit with me?" he asked. "Our siblings are doing homework at Zoey's so all is well until at least ten o'clock."

Cass scowled, filling her own cup and walking around to join him at a table where she could see everyone in the shop. "They'll eat all of that Black Forest cake she made yesterday. Every little bit including the crumbs."

He laughed. "That's what you think." He lifted a finger. "Hang on."

A few minutes later, he came back in carrying a plastic container. He noticed that Cass had freshened both her mascara and her lipstick in the time he'd been gone. He wondered how she'd done that so fast, but thought maybe that was something else he shouldn't question. There were a few things he'd learned from Rachel and Leah along the way. Not enough to keep him out of trouble, but some.

"Here you go. Got forks?" He set the container on the table and opened it. "I'm sure Zoey meant the big piece for me, but you can have it."

"You're all heart." She fetched two forks and paper napkins and returned to her seat around the corner of the table from him. Two bites later, she closed her eyes in sheer bliss. "Heaven in Tupperware, I swear."

"It is," he agreed. He ate slowly, finding as much pleasure in watching her as he did in the rich dessert, although Zoey's baking was seriously good.

When Cass had finished her piece and one of the last two bites of his, he raised his cup in a toast. "To Zoey and her cake."

She lifted her cup, but before she could clink it against his, he set his down abruptly, digging in the pocket of his jeans for the note Zoey had sent with him. "I was supposed to give you this because her phone was having a tantrum, and I forgot."

Cass unfolded the piece of lined paper and read quickly, frowning. "Damaris will be here either tomorrow or the next day and my father's bringing her." She leaned back in her chair. "We're ready for Damaris, but no one's ever ready for Dad."

Luke thought of his own father and how glad he always was to see him. Seth had mentioned that Royce referred to her dad as a "Great Santini wannabe." Luke and Seth had called theirs Sheriff Taylor from the old *Andy Griffith Show*.

"It will be all right, won't it?" he asked.

"As long as we don't all forget we're grown-ups. I'm not afraid of him anymore and I don't think Royce ever was, but I still call him sir and try never to upset him." She laughed, but there was more bitterness than humor in the sound. "When I got a divorce, Dad flew to California to tell me I was making a terrible mistake and that it was my fault because I didn't understand a man's needs. Even Tony, my ex-husband, was telling him that wasn't the way it was, but there was no stopping him. When I got sick then, almost right on top of the divorce, Dad was pretty convinced it wouldn't have happened if I'd just stayed married."

"Wow. And he and Damaris aren't married anymore, right?"

"No, not for years, but they're both military—it made a difference in their relationship. She outranks him, too. That was a little explosive."

Luke laughed even if he wasn't sure it was funny. "I'll bet it was."

Cass hesitated. "He won't like that you own half the orchard. He'll blame Zoey for selling it to you."

"Why should that matter to him?"

"He wanted to buy the whole thing from

my grandparents when he and my mother were married, then he wanted to buy her half after she and Zoey inherited. He even called me about the orchard after Mother died. He likes to have things, to have people, but he doesn't know what to do with them when he does. Does that make sense?"

"I think so." He lifted his gaze to meet hers. "I don't know you all that well, but I don't think you're like him."

It was the right thing to say. Her turquoise eyes lit. "I've spent thirty-five years trying not to be, so I hope you're right."

"Tell me about Damaris."

"She's like a twenty-years-younger Zoey, I think, although Dad went ballistic when someone mentioned that to him. I'm not sure how they ever developed a relationship, much less a marriage, but they were together for several years." Cass shrugged. "It's a sure thing you can never know what someone else is thinking."

Luke nodded agreement, then something occurred to him. "Is he going to stay at the farmhouse?"

She looked startled. "Good heavens, I hope not, but Aunt Zoey didn't say in the note. He'll want to, if for no other reason than his cheap streak." She grinned. "It's narrow but it's mighty. He's been retired for a good ten years and I think he's still wearing his fatigues. Not because he wants to, particularly, but because it saves him buying new clothes."

While Cass accepted payment from a table of patrons, Luke carried a carafe around and offered refills, the last ones of the night. When they were behind the counter cleaning up, she looked stricken. "I'm not sure I have coverage for the coffee shop in case taking care of Damaris requires more time than I've allotted."

"I'll take care of that." Scheduling and hiring were things he was good at. Not to mention, the people who worked at the orchard bent over backward to be accommodating when it came to emergencies.

"I can't ask you to do that."

"Actually, you can, even though you didn't. I know the shop is your baby, but we're partners. If I need extra help with the orchard, either retail or wholesale, I expect it from you without asking. Fair enough?"

"It is." She relaxed visibly, and the smile she aimed at him was blinding. "When was it you were going to ask me on that date?"

ONE OF DAMARIS'S ankles was broken, the other severely sprained, so she was in a wheelchair. Her right cheek and her left arm were bandaged and her short, dark hair was patchy where it had been trimmed away to repair cuts on her scalp. Cass and Royce, who weren't army brats for nothing, told her she looked great but she needed to see a different barber.

Zoey greeted Damaris kindly, made her comfortable near the bay window in the dining room and brought her a bowl of potatoes to peel.

Ken carried in Damaris's things, taking them to the maid's quarters and coming back to stand in the doorway between the kitchen and the dining room. Zoey was cooking and Cass was helping. Royce was setting the table and chatting nonstop to her mother.

No one paid any attention to him.

He cleared his throat. "Could I have some coffee?"

"It's in the pot. Cups in the cupboard above it." Zoey tossed him a brief—and not very friendly—look. "Are you staying for dinner?"

He looked startled, and Cass grinned down at the salad she was assembling. She wondered if he'd intended to stay at the farmhouse. Memory would have informed him there were empty bedrooms.

He walked over, selected a large cup and filled it. "If that's an invitation, I will." His throat clearing, a habit Cass had forgotten about, sounded strangled. "We need to discuss Damaris's schedule for rehabilitation. Her doctors were reluctant to have her staying outside a facility." He looked around, seemingly at a loss.

"Cream's in the fridge, Dad," Cass said. "In the door. Sugar and sweetener are there on the counter. Spoons in the drawer below."

"Thank you." He didn't sound grateful. He sounded irritated.

He'd been single for several years, living alone in the Idaho condo he'd purchased while still active in the military. Cass wondered who waited on him in the absence of wives or daughters. Maybe he had a housekeeper.

"We'll be able to get Damaris wherever she needs to go." Cass took pity on him and handed him the coffee creamer, hoping he knew how to prepare his own cup. "Zoey's and my schedules are both flexible." She hoped they were flexible enough.

"Royce can help, too. She has her license."

He nodded in the direction of his younger daughter. "The responsibility would be good for her."

"She also has school, a job and activities. She's busy enough just being sixteen," said Zoey crisply. She hooked a foot around the leg of a kitchen chair and pulled it out. "Sit down, Ken, before one of us trips over you."

He sat, and Cass grinned again. The chair Zoey had pulled out was a side chair, not at the head of the table where he would automatically sit if not otherwise directed.

"How will you get her into bed if I'm not here?" he asked. He sipped from his coffee and closed his eyes for a moment. Cass wondered if it was in appreciation or if he was thinking up a suitable criticism.

"We won't," she said crisply, when Zoey showed no signs of answering. "A nurse from home health care will be here for two hours in the evening. Someone else will come in the morning. It will be a long several weeks for Damaris, but she and we will all cope just fine." She raised her voice. "Right, Colonel?"

Her stepmother's voice floated back, laughter rippling through it. "Right, step-girl. Coping skills are in order."

"That's terribly expensive," Ken objected. "I could stay and help her in and out of bed."

Zoey turned to look at him, and the rest of the house fell silent. "Let's get something real clear," she said quietly. "This is our house, not yours. None of us are married to you. You have no control over any of us, even Royce, and that's the way it's going to stay. I can't stop you from staying somewhere at the lake, and you're free to visit Damaris and the girls whenever you like, but those are the limits, Ken. Do you get that?"

He started to speak, but she raised a peremptory hand. She wasn't finished. "If it's too expensive, we'll work that out, but as it is, Damaris has served our country admirably and deserves the best we can do for her. At this point in time—" her smile was downright wicked "—the best isn't you, Major."

Cass thought the reminder that not only did his ex-wife not need him but she outranked him as well was the final blow. He didn't say anything, only nodded.

"Now, take this platter of pork chops into the dining room and make sure Damaris is settled at the table. We'll eat in a few minutes."

The first meal as a strangely blended family started out fairly well. Damaris was anxious to catch up on what she'd missed with Royce, and even Ken sat quietly and listened. Most of the time.

"I notice the name Seth cropping up in nearly every sentence," he said at the end of a story about a football game, a familiar irritated ripple in his voice. "Is that something your mother and I should be concerned about?"

Cass nearly laughed. The only times her father had ever been concerned about any of his daughters' friends was if they were making noise or eating too much. He was of the seen-and-not-heard persuasion when it came to anyone either young or civilian or, even worse, both.

"He was my first friend here. Well, he and Mary and Isaac." Royce's tone was defensive, her blue gaze frosty when she met her father's.

"Sweetheart, will you bring in dessert?" Zoey requested. "It's already dished up in the fridge in the laundry room."

When Royce had left the room, Damaris said, "Back off, Ken. The only part you had in raising Royce was paying child support.

It's too late for you to start now." Her voice was even but weary.

"Do you want her marrying right out of high school the way her sister did?" Ken spoke to Damaris, but it was Cass's gaze he held, challenging her. "So she can be single in her thirties, living on inherited property with no money or future of her own?"

Damaris glared at him. "She could do much worse than to grow up like her sister."

"Those books that so embarrass you sell very well, sir," Cass murmured, anger making her stomach roil. "While I'm not rich, I do have a comfortable income. I believe my future will be whatever I choose for it to be." She wasn't sure of that at all, but her father didn't need to know that. "The same goes for Royce. If you decide to toss her out of your life unsupported if you don't like her choices, she'll receive sustenance of all kinds from the others at this table."

When Ken started to answer, she broke in, delighted with her own rudeness. "Please bear in mind that I haven't asked for anything from you since the day I left home, nor have you given me anything. I've survived marriage, divorce, Mother's death and breast cancer without paternal solicitude or support, so please don't come into my home and presume to scorn my life choices."

"This isn't your home," Ken said stiffly. "You lost your home in your divorce."

Cass almost reminded him that she and Tony had had a prenuptial agreement, something the major was all too familiar with, but neither her financial situation nor her personal life were his business. She leaned back in her chair, beaming with relief when her sister backed through the swinging door into the room carrying a tray filled with bowls of banana pudding.

"If you're arguing about me, let me just give you some new subject matter and bring you parental units up-to-date." Royce held the tray so Zoey could serve the bowls. "Sister Coffee Shop has kept me in line for the most part. I love living here except for when I want to buy new clothes. Aunt Zoey and I are best buds. I'm passing calculus   I think. I'd like to have a car of my own. I want a kitten. I rolled a stop sign the other day and got a warning from a really cute state cop."

Listening to the resultant laughter and argument, Cass thought this must be how conversation in Luke's family went. Regardless of the stiffness that always came with her father's presence, it was nice.

By ten o'clock, Ken had left for the bed-and-breakfast at the lake where he'd found a room and everyone except Cass had gone to bed. She gazed wearily at her computer. Surely she could come up with a few hundred words before falling asleep.

She'd just opened the file with Lucy Garten's latest adventure half written in it when her cell phone percolated a text.

I'm on your back porch. Want to walk in the orchard?

She grabbed a jacket from the mudroom. She thought about getting a flashlight, too, but decided to let the full moon do its job. The ladies at the coffee shop had talked about it today, but Cass had forgotten until now. She didn't think she'd paid attention to a harvest moon since the year she'd spent at the lake. She looked forward to seeing this one.

It was glorious, lighting the trees and the grass under them with a golden tone she'd never seen duplicated on canvas.

"So." Luke captured her hand, and she was

surprised at how sure her step was when she matched it to his. "How did it go?"

"It went okay after we got over the bumps." And it had, she realized. Ken had wanted to do his Great Santini thing, but it hadn't worked. "We were like that song Aunt Zoey taught Royce and her friends for the homecoming float—'I Am Woman.' There's a line in there about roaring, and all four of us roared very quietly right over the major. It felt pretty good."

At the end of a row of trees, they paused to look up at the great orangey moon. Cass's throat tightened. She looked at Luke's profile and had the inane thought that she would probably be okay with looking at him every day for the rest of her life. But something about the set of his jaw disturbed her, made her wonder if… "Are you happy?" she asked.

He hesitated. "I'm content." He kept his gaze on the moon. "I like my life for the most part. Happy?" He shook his head. "I don't think so. Jill wouldn't like me saying that, but it's true. I had happy with her and I just don't think I'm one of those people who gets that again. At least not that kind."

"You still miss her."

He nodded. "I do, but I'm not holding on

to her memory or anything like that. I can't really remember the sound of her voice." He lifted his hand, the one that held Cass's. "I don't recall how her hand felt or the scent of her skin. But I remember how *I* felt when I was with her—that's what I think won't happen again."

She and Tony had loved each other, but it had never been that way for either of them. She'd probably wanted his family more than him, and he'd cared more about how she looked than who she was.

"I don't think my ex and I ever had that feeling," she confessed. "But contentment—that I understand."

Luke looked at her then. "You've had a rough few years. Are you content now?"

She thought about that, falling into step beside him again. She saw the round barn silhouetted against the sky, the barns beyond it, and remembered the big farmhouse behind her. She thought of Ground in the Round and sitting at its corner table writing. She thought about the warmth of days with Zoey and Royce and how glad she was to have her stepmother in the house. "No," she said, surprised, "I'm way beyond that."

Saying that, and smiling with the rush of

pleasure that came with it, she also felt heaviness still resting in the back of her mind. It warned her not to uncross her fingers.

CHAPTER TEN

"REALLY, ROYCE, ISN'T there enough going on?" Cass focused her irritation on her sister's hopeful face. She knew if she looked at the kitten lapping hungrily from the saucer of milk she would be lost. "And how's it going to look if a customer comes in and sees a cat sitting on one of the tables drinking from the same dishes we use in the coffee shop?"

Royce rolled her eyes, doing nothing at all toward assuaging Cass's annoyance. "It's a cardboard saucer—we use them once. And it's time to close—no one's here." She stroked the kitten, a tiny black thing almost certainly too young to leave its mother. "Aunt Zoey doesn't care—I asked—and I'll take care of it and empty its litter. I'll even buy its food."

"And what if it trips your mother? She's getting started on crutches, but it would only take one tumble to put her back in that chair. Plus Dad hates cats and he'll complain every time he comes over."

"Dad hates everything."

Cass stopped typing. Making her deadline had become little more than a distant dream anyway. "He doesn't," she said wearily. "He just doesn't know how to show affection." *Or any other kind of emotion other than disapproval.* "He's the only father we have, kiddo, so we may as well make the best of it."

The kitten finished its milk, stepped daintily onto the computer's keyboard and began to wash its feet, casting covert glances at Cass as it did so. As if it was saying, "Look at me. Aren't I cute?"

"Yes, you certainly are."

"What?" Royce came over to the table with steaming cups. "Oh, no. She's on your keyboard."

"She's a girl? She won't hurt it." Against her will, and with a glower at her sister, Cass scooped the kitten into her hands. "What's your name, sweetheart?"

"Misty. Look at her eyes. They're like looking at the sky at night when it's raining." Royce grinned, hope like a mist in her own eyes. "I won't ask for another single thing. At least until the winter formal in December, when I want a new dress."

"Are you going with Seth?" Cass had wondered about that but hadn't asked. She didn't want to usurp any territory that belonged to Damaris.

Mist covered Royce's eyes again and spilled over. "No. He'll be on the king's court even though he doesn't want to be—he thinks it's lame. So, anyway, he really needs to take one of the senior girls on the court to the dance because the pictures work out better that way."

Cass set the cat down, watching her curl into the cloth napkin on the table. While she didn't want a customer to see that, she had to admit it was really cute. "Did you really just say that? And does he feel that way? That the pictures are important?"

Royce sat down so suddenly Cass thought she heard a thump. "Aren't they?"

Cass hit the save button and closed her laptop. "What do you think?"

"I went to a school where things like that mattered more than they do at this one, and I don't exactly know what to do here. Seth and I are going out, but we've never said it was exclusive." Royce chewed the edge of her thumbnail, a gesture Cass was still guilty of when she was being thoughtful. "I was ahead in my classes when I started the school year—you knew that, didn't you?"

"I knew." The guidance counselor had called her with the information within the first week of school. Royce had gone straight into advanced placement classes and was still ahead—most of her senior year would be credit-earning college courses if she stayed at the lake. "Your school in California was an academic wonder. Miniagua is…well, it's good. But it's small and its curriculum is on the small side, too. You might not be as ready for Berkeley as you'd like to be."

"I don't care about Berkeley."

Cass frowned. "Excuse me? You've talked about it since first grade. I got you a cheer-leading outfit for Christmas when you were seven. It's where everyone in your mother's family went to college." She caught her sister's gaze. "How much does this have to do with Seth? He's going to Purdue, isn't he?"

Royce nodded. "Maybe—or Penn State. He hasn't decided. But he's not why. At least not the only why. There's Aunt Zoey, too, and the orchard. I love the house—it feels like the one in the *Anne of Green Gables* movies on TV. You and Aunt Zoey even sit on the back porch and peel things the way Marilla and

Rachel Lynde did. Then there's Mary—I've never had a friend like her."

Cass's heart ached. Once upon a magical time, she'd had a friend just like that. Linda Saylors had been the other half of her angst-ridden teenage soul. While she'd had many friends in the years since, no one had come close to filling the empty place left by Linda's death.

"It's weird that we're the same age and she doesn't go to school anymore because she's Amish. We both read the same books, though—she loves yours even though she doesn't know who you are. I want to tell her, but I know it's still this big secret." Royce gave Cass a mildly resentful look before returning her attention to the kitten. "So, about Misty?"

"You can keep her." It would be another first for them. Neither of them had ever had a pet. Tony had liked animals as little as her father had, and it hadn't been a battle she'd cared to fight.

"What if I have to go back to California? They'll probably make me when Mom is well enough." Royce took the kitten back into her arms, holding it close to her face. "If they know my classes aren't as advanced, they won't let me stay here."

"I can't promise you they will." Cass reached across the table to push Royce's hair back from her face. "But for what it's worth, I'll do all I can to keep you here. If you *do* have to go back, I'll keep Misty for you wherever I am until you can have her. Deal?"

Royce nodded, tears dampening her lashes. "And do you think the pictures don't matter? I was the one who told Seth they did."

Cass had to blink back some moisture of her own. "No." She shook her head and opened her laptop again. "Pictures don't matter. The people in them—they matter. I suppose there are times and places that call for that kind of correctness, but not high school dances. Has Seth already invited one of the court?"

"No."

"Then tell him you've changed your mind."

Royce looked uncertain, and Cass remembered, out of nowhere, the panic-laced night before her wedding. She'd sat down between her divorced parents and told them she was sorry, but she couldn't go through with it. She'd told them she liked Tony, but that wasn't enough. It would never be enough.

They had told her in no uncertain terms that it was too late to change her mind. That, yes, she could go through with it. So, even though she'd seen her own terror reflected in Tony's eyes, that's exactly what she'd done.

"It's never too late to do the right thing," she said briskly, and waved her hand in a pushing motion. "Now go, and light the closed sign and lock the door. I have a scene to finish writing before I go home."

Royce got up, carrying the kitten, and went to rinse her cup. She came back to kiss Cass's cheek. "Thanks, Sister Coffee Shop. I love you."

"Take my car home. It's gotten completely dark while you've been bothering me. I love you, too."

As soon as the door closed behind a laughing Royce, Cass snatched a paper napkin from the dispenser and buried her face in it. She wasn't sure why she cried, whether it was for her sister's teenage angst or for her own. Or for Linda Saylors, who'd wanted the end seat in the van so that she wouldn't crush her prom princess dress. Cass had wanted to sit there, too, because her legs were longer, but Linda had insisted and she'd given in. Sam had sat behind the driver's seat and Jesse had taken his. Cass was beside the window, looking out into the rainy night and wishing they'd hurry up and get home. The dance had been fun, but there wasn't room in their seating arrangement for both Jesse's and her long legs.

She'd been irritated with Linda, but the night had been too much fun to let it become an issue. Linda had never known her best friend was annoyed with her.

Cass didn't know why the prom night memories bothered her so much right now. It was autumn instead of spring, and from everything she'd heard and seen since coming back to the lake, all the accident's survivors were well and happy.

She gave up on writing and got the coffee shop set up to reopen in the morning, then locked it behind her and walked through the orchard to the farmhouse, amazed at herself for being so comfortable alone in the dark.

"I DON'T THINK it's going to make us rich." Cass frowned at the bottom line from the week's receipts after closing on Saturday night.

She looked too tired. She was working too many hours—between the orchard and the coffee shop, she was at Keep Cold more than he was. Luke would love to send her home with orders to put her feet up the way he would anyone else who worked for him, but he wasn't her boss. No, he was her partner, which he really liked, but still. Yeah, still. She needed some rest.

He filled his cup and joined her at the corner table that seemed to have become the permanent home of her laptop. He wondered why the little computer was so important to her that she had it with her virtually every waking minute, but something kept him from asking. He would never have considered himself intuitive, but in this case he was going with that.

"Was that the idea?" he asked. "Getting rich?" If it was, maybe she was more her father's daughter than he'd have thought.

She grinned at him. "No, the idea was that you would realize I was brilliant and that the coffee shop wasn't a fiscal mistake. I'm still brilliant, but the fiscal part… I don't know." The grin slipped away. "Did we even break even?"

He reached for the printout. "Not this week, but look at last week, when you made a killing. You're staying open after the football games on Friday nights so kids won't be all over the place in cars. A little bird told me you sell everything at half price unless the kid doesn't have any money, in which case he gets it free. Sometimes good will is better than good profit."

She shook her head, color creeping up her cheeks, and he went on, wanting to make her feel better. "You're featuring new fall flavors going into Halloween—you'll make it back then. That's the way business goes. You know that." He stood just enough to lean across and kiss her. Lingeringly. "Because you're brilliant."

She laughed and closed the book on the week's paperwork. "I don't think I've ever worked this hard or been this tired or had this much fun in my whole life—well, since junior year in high school anyway."

"How about a late dinner at Anything Goes?"

"I'd like that."

She frowned when she got to her feet, and rubbed her upper arm.

"You okay?" he asked.

"Fine. Just not used to physical labor, and between the coffee shop and the orchard, it gets pretty physical."

"It does," he agreed, holding her jacket for her. "Just think, you're not going to get rich, either. What more could you ask?" She hesitated before slipping her left arm into its sleeve, dipping her head and catching her breath. "Cass? Are you sure you're not hurt?"

"I'm sure." She smiled, the corners of her mouth tucking into her cheeks. "However, I am really hungry. Did you say you were buying?"

"I'm buying, but this meal may be a lesson on scheduling. Keep Cold is lucky in the help it has. You need to give them more hours in the coffee shop and yourself fewer."

"Is that the pot calling the kettle black? You leave the orchard last every single day."

He was silent a moment, then he nodded. "You're right. I need to work less, too. If you will, I will. How does that sound?"

"Sounds good."

He thought it did, too, but he doubted either of them would stick to it.

On the way to Anything Goes, Luke reached for her hand and held it loosely against his leg. "Does it feel odd to you to be dating someone? I get the impression you haven't done a lot of it since your divorce."

"Try none. And it does seem odd in a way. How about you? Have you dated much?"

"Off and on—Jill has been gone a long time. But I've only had one serious relationship. Then I figured out it wasn't fair to ask for more from a woman than I was willing to offer in exchange." He wondered as he spoke the words which one of them he was warning.

She turned in her seat, taking back her hand and laying it on her other one in her lap. "What do you mean?"

"I'm not sure I can explain it without sounding like a complete loser, but mostly I don't want to be in it for the long haul."

Cass shrugged. "Most men don't, do they?"

"Most of the guys I know who are married like it that way. I liked it, too, but I'm not willing to do it again."

"That's understandable. I feel the same way. I liked marriage, or at least the idea of it, but I think I'm like my parents and just not good at it." She chuckled, although her eyes had that haunted look they occasionally got. "That's what Tony said, too."

"Was he good at it?"

She hesitated. While she thought most of

the anger over her marriage had left her, the sense of failure was still healthy and strong. Sometimes it was hard to separate the two. "I think he may be better at it with someone else. He's married again, to someone he met while we were supposedly together. They have a little girl and are expecting another. He calls me a couple of times a year to make sure I'm all right, and I don't know whether it's guilt or because his wife is a nice woman who makes him do it. But, no, he wasn't any better at it than I was."

He pulled in at Anything Goes, turned off the car and looked at her. "How long did it take you to know that?"

She reached for her door handle. "What's the date today?"

He started to answer before he realized what she meant. "You thought it was all your fault?"

"Sure, I did. Sometimes I still do." She let go of the door handle and pushed back her hair.

He had to bite back irritation. He'd been single for ten years, but even so he knew relationship failures were seldom one-sided. "Don't you think that's a little on the martyrdom side?"

"No," she said mildly, "it's a *lot* on the martyrdom side. Doesn't change how I feel some days. I *know* we were the textbook couple who married too young and for the wrong reasons, but I still feel like a failure because we couldn't make it work."

He thought back to when he'd visited the cemetery in Pennsylvania the week before, placing colorful chrysanthemums on Jill's grave. He'd remembered, stroking a hand over the wind chime that hung from a shepherd's hook beside her marker, how deep their love had been. And how punishing the grief when she'd died. For a moment, standing there in the chilly afternoon sun, the old pain had revived and seared him like a slow-motion streak of lightning. Unable to move with the force of it, he'd spoken aloud to her, which he never did. "Why, Jill?"

Just as there'd been no answers ten years before, there weren't any then. By the time he'd gotten in the car and driven away, he'd been all right again. Thinking about the orchard and Seth's football game and—before he knew it was happening—seeing Cass later that day.

"You're right." He smiled at Cass. "We do all have our days, don't we?"

"SOMETIMES I HAVE to be hit over the head." Alone with Damaris at breakfast the following morning, Cass took a bite of the applesauce Zoey had just made. It was still warm, redolent of cinnamon and so smooth she had to stop herself from groaning with the satisfaction of it. "I never *knew* applesauce was ambrosia."

Damaris laughed. "That's what you had to be hit over the head with?"

"No. I think I figured out that Lucy Garten needs to take a sabbatical. She went so far outside the lines in the last book that I don't seem to be able to reign her back in."

Her stepmother looked thoughtful. "When are you going to let Cassandra come out of the family closet?"

Cass shrugged. "I don't know. What's the point after all this time? Cassandra G. Porter's been around for twelve years. Dad and Tony—"

"Your dad and Tony aren't the point here," Damaris interrupted, sounding every inch the officer she was. "Although they had a lot to do with how you became who you are, they no longer have any power over you unless you *let* them have it. You owe it to Cass Gentry to *be* Cass Gentry."

"Got any real idea who that is? Because I surely don't." Cass's arm hurt again, and fear feathered through her. "I was just thinking the other day about how happy I am right here and right now. But I'm not even sure it's the real me who's happy. There've been too many losses, too much illness and too much of the crap that goes with it. What you have here—" she raised her right arm dramatically "—is the empty shell of a person. Every loss has taken its toll, whether it was physical, emotional or mental. Or, to be really poor-me about it, all three." She lowered her arm and met Damaris's eyes. "But Cassandra G. Porter remains intact. She has the body parts she was born with. She doesn't have an un-successful marriage in her back-of-the-book bio. She wasn't a grievous disappointment to her parents." Cass smiled, but she didn't re-ally mean it. "Let her live."

"Which one of you comes home from dates with Luke Rossiter with stars in her eyes?"

"That would be my little sister, and it's Seth, not Luke."

Damaris shook her head, smiling. "I wasn't born quite yesterday, Cass."

"It's just not a place I'm ready to go. I like Luke. I even like dating—who'd have thought it? But it's a nice, safe thing. He doesn't want to become involved with anyone and neither do I. Not only that, we're business partners—that's not a good basis for a personal relationship."

"So, which one of you is it?"

Cass got up to get them more coffee. They'd both stayed home from church and had been enjoying the quiet time. Even Misty was sleeping on the windowsill instead of chewing their toes as the kitten had shown herself prone to doing.

She thought about her stepmother's question, trying to separate the two selves she claimed in her mind. "I'd like for it to be Cassandra—her life's in pretty good order, you know?" she said finally, stirring her coffee. "But I'm afraid it's probably me in my best screw-up mode. We'll date and have a good time and keep an eye out on each other's siblings, but eventually something will pound a wedge between us and we'll go on separately. That's the way life is. You know that as well as I do." The words were agonizing to say. She could hear her voice shattering from the effort. She kept stirring the coffee. And stirring. *What if Luke knew*

*her as Cassandra? Would "the long haul"
look better to him then?*

Damaris lifted the papers in front of her
and extended them toward Cass. "See these?"

Cass set down the spoon, frowning at
her trembling hand, and leafed through the
printed sheets. She'd seen them before. She'd
signed them several times since Damaris and
her father had divorced. They granted Cass
temporary custody of Royce in the event neither parent could make a home for her. It also
gave Cass full power of attorney.

"What about them? Do I need to sign
something else?" *Do you want someone else
to take care of her?* The thought ripped a new
place in the list of wounds she'd just reeled
off. That particular loss was one she couldn't
bear to consider.

"No. They're all in order. I was just checking over them, because Ken has a way of
hammering in those wedges you just mentioned at the most difficult of times." She
shrugged. "What he doesn't tear asunder, the
army does. I have loved one or both of them
most of my adult life, but there's no denying
the truth of that."

Concern made the short hair on the back of
Cass's neck stand up. "What are you saying?"

"That things happen—I have these lovely broken bones to attest to that—and I have to know Royce will be with you no matter what. And I want to know she's with the complete you. You might see yourself as two people, stepgirl, but you're not. Until you know that, I'm worried about you not only as yourself but as Royce's next-in-line parent."

"I'll always be Cassandra for Royce. I can do that. Grouchier sometimes than I'd like her to be, but still Cassandra." *I won't let anything happen to her. I'll never leave her because I don't know how to stay. I can learn, here in this place. I can learn how to stay.*

"That's not what I want," said Damaris gently. "I don't want her to be afraid to make mistakes or love the wrong person or to not have a best friend because that's how a girl gets hurt. Did you ever think how odd it is that you turned Cassandra G. Porter into the person you thought your parents wanted you to be?"

Cass drew back, feeling as though she'd been slapped. "That's not true." She glared at Damaris.

Her stepmother laughed, a gentle sound that eased the hurt. "Of course it's true. Cassandra's beautiful, although no one would know for sure because your author photo is so doctored that you're completely unrecognizable in it."

"That was on purpose. You know that. The publisher insisted on a picture, but they never minded that no one could tell who I was in it. It worked to their advantage to have the mystery writer be a bit of a mystery herself." Cass took a sip of coffee, spilling it down the sides of the cup because her hand was still shaking.

Damaris was calm. She always was, something Cass usually appreciated and envied, but not now. Now was not a good time for calm. "Yes, I know that. And you said the rest of it yourself. No bad marriage. No reconstructed breast. No guilt over an accident you had no control over or because you couldn't satisfy parents who were, quite frankly, not satisfiable."

Cass had written about seeing a red wave of anger before, but she'd never experienced it herself until now. She set her cup down so hard the table trembled from the force. "Linda died, Damaris, remember? She was in the seat I should have been in and she *died*. You think a little guilt isn't called for?"

"I'm a colonel in the US Army. I've made

decisions that have caused people to die. Relatives, especially you, have raised my only child more than I have. I had one of those bad marriages you're flagellating yourself about. I know all about guilt." Her eyes, dark brown and shadowed with the pain she still suffered from her injuries, held Cass's gaze. "I also know when you separate what you consider the bad from the good in yourself, you're left with two incomplete identities."

"I don't hurt anyone."

The other woman laughed, a soft and unexpected sound. "Yeah, you do. It's fine that Cassandra is this exemplary human being, but it's Sister Coffee Shop and Sister Chemo Brain and Sister Two-Left-Feet that I love best, that Royce loves best. She may be the one who's made some mistakes and who's a guilty mess over stuff that wasn't her fault, but she's the real thing. If you combine Cass and Cassandra…well, that's who I want taking care of Royce if I can't. That's who my stepgirl is. Five'll get you ten that's who Luke Rossiter likes, too."

LATER THAT DAY, walking through the orchard with Misty keeping her company, Cass looked through the branches of a pear tree, loving the picture the nearly leafless limbs made against the pale blue sky.

She eyed the tree trunk where it divided. It made her wish she had one of the orchard's ladders out here. It had been a while since she climbed a tree just for the sake of climbing it. The last time had probably been when the volleyball team camped near the creek at the back of the Worths' farm.

There weren't enough leaves left on the tall Bartlett pear tree to offer the whispering accompaniment to her thoughts she remembered from those days, but still...it had been a while.

A few minutes later, she knew she hadn't lost the knack. With only one slightly scraped anklebone, she settled into where the tree's trunk divided, giving herself a back scratch against its bark in the process. Misty crawled into the kangaroo pocket of her sweatshirt and fell asleep. Cass pulled out her phone and opened a notes app. She never used voice-activated programs, but her fingers were so slow on the phone's keypad that she tapped the little microphone on the screen and dictated story thoughts.

She didn't know how much time had passed, but the sun was dangling low over the western horizon and the kitten had wakened and was sitting on her shoulder grooming herself when a voice came from below. "Please tell me you don't need to be rescued."

She loved the sound of Luke's voice. Even with an ear of tin like hers, she thought she could hear the music in it. "I'm good," she called. "I'll be right down." She scrolled through the notes on her phone. And scrolled and scrolled.

So this was why she couldn't finish the book she'd started. Evidently Cassandra G. Porter needed some time off. The words on the screen came directly from Cass Gentry's heart. There were a lot of them, and she could hardly wait to get to her computer to put them to good use.

She climbed down, Misty clinging to her shirt. "What's up?"

"Nothing. I was at the apple barn pleading with the cider press to get us through this season. So far, it's agreeing, but there's no telling how it will go tomorrow. If our relationship were a marriage, we'd have been divorced years ago."

She grinned at him. "Too high maintenance for you?"

"Sure is." He flinched when Misty made

the leap from Cass's shirt to his shoulder. "Want to go to a movie tonight?"

She started to agree, then stopped. "Actually, I've got some paperwork that won't wait. I know we talked about reducing our hours, but we haven't done it yet. You worked this afternoon and I'm opening the coffee shop in the morning. I really need to do this tonight."

"Okay. Not a problem."

He looked disappointed, which sent a happy chill scampering down her back. "Aunt Zoey's teaching Dad and Damaris how to play euchre. I'm sure they'd be glad for a fourth if you're not doing anything. Royce hates it, plus she's always grumpy when Seth spends the weekend with your parents."

"He is, too. He'd rather Mom and Dad stayed down here every weekend. He doesn't quite get that they have a life up there."

Cass scooped Misty into her hands and tucked her into her pocket. "Want to come home with me for supper even if you don't play euchre? Aunt Zoey's cooking, so it will be good."

"You talked me into it." He caught her hand as they walked. "How's it going with your dad? Is he going to stay here until Damaris is well?"

"It's all right, I guess. He's leaving this week. He wants to have dinner with Royce and me by ourselves before he goes. That should be quite an experience."

"Think he's trying to make up for time lost while you were growing up? I don't know him well, and neither you nor Royce says much, but there's no sense of warmth in the conversation. All your memories seem to revolve around your mothers—or in your case, Zoey and the lake."

"I don't know." Cass shook her head. "I keep telling Royce he loves us the only way he knows how, but I'm not sure he does." It was no wonder she was weird about men. She'd never been loved by one. Not exactly the norm when a person's father was living and she'd been married as long as she had.

Luke didn't argue her point. "It happens, although I admit I don't understand it."

Cass thought fleetingly of her perfect alter ego who didn't have issues like unloving fathers or debilitating guilt. If Cassandra had shown up in childhood, life would probably have been much easier.

"Wait!" Luke drew them to a halt, standing still in the crunchy autumn grass. "Do you hear it?"

"Hear what?"

"The music. Somewhere, someone's playing an apple orchard waltz." He swung her into his arms. "Come on, let's dance."

She tried to pull away, both laughing and embarrassed. "Don't tell me you've missed Royce calling me Sister Two-Left-Feet. She's not kidding."

"Don't worry about your feet." He held her closer and smiled into her eyes. "Dance from your heart—that's where the music is."

CHAPTER ELEVEN

"YOU AND JILL were serious while you were still in high school, weren't you?" Seth closed the dishwasher door on Monday night and took his guitar from its stand. He sat down with it, his eyes on Luke's fingers. "Show me how to do that."

"We were." Luke stilled his fingers on the neck of the Gibson so his brother could replicate the complicated chord.

They had played together since Luke and Jill had bought Seth his first guitar for his sixth birthday. It was how the brothers were always able to communicate when the only alternative was shouting.

"Was it a good idea? Was it hard?"

Luke slipped into "The Wreck of the Edmund Fitzgerald," knowing Seth loved playing the lead in the song. "It wasn't an idea. It just was. It probably wasn't overly smart, but we were seventeen—nothing we did was very smart. Everything was hard for Jill and me because she was sick."

He smiled, thinking of those days with his wife and the little brother they'd both loved. It used to hurt too much to call back those particular photographs of the heart, but now the memories were just sweet. "We had ten or eleven years to do what we anticipated having a whole lifetime for."

"Have you ever wondered if you'd have ended up together if she *hadn't* gotten sick? You guys had extenuating circumstances that led every inch of your lives together. What if you hadn't had those?" Seth moved into the difficult lead, and for a moment concentration on the music kept him from talking. Then he said, "Would you do it again?"

Luke didn't answer, concentrating on playing the song, the rhythm he strummed adding fullness to his brother's lead. He shook his head when Seth started to speak. "Come on. Sing." The song about the doomed freighter was a long one. Maybe by the time it was done, Seth would have forgotten his questions. A guy could hope, anyway.

He wasn't big on hope, to tell the truth. He didn't think he was negative, although his sisters were unrelenting in telling him he was, but he believed unfettered optimism was foolish. He worked hard to make good business decisions, even harder to bring those ideas to fruition. He enjoyed his personal life as it was, but he wasn't going to hope for more than he had.

"Sing with me." Seth started again, so the song was even longer, and Luke couldn't think when he sang. There were too many lyrics to remember.

But he thought anyway, fumbling one of the verses enough that Seth scowled at him before bursting into laughter that forced them to start the stanza again.

"I'm proud of you," Luke said, when the notes of the song finally faded away. "At the orchard, on the field, in music. You're the go-to guy for things, and I've spent enough time in the workplace to know that's irreplaceable. Jill—" He cleared his throat and went on. "Jill always said you would excel at whatever you put your mind to doing. She was right."

He set his guitar on its stand and got to his feet. "Understand, if you ever tell anyone what I just said, I'll deny it right down the line, but I mean it."

Seth fingerpicked quietly. "Thank you. That's cool to hear." He waited. "So?"

Luke sat back down and reached for his shoes. "What?"

"Questions, bro. The ones I asked. You didn't answer them."

"You are a pain in the—"

"Yeah, yeah, I know." Seth picked out a familiar-sounding melody, then silenced the strings. "I'm waiting."

"Fine. Number one, yes, I think we would have ended up together. We'd have had half a dozen kids and it would have been the best life imaginable. Not because of me but because of Jill—she was that great. Second, life always offers extenuating circumstances— it's how you handle them that makes all the difference. Dad told me that when we first found out Jill wasn't going to make it, and he was absolutely right."

"And?"

"And we just talked about this not two months ago. Weren't you listening? Yes, I would marry Jill again. I would live every minute with her I could, just like I did. And, no, I probably won't let myself fall back into the same situation with someone else." Even now, he sometimes woke with the expectation that Jill was there. Not in bed beside him, surely, or even in the house, but in his life. In his heart. In his mind, she'd never aged, so even though he was thirty-eight with silver starting to work its way into his hair, she was forever twenty-seven.

"It's probably naïve to say I can avoid it, because I know you don't always choose who you love, but you can choose the life you live. I imagine at some point I'll love someone, but I don't plan to share a life or have a family. I'll never say it wasn't worth the pain with Jill, because it was, but I will say I'm not going to go through it again. Does that make sense and can I count on you not asking me that question again?"

He tied his second shoe and regarded Seth, sitting silent and somehow watchful on the couch. "Are you thinking about Jill and me or about you and Royce?"

"Maybe both. I like her more than I meant to. I think she feels the same way."

Luke hesitated, not sure what his brother was asking and even less sure of what to tell him. "You know to be careful, right?" he said quietly. "To protect both her and yourself so that you don't have to be a grown-up before your time?"

"I know."

The quiet dignity in the answer convinced Luke to back off. Seth might have his faults, but he was never less than honest.

"We had to hurry with everything." Luke held his gaze. "If you want my advice, or even if you don't, that's it. You don't have to hurry, so don't."

Seth nodded. "You going out?"

"Cass and I are going to try to figure out scheduling for both the orchard and the coffee shop. It'll change as we go into winter, but at least we can create a workable base."

Seth looked thoughtful. "You see each other almost every day, don't you? Besides at work, I mean. You're going out."

"Back in the dark ages, we called it dating, and yeah, we are. But that's all there is to it." He realized as he said the words that they weren't quite true. But that they needed to be.

He and Cass met at Anything Goes a half hour later, sipping hot chocolate and sharing an order of French fries. She had her omnipresent laptop, so she typed in their schedule as he wrote it out in pencil on a yellow legal pad.

"I think it will work," she said happily

when they were finished. She closed the computer and beamed with satisfaction.

"Except that by the end of no more than two workdays, something will have happened to make half this schedule null and void."

She propped her chin in her hand and gazed across the table at him in somber silence. "You do know there's nothing wrong with thinking positively sometimes, right?"

He met her eyes, thinking how beautiful they were. She'd suffered divorce, cancer and the loss of her mother in a two-year time span. That she was still haunted by things he didn't understand and secrets she didn't share showed in the shadows in those eyes. He was almost certain thinking positive was no more natural to her than it was to him.

"I do, sometimes," he said, because he wanted to lighten those shadows if only for the moment. "That's when I dance in the orchard with my best girl."

"AT LEAST I'M old enough to not be disappointed anymore." Royce looked at the table they'd set in anticipation of their father's arrival for the dinner with just the two of them he'd requested.

Ken had just left, after bringing envelopes

for each them and begging off dinner. He could catch a military flight from Grissom, the nearby air reserve base, so had to leave earlier than anticipated. He'd been sorry to spoil their plans.

Of course, he'd *always* been sorry to spoil their plans. He'd flown to Indiana the day after the prom night accident, determined Cass was going to live and be relatively unscarred and flown out again the same day. He'd missed her high school graduation and been late to her wedding. He'd missed both their births.

"You think that's bad," said Royce, when Cass reminded her of those facts. "He was supposed to be my show-and-tell person in the third grade and didn't show up. Mom was TDY somewhere and I was staying with him and a live-in nanny. The nanny came and brought some really great cookies, so in the end, I guess I was relieved. All Dad would have done was scowl at everyone and tell them to do their duty."

Zoey pushed Damaris's wheelchair into the dining room. Regret showed on both the older women's faces. Regret, but not surprise. They knew all about being let down by Ken Gentry.

"Well," said Cass, "let's set another place." She smiled at each of them in turn. "This is a family dinner, right? I'm happy you're my family."

"Me, too," said Royce. "But I lied about not being disappointed. It would be nice if he followed through sometimes."

"We're glad he followed through at least twice." Zoey took her usual seat at the head of the table and nodded at Damaris at the other end. "I think we're both pretty pleased to have you girls as our family."

Damaris smiled. "And grateful. I'm glad not to be married to your dad, but I can never be sorry I was."

They talked about gratitude all the way through dinner. By the time dessert was finished, Cass thought Royce's disappointment was forgotten.

The others shooed Cass out of the kitchen after dinner. "Go work on the book you're supposed to be writing," said Zoey. "We're going to the movies. Damaris needs practice with the crutches and the boot."

Cass was glad to go into the sunroom she used as an office. She needed to decide what to write. What had gone so wrong with *Murder on Market Street*? She knew Lucy

Garten as intimately as any flesh-and-blood friend she'd ever had, yet suddenly the sleuth seemed to be going out on her own. Falling in love and selling the condo she'd lived in ever since *Murder Downriver*, the first book in the series. The next thing Cass knew, the character would be insisting on getting rid of her MG in favor of a minivan.

Frowning, she typed an email to Holly.

How did you know it was time to change from contemporary to regency romances?

A few minutes later, an answer popped up.

When I found myself bored with my own writing—I knew that couldn't be good!

Cass frowned. She wasn't bored. She loved Lucy's stories, including the one she seemed unable to finish. But something wasn't right in the telling of it.

Another email came through.

Anything you'd like to talk about? I can come over.

Cass typed, I'm good. Thanks anyway, but

deleted the message and wrote another. I'll put the coffee on. And she hit Send.

THE COFFEEMAKER HAD just finished its gasping, throaty process when the light knock came at the back door. Cass opened it with a smile, surprised when Holly pulled her into a hug. The other woman was shorter by half a foot and probably two sizes bigger around. She smelled sweetly of the snickerdoodles she was carrying in a paper sack. "I made these because when I'm trying to plot, I need calories to get me through. Then when the book's done, I have to go to the gym for a couple of months."

Cass nodded. "Sounds reasonable. Can we eat them now?"

"You bet."

They had just taken seats at the kitchen table when Holly said, "Wait a minute. Show me your office. I want to see if you're as big of a slob as I am."

Cass met her glance. "My office?"

Holly grinned at her, although her dark eyes were serious. "Yes, Cassandra, the room where you and Lucy do your creative thing."

"Cassandra?"

"Yes, as in Cassandra G. Porter, author of

The Case of the Missing Footprint in which a certain ex-cheerleader with a prosthetic foot is accused of a really yucky homicide—"

"How long have you known?"

"How many former cheerleaders do you know with prosthetic limbs? I caught it right away."

Cass led the way into the office. "But you never told? You never contacted me?" She gestured toward the chair on the opposite side of her desk from her office chair and set the plate of cookies between them.

"That was what you wanted, wasn't it?"

"It was."

Holly tilted her head, and Cass remembered with an inward giggle how much she'd envied those long, thick lashes when they were in high school. Jesse, ever the artist, used to threaten to cut them off and use them for paintbrushes.

"But now you don't?" Holly asked.

"What makes you say that?" Cass bit into a snickerdoodle.

"Did you call me tonight? Did you ask me a question about writing no one else on the lake has *ever* asked? Is the top of your desk not a maze of cryptic notes that would make no sense to anyone besides yourself?" Holly laughed. "Have you ever sat in a fast-food place with your writers' group and plotted a murder in full hearing of half a police department?"

"My writers' group is online, so that last one is a no. Did that really happen?"

"Not to me—I don't do mystery—but my friend Terri does. I thought she was going to get us thrown out of the place. Or arrested." Holly stopped midlaugh. "Where on earth did you get that author photo on your back cover? Have you thought of suing the photographer?"

Cass nodded. "Terrible, isn't it? It was to help satisfy curious readers at the same time as it kept me out of the public eye. It helped."

Holly looked thoughtful. She took a drink of coffee and another cookie. "Why?"

"Why what?"

"Why any of it?" Holly held up a hand. "And, yes, I know it's none of my business, but way back in school when we started the Write Now group, we talked about how a writer's curiosity wasn't mean or even nosy— we just want to know how stories turn out. I'm thrilled to pieces that you're back on the lake, but I don't have enough of the middle to put together how your story is turning out.

You know, the part we all struggle with when we're writing it?"

"I don't think it makes sense. It would need a horrendous amount of revisions."

Holly rolled her eyes. "There were…how many? Thirteen of us in that wreck that night, counting the guy who caused it, Jack and Tucker's dad? Not much of what's happened in the years since has made sense. Even those of us who stayed here had trouble putting things behind us. Not just some things, but all of them. All of our dreams changed. No one became what they planned on being. There was so much guilt—"

Cass's voice was harsh when she interrupted. "What?"

"Guilt."

"Why would anyone have felt guilty?" *Anyone but me, that is.*

"We all had our reasons. I felt guilty because as much as I loved Daddy, I knew he was Arlie's birth dad, so she had to feel worse than I did when he died."

"That's crazy. Dave loved you both the same, just like Gianna did. I was so jealous."

"It is crazy, but that's how I felt. We all had different things."

"Like what?"

Holly shook her head. "Their stories belong to them. There aren't any real secrets anymore, other than yours, but it's up to them to tell you. If you tell me yours tonight, it will stay with me. I know you go to Arlie's clinic, but she's a professional—if she knows anything about your life, she keeps it to herself."

"You wanted to be a dancer and to teach dance in your own studio," Cass remembered. "But first, you wanted to be a cheerleader at Ball State."

"Right. I did go to Ball State and I do teach dance in classes at the lake's summer camp. But while I was in rehab, learning to walk on a prosthesis, the English teacher from high school—remember Mr. Andrews?— brought me a notebook and some pens. He told me I had plenty of time to get a jump on the next year's writing assignments. But I didn't. I read a Nora Roberts book—the first of a gazillion or so—and thought writing romance novels looked a lot more interesting. I filled that notebook with the most horrible manuscript ever conceived of."

Cass laughed, delighted with the story. "No, no, that would be mine. I wrote it the first year I was married, when I had absolutely no idea what to do with myself. It was so bad my husband couldn't even finish reading it, and he *liked* mysteries."

Holly chuckled, as she'd meant her to, but the other woman's expression was one of waiting. Patient, but waiting nonetheless.

Cass went into the kitchen for more coffee. She filled their cups, set the empty carafe to one side and sat down. "I never came back because of that guilt you mentioned. That and family issues. Nana and Grandpa died. My mother and Aunt Zoey were pretty much estranged. I got married at eighteen." She shrugged, looking down at the top of her closed laptop. "Lots of reasons. Lots of excuses."

"Was that why you used a pen name? So no one from the lake would know?"

"No. I used the name because my father was embarrassed by what I did. Tony, my husband, didn't want business associates to know about it, either, although I think he might have liked it if I'd become famous. It was just easier to use the pseudonym, although social media made keeping it a secret quite a challenge."

"Were *you* embarrassed by it?" Holly's smile was only half there. "I gotta admit I've had a few covers I'd rather not talk about. But let's talk about writing. You having trouble?"

"I am. You want to read a couple of chapters and see what you think?"

"Sure do, if you'll make more coffee."

"I can do that. Or open a bottle of wine."

"Even better."

Zoey, Damaris and Royce came home while they worked, waving goodnight through the French doors that led inside.

Royce, wearing pajama pants and a ragged sweatshirt, came back down with Misty and a few of Holly's books and begged her to sign them. "My friends in California won't believe you live here on the lake."

Holly's dimples flashed. "I don't. I live in a duplex in Sawyer with my cat. But don't tell them that. It's not nearly glamorous enough."

Royce nodded wisely. "I know author glamour. I live with Sister Fuzzy Socks." With a gasp, she stepped back, her eyes wide when they met Cass's. "I'm sorry. I don't know what made me forget. I know it's a secret."

"Holly made you forget. Getting to know her is pretty exciting." Cass got up and hugged her little sister. "It's been a secret long enough. If Dad can't deal with it by now, it's too bad, isn't it? We don't have to make any public announcements, but if word gets out, it just gets out."

"Maybe your sister and I could pay a visit to a Write Now meeting one of these days," said Holly. She beamed back at Cass's glare. "Just saying."

Royce left the room laughing. Holly went back to reading and Cass returned the favor. Neither of them went anywhere without a laptop in tow, so it was easy to exchange stories.

A bottle of wine and a pot and a half of coffee later, Holly closed the file she was reading. "You have an alarming tendency to use the word *look*, don't you? With me, it's *just*. I always say I have to write an extra two chapters to make up for all the overused words I have to take out."

"Yes." Cass waited a beat. "What do you think?"

"I think Cass Gentry's writing this book, not the oh-so-perfect Cassandra, and I think you should let her rip the way you did in *The Case of Daisy's Ashes*." Holly laughed. "Even the coffee shop Lucy goes to is *your* coffee shop, not some generic one on a nameless street somewhere in central Indiana. She's sold her condo and survived breast cancer and fallen in love. Bring her to the lake and give her a new and better life. This is your best ever."

"She hasn't *really* fallen in love." Cass shook her head. "She's just met this guy she likes."

"You just keep telling yourself that." Holly got up, stretching. "I can't believe how long we've sat here. It's been great talking to another writer."

It had been great. Friendship with other writers was a luxury Cass's secret self had been denied too long. Being reassured was another one.

"Do you think so? That this is my best book, I mean," she asked. "Really?"

"Really. And I've read them all." Holly grinned at her. "Looking for more references to that cheerleader." She nodded at Cass's open laptop. "Or to an orchardist who plays guitar."

"Not going to happen." Cass lifted her hands in supplication. "What would happen when we break up? He'd sue me for defamation or something, right?"

Holly clapped a dramatic hand to her forehead. "Oh, no, that means I shouldn't have written the book about the vet!"

"Speaking of the vet, will you give him a message for me?" Cass couldn't face Jesse with what she wanted to say, but maybe if the words came from the woman he loved, he'd forgive the loss of the girl he'd loved first.

Holly looked thoughtful, and softened her eyes. "No," she said. "We survivors have had to learn to talk to each other, to say what needs saying without a go-between. You made a big first step, asking me to come over tonight. I don't know what you want to say to Jess, but I imagine saying it to his face needs to be your next big step."

"I thought…" Cass's voice trailed off when she hesitated. "I thought coming back was my first big step."

"I don't think so." Holly hugged her. "In your heart, I don't think you ever left."

CHAPTER TWELVE

"SHOTS?" CASS LOOKED dubiously at the little cat sitting on the windowsill beside her desk. "Surely she's still a baby."

"I looked it up. Just like a people baby, she needs shots." Royce grimaced. "She might need a hysterectomy, too, but it seems awfully early for that."

"I don't think they call it that in cats." Cass *knew* they didn't, but she was too entertained by her sister's serious devotion to Misty to come right out and say so. "Maybe we could give her some hormones instead. You know, to control the hot flashes and mood swings."

Royce picked up Misty and cuddled her. "Sister Snarky Person is in high gear, isn't she, kitty?" She looked at the clock and set the cat down on the desk. "I got an appointment this afternoon for her shots. But Aunt Zoey has to take Mom to rehab and I need to stay after school for a Write Now meeting. Can you take Misty to the vet? It's just out on Lake Road by the winery."

Cass knew very well where it was. And who it was. Jesse Worth had been very polite to her the few times they'd met since she'd come back to the lake, but others had always been around. Would he be able to bear the sight of her on his home turf?

"Oh, honey," she said, "I was going to write this afternoon. I'm still trying to make that deadline."

Royce's face fell, but only for a moment. "I didn't even think of that," she admitted. "I'll call and change it."

I don't know what you want to say to Jess, but I imagine saying it to his face needs to be your next big step. Holly's words were as loud and clear as Royce's.

Maybe louder.

And maybe there wouldn't be that many more opportunities. Her appointment for blood testing and scans was coming up. She felt all right except for the persistent arm pain, but good health wasn't something she took for granted. Not anymore.

"No." Cass shook her head. "I'll take her. It's okay. You go on and have a good day. What time's the appointment?"

"Four. I think it's the last one of the day, but the lady on the phone said sometimes they run behind."

"I can do that. I get off at the coffee shop at four. I'll just take Misty to work with me and save time. She loves it there, anyway." She shook a finger at her sister. "But when I get home, the rest of the night is mine. If it's my turn to help with dinner, you're taking it. Deal?"

"Deal." Royce blew her a kiss. "But does Luke know the rest of the night is yours? I've noticed that whenever he calls or comes over, you drop everything."

"He still doesn't know about Cassandra and the books." Cass felt heat in her face. She was embarrassed that she hadn't told him. "I'm afraid he'll look at me differently."

"Oh, Cassie, you know that's not true." Royce suddenly looked both older and wiser than she should have at sixteen. "He's not Tony, you know. Or Dad."

"I know."

"If I told Seth I changed my mind about going to the holiday dance, you can tell Luke you write books."

"It's not the writing books. It's that thing of being two people. I've been showing him the Cassandra persona for the most part—the businesswoman who doesn't screw up. What if he doesn't like Cass?"

Royce frowned, stroking Misty's fuzzy belly while the kitten went into paroxysms of ecstasy. "Do you only like me when I'm like I am in California, or do you like me now, too?"

Cass returned her scowl. "That's just silly."

"Uh-huh. It is, isn't it?" Royce set the cat on the desk and waved, winking broadly in the process. "See you later, Sister Silly. Thanks for taking Misty to the vet."

Cass put Misty into the quilted carrier Lovena Beiler had made and rode her bicycle to work with the kitten riding peacefully in the basket on her fender. It was only a few miles to Jesse's clinic, and the blue sky promised a beautiful day. October had been kind this year.

The day at the coffee shop seemed to drag, something that had never happened in the weeks since it opened. She had time to think more than she liked, recalling Linda's crush on Jesse in heartbreaking detail.

He was so quiet no one knew for sure how he really felt, but Cass still remembered him placing Linda's prom princess crown back on her head after the accident. He'd bent his head and kissed her and held her until Father Doherty had drawn him away so the emergency personnel could prepare her body for transport.

Half a lifetime later, Cass's heart broke again with the memory. When she pushed her bike into the rack at the barn that housed Jesse's veterinary practice, she had to stand for a minute and look over at the grapevines growing where the vineyard abutted Worth Farm. It was a peaceful view and she was glad for it.

The clinic was a busy place. "We're running behind," said the office manager apologetically. "We're *always* running behind. I warned your sister on the phone, but she said you needed to sit down and take a break more anyway."

After Misty weighed in at two pounds, seven ounces, and had her personal fact sheet created on the office computer, Cass took a seat beside a man with a miniature dachshund in his lap. A few minutes later she found herself to be a contributor in a discussion regarding the changing school schedules. She was surprised to have her opinion asked and even more surprised to discover exactly how strong her opinion was. Had Royce been there, she'd have been calling her Sister Long-Summer-Advocate.

By the time Jesse stepped out and beckoned her to follow him to an exam room, it was over an hour past her appointment time and the waiting room was empty. Misty had already used the litter box behind the desk and taken a rude swipe at the dachshund when he tried to be friendly.

Cass wasn't sure how people did it who had to take recalcitrant children to pediatricians. Especially in small communities, where before you knew it you found yourself volunteering to work for the blood drive because a woman with a Siamese cat who'd supported her school schedule views was with the American Red Cross.

"I'm sorry to be so late," said Jesse. "It gets crazy in here sometimes." He took Misty from her and smiled into the cat's face. "I see where you got your name, kitty. You're a pretty little thing, aren't you?"

While he examined ears and gave injections, they talked about Cass's return to the lake, about both his and Holly's and Libby and Tucker's upcoming weddings and about the orchard and coffee shop. Admittedly,

Jesse listened much more than he talked, but he was friendly. If he held a grudge against her, it was hidden under a professional demeanor.

"Luke's a nice guy," he said at one point. "It's really cool what you and he are doing at the orchard. Holly's getting me attached to your coffee."

"Thank you." She looked around. "This is great, too. I never knew—was this always your plan?"

"No." He smiled, but there wasn't any humor in it. "I was going to go to Paris and be a starving artist until I made a lot of money and became a rich one." He shrugged. "Life got in the way. You know how that goes."

"I do." *Just tell him you're sorry. Don't make a federal case out of it.*

He stroked the cat, not meeting her eyes. "Holly said you wanted to talk to me."

Cass chuckled, although it sounded hollow to her own ears. "Actually, I wanted to just have her give you a message, but she wouldn't do it."

"Yeah. Come on up front." He led the way to the office area behind the counter in the now-empty waiting room, gesturing for her to take a chair on one side of the partner desk while he sat in the one across from it. "Most of us who were in the accident have learned that we're better off with the direct route."

"Better, maybe, but it's still hard." Her voice shook in spite of herself. "I just wanted to say I'm sorry. I know it's a long time after the fact, but..."

He set Misty down and leaned forward, his elbows on the polished surface of the desk. "What are you sorry for?"

What was he saying? How could he not know? "Linda. I should have been sitting where she was. You lost her because of me."

He was silent for so long she thought he wasn't going to even acknowledge her apology, much less accept it. She started to get up, reaching for the kitten who'd made herself at home in the in basket on the desk.

"Please." He made a downward motion with his hands. She sat back. "Tell me that's not the reason you've stayed away from the lake all this time."

She shrugged. "It's not all of it. Like everyone else, my family has its share of dysfunction, so that's some of it, too. But feeling responsible for your best friend's death..." She had to stop and take a deep breath, and when she went on, she looked past Jesse at the painting on the wall behind him. "It takes its toll. I've made sure to never be best friends with anyone else. It was years before I'd drive or ride in a car my little sister was in. When I was married, we made the decision not to have kids and it was a relief because I couldn't stand the idea of being that responsible for someone's life."

She felt tears pushing at the backs of her eyes and had to stop again and focus on the painting. It was of a scene inside a tearoom. Not the one Neely ran, but somehow familiar. Cass would like to go there.

Jesse turned his head to follow the line of her vision. "That was Seven Pillars," he said. "Libby owned it for years. The tornado last spring destroyed the building. She reopened it where Just One of Those Things is, then sold the business to Neely." He chuckled. "She's going to college now, studying astronomy."

"It looks familiar. Probably because Libby designed the layout in both tearooms."

He nodded. "It surprised me when she sold it, but she had other dreams to follow, including marrying Tucker." He smiled, the quiet expression she remembered from high school days. "Don't change the subject. It sounds to me as if you *did* stay away for that reason."

"Sort of. After the accident and the funerals, I couldn't face anyone. I couldn't stand to think about it. I used to go to the cemetery and make sure flowers were always kept there, but one day when I went, Linda's mom was already there. She was lying on the ground beside the grave crying. I knew I'd done that to her because I changed seats with Linda." Cass gestured at the clinic surroundings. "You're here instead of in Paris with Linda. Because I changed seats." She laughed, the sound ragged. "And you don't have to tell me that's extreme. It's goofy. I *know* that, but it's not a feeling that goes away. I went home the next day—back to my mother's, I mean—and thought I'd make it easier if I just never came back."

"Holly and I didn't start seeing each other until last year," Jesse said without preamble. "But eighteen years ago I had it all planned out. Linda and I were going fishing the day after the prom and I was going to tell her I liked her a lot, but I wanted to see other people. Actually, the only other person I wanted to see was Holly, but I wasn't going to say that." He met Cass's eyes. "I was so ticked off at Lin the night of the accident. She took the whole prom princess thing so seriously she didn't even want to slow dance because she didn't want to mess up her dress, the same reason she wanted that seat in the van."

"I remember how much it meant to her."

"It did. And I felt guilty about wanting to break up with her. About being mad at her. Guilty enough I wouldn't ask Holly out no matter how much I wanted to. She asked me instead, finally—well, actually, she *told* me—and now we're going to have one of those happily-ever-afters she writes about. And she's going to make me dress weird in the process—I know dang well she is."

"You mean you don't blame me?"

He reached across the desk to grasp her hands. "Listen to me. Almost all of us who were in the wreck felt some sense of responsibility for it. A few of us, like Jack and maybe you, were driven by that culpability, no matter how wrong it was. We *all* carried that adolescent guilt into adulthood with us. I remember Nate Benteen telling Libby that we didn't take ownership of our lives—we just rented them until they became painful and then we let them go for something else."

Cass flinched. That came way too close to the bone for comfort.

He squeezed her hands. "No, I don't blame you. I'm sure Linda's mother doesn't, either. So, let it go—that's a mantra several of the survivors have latched on to. Remember something else, too. Linda would never have blamed you. She loved being best friends with you."

The tears slipped onto Cass's cheeks then. "I loved it, too."

He let her go and pushed a tissue box toward her. "Are we okay now?"

She blew her nose and smiled at him. "Yes. Does this mean you're going to talk to me when we see each other?"

He laughed, the sound so quiet a person couldn't have heard it more than three feet away. "Not a lot, but we're still friends." He picked Misty up and stroked her head. "Bring her back in next week to be spayed and don't let her eat from the table."

They walked outside together, Misty already snoozing in her carrier by the time Jesse put it in the bicycle basket. Cass was surprised when Jesse pulled her in for a quick hug. "Own your life," he said, holding her gaze. "It may not be the one you planned, but that doesn't mean it can't be good."

They both looked up in surprise when the orchard truck pulled up beside them. Luke rolled the window down, looking a little embarrassed. "I was afraid you'd be riding home in the dark." He waved at Jesse. "I know how this guy can talk your arm off."

Jesse grinned at him. "I talk about as much as you climb trees. Want the bike in the back?"

"I can ride home." Cass frowned at first one and then the other.

"You can," Luke agreed, getting out and walking around to drop the pickup's tailgate. "But why would you when I'm right here and you can probably talk me into pizza? Everyone else in our respective families is eating somewhere else."

"Well, then." A tremor of glee made the hair on the back of her neck stand up. "I'd be foolish to turn that down, wouldn't I?"

As if she'd ever want to.

CHAPTER THIRTEEN

"I THINK WE should have a festival."

They were in the middle of what Luke and Cass had placed on their new schedule as their Monday morning business meeting, only it was happening on Halloween night after closing at Ground in the Round. They'd somehow missed Monday, and it had been a busy week. Many people, including several who worked for the orchard, equated Halloween with apples, so Keep Cold had held a party in the retail store and opened the parking lot to a Trunk-or-Treat celebration. If Luke never saw another piece of candy corn, it would be way too soon.

Zoey, Luke and Cass sat at a table with Luke's yellow legal pad, Zoey's leather-bound notebook and Cass's laptop. They were drinking the last of the day's coffee and talking about winter plans for the retail store.

They certainly hadn't been talking about festivals. They hadn't even cleaned up the

Halloween mess yet. Not that there was all that much, but still...

Luke put down the cup he'd just picked up and stared at Zoey. "You do know this is the wrong end of apple season for that, right? A festival would have been good a month ago or two weeks ago or even right now, but we should have planned it last year or at least this spring. Am I making sense?"

"Of course you are." Zoey waved a dismissive hand at him. "What does that have to do with anything?"

"Zoey, do you know how much work a festival would be?"

"I do. Do *you* know we've been cutting back hours enough that people would be glad for more of them? Besides, festivals are fun. We have plenty of apples and we've been keeping the retail store stocked to stay open all winter. We could have things like face painting and a coloring contest. Maybe even bob for apples the way people used to do all the time—is that even legal anymore? And a wine tasting! I'm sure Sycamore Hill would be glad to set one up and staff it."

He hated to curb her enthusiasm, especially since he could see interest brightening Cass's blue-green eyes, but the idea of creating a festival out of thin air was just crazy. Admittedly, opening a coffee shop had been crazy, too, and it was going great guns, but there just wasn't time for a festival. Not this late in the season, with Thanksgiving just over the horizon and Christmas a mere heartbeat after that. Tourism died almost completely away from the lake during the cold winter months, so local businesses made the most of the holidays.

"I don't think it's reasonable," he said firmly. He hated doing that; it reminded Zoey that she was no longer actually a voting member of Keep Cold Orchard even though he and Cass always included her in business discussions. "We've had a good financial year, especially with the addition of the coffee shop. Taking a chance on the spur of the moment like this would be too…chancy."

Zoey frowned. Cass drained her cup and refilled it. Luke refilled his, too. Misty jumped onto his knee, but only stayed long enough to bite his index finger before leaping lightly into Zoey's lap and settling in.

He thought it would be a good idea to make the coffee shop a cat-free environment, but he was almost positive that suggestion wouldn't go over well. He'd be lucky if Cass didn't throw in with her aunt on the crazy festival idea.

"I think we could do it."

And maybe he *wouldn't* be so lucky.

Cass's words were laced with challenge. Her chin had a little extra lift to it, too. He remembered the evening before, when they'd watched movies and eaten popcorn and laughed in his living room. Afterward, they'd put on sweatshirts and gloves and walked the lit path around the perimeter of the lake. There'd been much kissing and conversation involved, and when he'd stood lakeside with her held firmly in his arms, he'd had to remind himself that neither of them was interested in a serious relationship.

Sometimes, when the challenge in both her voice and her chin presented themselves, he thought a business relationship wasn't such a great idea, either. Other than the coffee shop thing—which had exceeded even Cass's expectations. And the fact that he got to see her every day.

The fact that he never *didn't* want to see her planted a little seed of concern in the back of his mind. Just a small one that he was doing just fine at ignoring. Just fine.

"We don't have time," he said again.

The chin lifted higher. She had the most amazing profile. "*You* may not. I know you have much to do with winter coming on. But the rest of us can certainly make time. When, Aunt Zoey?"

"The weekend after the one coming up. That will give us two weeks. What do you think?"

Cass's eyes widened and she swallowed, but then she nodded. "Okay." She turned her head enough to meet his eyes. "Okay?"

He frowned. First at her, then at Zoey, then at her again. "It's crazy. Where did it come from and why now? The holidays are coming. Football's still going on. Whatever you do on that computer of yours takes up a ton of your time. We didn't allow either hours or money for anything like this when we made up the schedule and the budget. It's…well, like I said, it's crazy."

"That may be, but it's personal," said Zoey. "Damaris and Royce might not be here next year and we want to show them everything about lake life we can. And you know it would be good for business for everyone, not just the orchard. The tourists might stay around for another weekend to see what's going on."

He sighed, got no reaction and sighed again. "Okay. I won't stand in your way." He sighed one more time, thinking surely one of them would realize they were being both unprofessional and manipulative, but they just looked at him. "How can I help?"

"We'll take care of it," Zoey assured him. "If you'll make sure the little field beside the parking lot is mowed so vendors can set up tents, we'll try to leave you alone."

He nodded and smiled. But he didn't believe a word of it.

"I THINK MAYBE we unleashed a monster." Three days later, Cass and Luke walked between the rows of leased vendor tents in the little meadow. They'd rented ten, hoping they'd be able to fill that many, but had ended up getting five more. Three other vendors had rented the empty spaces in the round barn.

"We?" He raised an eyebrow and moved his shoulders with an exaggerated groan. "She's been working us both to death."

She laughed. "Not only us. It's everyone she's come in contact with. She dropped Misty off at the vet clinic to be spayed and ended up talking Jesse into an art show in the barn. He got the Miniagua Arts League involved, so it'll be a good-sized show. Damaris is pleased because that's something she can help with even though she's not very mobile yet." She beamed at him. "Your sisters rented a tent. I didn't know they made jewelry."

"I hope you charged them extra."

She smacked his arm. "I didn't want to charge them at all, but they were insistent on paying. Said it was a business expense and that you'd pay it for them."

He snorted. "Like that's going to happen. But I'd have charged them more just for the trouble they'll cause."

"That's what Rachel said." Cass laughed, remembering the conversation from the day before. "She said some other things, too."

"Don't believe them."

"Where do they live?" She'd met his parents when they'd come down to watch Seth play football, but Rachel and Leah hadn't visited since Cass had come back to the lake.

"Pennsylvania. The same community where we lived until I was in college and the girls were in high school. They're both married and have kids. Rachel's a teacher and Leah's a pharmacist."

"What do your brothers-in-law do?"

"They're farmers, plus Abe does financial consulting. Both girls had always said they'd never marry farmers, because spending their teenage years in a rural area convinced them Philadelphia was in their future, but now they live on opposite sides of their husbands' family farm about three miles from where we grew up and nothing would ever move them."

"I can understand wanting something different. Growing up on military installations convinced me I never wanted to do that again." Tony and his family had always lived in cities, and she'd loved that. It still amazed her that a lake in the middle of Indiana farmland was the place that held her heart. "Do they like it here?"

He shrugged. "They've never spent much time here. Their kids are busy enough, and the farm and the girls' jobs are demanding enough that they don't get away all that often. I have no idea what's bringing them here now."

"Rachel said on the phone that they crossed their fingers and the stars aligned." Cass thought maybe there was some curiosity involved with the visit, too, that the sisters wondered about the unknown females their brothers were spending time with.

Luke smiled then, his chocolate-colored eyes softening with the expression. "They're good people," he said. "I'll be glad to see them."

"I was thinking…" But Cass's voice faded away when she looked at him. It was there in his face, in the sweetness of his expression, the slashes on either side of his mouth when he smiled. She could see it in his eyes when they met hers—especially right before he kissed her. They changed then. Darkened and lit at the same time as if they were relating the same message as his lips did when they covered hers. This was a man she could love. Or more than love. This was someone she could weave the parts of her life with the way they tangled their fingers when they held hands.

As if on cue, pain rippled down her arm. She knew it was from lymphedema, a buildup of fluid resulting from her mastectomy, but it reminded her of what had been and might be again. While fear of recurrence didn't dominate every day of her life, it did influence thoughts of her future.

She looked at the man walking beside

her, who'd already lost one woman he loved to disease. Cass thought his feelings mirrored her own—it showed in those eyes she couldn't stop looking into—but she was almost certain he wouldn't be willing to risk loving a cancer survivor. Even if she was his business partner.

Especially if she was his business partner.

She rubbed her arm.

He frowned. "You all right?"

"Yes."

"What were you thinking?"

She frowned. "About what?"

He laughed. "I don't know. You said you were thinking, but then you stopped."

"Oh! Good heavens, where is my mind?" She knew very well where it was, but it wasn't information she was going to share. "I was thinking about having some music in the coffee shop during the festival. Just for a few hours in the afternoon. What do you think?"

"Good idea. Music is always popular. It might be hard to find someone this late in the game, though."

"Oh well, yeah, that was the rest of what I was thinking." She ducked her head, feeling more adolescent than she had when she *was* an adolescent. "And what Royce, Zoey and Damaris were thinking, too. Seth was playing his guitar at the house the other night and we thought you and he might like to play for a while. And sing."

For a moment, she wondered if she'd made a mistake. Although she'd seen the four guitars that sat on stands in his living room, he'd never mentioned them, much less picked up an instrument to play. She'd been curious, but was reserved enough to respect the fact that he'd never talked about music. Maybe she should have asked—not everyone had a privacy gene as developed as hers. "Have I crossed a line?"

"No," he said quickly. "No. There's no secret. We could do that if it's okay with Seth, I guess. We might be on the rusty side. Other than church at Christmas and at family reunions when Rachel gets insistent, we don't play in public very often. We play every day, but that's different than practicing for performance."

"It is?"

He laughed. "Sure it is. We don't use a playlist at home, and if we blow a song, we stop in the middle and go back to its beginning. Ten times, if that's what it takes, or even more. Seth only changes his guitar strings when his are so dead the music's all gone from them. We both have stage fright to the extent that we have to play a few instrumentals before trusting our voices to sing."

"I had no idea what was involved." She couldn't write with music in the background, although having Royce in the house had taught her to block it out. Cass never even turned on the car radio. She'd been pleasantly surprised at Seth's first football game to discover she still remembered all the words to Miniagua's school song. "I'm afraid I'm not musical. My tin ear matches my two left feet." The admission made her feel even more awkward than she actually was.

"Everybody's musical." His smile crinkled the skin around his eyes, and she found herself unable to look away. They'd stopped walking at some point and were standing close enough that she could feel his body heat as they faced each other in the crisp intimacy offered by twilight.

She shook her head, looking down. "Not everybody."

"Oh yes, everybody. You just haven't heard the right song yet." His hand shaped her face, lifting it to his, and he kissed her. She was reminded of when they'd danced right here to the imaginary tune of the apple orchard waltz. He'd told her the music was in her heart. She'd laughed, enjoying being in his arms.

She enjoyed it again now, the warm, leisurely sharing of kisses taking her breath away. "Maybe someone was right a week or so back," she whispered, her mouth close to his, "when he told me to dance from my heart. I think that's where I need to listen from, too."

"Oh, yes, Sister Dances-in-the-Orchard," he whispered. "You're absolutely right."

And so she danced. And she listened.

CHAPTER FOURTEEN

CASS HADN'T INTENDED to spend so much of the festival walking around in a Keep Cold Orchard baseball cap and a Ground in the Round hooded sweatshirt with a clipboard on her arm taking notes. She'd tried to give the clipboard to Zoey, who'd played her senior citizen card and said she needed to run the cash register in the orchard store during the festival.

"Aunt Zoey, this was all your idea. The least you can do is check its progress."

"But it's your business. You'll want to know what to do and what not to do next year." Zoey beamed at her. "And the year after." She counted change back to a customer with thanks. "Besides, walking around the whole area is a little more than my sciatic nerve will allow."

"Your sciatic nerve is pretty selective about when it shows up, isn't it?" Cass raised a skeptical eyebrow, but spoiled the effect by grinning at her aunt. "Have fun. I'll catch up later." She snagged a cup of hot cider and moved on.

The crowd was surprisingly large given the last-minute organization of the event. What was also surprising was how many people she knew. By the time she'd perused all the tent area, making notes all the way, she'd talked to half the survivors of the accident, promised Gianna to come for dinner one night the following week and agreed reluctantly to speak to the Write Now group at the high school.

Royce was going to just love that.

Kari Ross, walking with Arlie, reminded her that her appointment would be Tuesday at the Indianapolis office. She'd have all the results of the testing ready to talk about. Had she gotten her blood work yet? Was she worried about anything?

Cass hadn't been—at least, not much— but after seeing the gynecologist, she had to switch the clipboard to the other arm for a while.

All of the vendors in the tents seemed to be happy with both attendance and sales. Luke's sisters presented her with a necklace and matching earrings. When she dug into her pocket for money, they shook their heads.

"It's a sympathy offering." Rachel looked woeful. "He may seem like a nice guy, but the minute your back is turned, he'll rat you out to our parents."

Leah elbowed her. "He only did that to you because you wrecked the car and blamed him." She turned a very familiar smile on Cass. "He really is a nice guy, and we're seeing a look on his face we haven't seen in far too long. We love him and we're grateful."

Cass walked on with a little extra bounce in her step, the pain in her arm forgotten for the time being.

She supplied a couple of extension cords, made change for a woman selling Christmas ornaments whose first customer had paid with a hundred-dollar bill and handed out coupons for free cups of coffee from Ground in the Round. When she was unable to talk Mary Detwiler's little brother down from a Golden Delicious tree, she climbed up after him, bowing red-facedly to the applause when she descended with the little boy and the clipboard both intact.

She was still blushing and brushing leaves from her sweatshirt when she reached the coffee shop. It was packed, with Royce, Mary and Libby Worth all serving customers. Cass stopped short—Libby didn't even work there.

"Royce said I could have all the pumpkin spice latte I could drink if I helped through lunchtime." Libby handed Cass a cup of coffee. "I was having so much fun, I just stayed."

The sound of guitars tuning up behind her made Cass turn to find its source. A stool beside her emptied and she slid onto it, fanning herself against the warmth generated by the number of people in the room.

Luke and Seth sat side by side on barstools with microphones in front of them. They both wore faded jeans and boots. Seth's shirt was denim, Luke's flannel.

Cass thought they would look spectacular on the cover of a magazine. Any magazine. It had been a long time since she'd seen that much gorgeous in one spot. A look at her sister, standing spellbound with a tray of empty cups in her hands, indicated the fascination with the Rossiter brothers seemed to be a family affliction.

They played and sang for two hours, their play list both eclectic and flexible; when a seven-year-old asked them to sing her favorite song from a Disney movie, Luke and

Seth pulled up another stool so she could sing with them. When the audience cheered and clapped enthusiastically, they performed for another fifteen minutes before getting to their feet and stepping away from the corner that had become a stage for a magical space in time.

Cass, who should have made another round of the premises with her trusty clipboard but had not, smiled when Luke approached. "Well, Brother Six String, keeping secrets, were you?"

He grinned at her, taking her cup from her hand and finishing her coffee, a gesture so intimate it took her breath away. Of course, he in his flannel shirt with his mellow voice and nimble fingers on guitar strings had already done that pretty well. "You knew I played."

"I did," she admitted, "but you never talked about it. I assumed you were a living room musician."

"I am," he said. "I'm what I call a banger, and bangers come in different degrees. I'm better than some, worse than a lot of others. Seth has a better ear, I think, although I'm not going to tell him that anytime soon."

"And your singing?"

He shrugged, color creeping up his cheeks. "I like to sing."

She thought for a moment about her writing, about the fact that she did it every single day whether the words were flowing or not. On the days she missed—which she'd had more of since coming back to the lake than she'd had in years—there was an unfilled place inside. But if anyone asked her, she knew she'd answer just as he had. She'd just say she liked to write.

She hadn't thought liking and passion were intended to be synonymous, but sometimes they were. She wondered, as he sat beside her and laid a casual arm over her shoulders, where love came into the equation. Or if it did.

LUKE SQUINTED AT the bottom line on the handwritten ledger sheet Zoey handed him. "I think I'm going to give up any pretense at management and just be the cider-press-and-tractor fixer in the future of the orchard. I have been so completely wrong about everything this season." It was there again, the doubt that had come to Miniagua and Keep Cold Orchard along with Cass Gentry. While he had to admit that going from a one-man show to a man-and-woman management team was working, the near certainty that it wouldn't continue to do so was a daily concern. If their business relationship became a problem, what would happen to their personal one?

"It was great, wasn't it?" Zoey beamed. "The people who had pieces in the art show were ecstatic. Jesse sold two paintings and he wasn't the only one. A gallery owner from Indianapolis who attended the festival offered solo shows to a couple of artists, Jesse included."

"The vendors were all happy, too." Cass held up her clipboard. "Even the ones who didn't sell as much as they'd hoped wanted to put their names in for next year."

"And, finally, if you decide the cider press needs to be replaced instead of repaired, we can do it without breaking the bank." Triumph rang through her voice, but then Zoey's cheeks grew pink. "I'm sorry. You two are way too good at including me in things. I forget I'm no longer an owner."

Luke and Cass exchanged glances. "You know," he said, "it will always be your orchard whether your name is on the deed or not." He grinned. "If for no other reason than

I won't have my half paid off any time within the next decade or two."

Luke was happy for Zoey and Cass. Happy for the orchard and its employees. The festival had padded the operations account enough that investing in new equipment wouldn't signal a financial disaster.

He wasn't so sure he was happy for himself, but he hadn't figured out why. This was what he'd wanted for Keep Cold, wasn't it? He'd wanted the orchard to prosper and grow. He and Chris Granger were well on their way in the development of the Keep Cold label for Sycamore Hill Winery. Luke had talked with a grower from Southern Indiana who was itching to sell his fifty acres of apple trees and retire to Arizona. Those were the kinds of progress his engineer's mind embraced. Not coffee shops and festivals or the weekly competitions that had started with the naming of the coffee shop. The last contest had been to see who made the best apple dumpling, where Cass's had come in not only last but *very* last. The one before that had been jack-o'-lantern decorating.

Was he jealous that the things the women had seemingly thrown together were working so well while his ideas seemed to take years? He'd been fighting the cider press ever since he'd taken over the orchard, yet the festival had been instantly successful. The coffee shop, even with all of the requisite new-business hiccups and a few expenses that had been both unexpected and shocking, was holding its own nicely.

He thought of the phone call he'd gotten that morning, from the structural engineer who'd mentored him through his first job and been there for advice through the two that followed it when Luke had moved on to larger firms. Usually Dan Graham just called to talk—this morning he'd called with a job offer.

Was it time to go back to the profession he'd once loved? It wasn't like it was a new idea. As much as he enjoyed the orchard, he'd never planned to make it a career. The fact that it had become even an interim one still surprised him.

"Your sisters said to put them down for a booth next year," said Cass. "Rachel said for you to hurry and get your bathroom done so they could stay at your house."

He frowned, trying to bring his attention back to the conversation. "I've lived with Rachel. We had to share a bathroom when we were kids. I'm not doing it again."

"I don't think she intends for you to be there. She mentioned the campgrounds across the lake."

"I'll bet she did."

And Rachel had a point. If he finished the bathroom and a few other things during the coming winter, the lake house could become the rental he'd once intended it to be. The new job, if he took it, would be a financial boon. The price of his health insurance would go down when its premium costs were subsidized by a company, and he could once again support his retirement account on a consistent basis.

For a moment, even with the pleasant sounds of Cass and laughter in his cars, he heard another voice.

Really, Luke? Your retirement account? A rental house? You haven't even been to Europe or skydived yet and you're thinking about retirement? I'm the one who died here, not you.

He wondered why it was that when he tried to recall the sound of Jill's voice, he couldn't do it. It would remain frustratingly out of reach. Just when he'd think he had it, the sound would float away. But now, when he wasn't looking for it in the least, when he was in fact thinking about another woman, his wife's impatient rebuke rang loud and clear.

You're wrong, Jilly. I know it worked for us, but it won't work again, and I couldn't go through that kind of losing again. You know that.

For a moment, he thought he'd spoken aloud, and felt familiar color rise in his cheeks. "It's going great," he said, putting down the ledger sheet and smiling at both his partners. "Keep Cold's best season yet."

He'd worry about *his* season later.

"JUST LET ME skip school tomorrow. That way, if you're not feeling well after your appointment I can drive us home, and if you *do* feel well we can go dress shopping."

Royce rarely wheedled, although she was doing a creditable job of it now. It was hard to turn her down when she seldom asked for anything other than the daily request for a car of her own, but Cass didn't want her little sister there if the visit with Kari Ross didn't go as she hoped. She knew "not feeling well" was a polite euphemism for bad news.

"Sorry, Roycie." She shook her head.

"Luke's taking me. It may not be the most romantic date ever, but it's still a date." Luke sat at the counter, and she cast him a pleading glance. *Just go along with me.* "We'll go shopping for your dress over the weekend."

"In Indy?"

Cass sighed. "Indy or Fort Wayne. Your choice."

"Can I take a friend with me?"

"Yes. I will, too, and we can stay in town for dinner."

"How much can I spend?"

"Up to your mother, but remember—if you want another new dress for the Valentine's dance and one for the prom, too, you might want to keep things reasonable." *You're welcome, Damaris.*

Royce sighed. "Okay." She gave Cass a hug. "Can I leave now? Seth and I are going for pizza. Mom knows. She and Aunt Zoey went to the movies."

"Go ahead. Luke will help me close up."

"Okay. Thanks, Luke!" Royce waved at Luke and left the coffee shop, turning off the open sign on the way out.

Cass finished cleaning while Luke washed the tables. "You don't have to take me," she said, avoiding his gaze when they both found themselves in the same space between two tables and ended up face-to-face. "I just wanted to appease Royce."

"I'll take you." He didn't meet her eyes, either. Instead, he closed his and bent slightly to kiss her gently. Warmly. His hands came to rest on her shoulders. More warmth.

Is this what it was like to feel completely safe? She'd never felt like this with Tony. Or at any other time. Ever.

"No." She shook her head and moved one foot, then stood still so he could kiss her again. Longer. Warmer. Maybe not quite so gently. "Luke." She put her hands on his chest and tried not to think about how much she'd just like to leave them there. How much she'd like to be just Cass Gentry and hang on for dear life because, heaven help her, she was so scared. She shuddered, hoping he wouldn't feel the tremor, and said, "Really. I'm better doing this on my own," although the words rattled on their way out. "I'm used to it."

She wasn't. No one got used to it. They just lived with it. Or died with it.

"No one's better doing that on their own."

"Did you used to go with Jill?"

"I did. Every time."

"Did she want you to?"

"Not always. She used to get mad about

it sometimes. She'd say she had few enough choices in life without me taking more of them away."

"She was right."

"Probably. I still went with her. Those days were some of the best and some of the worst ones we ever had together and I wouldn't give up a single one of them. I'm pretty convinced she wouldn't have, either."

Relief was weakening both her legs and her resolve. "We shouldn't both be away from the orchard at once."

"Haven't you noticed that the orchard's employees are the best ones anywhere? They only put up with me hanging around to make me feel good about myself, and I assume Zoey can run the coffee shop."

"She could, but Libby's going to do it. She misses her tearoom—not enough to have another one, but enough to spend a few days here and there at Ground in the Round." Cass took a deep breath, feeling it flutter inside her chest. "I really don't mind—"

"I do." His fingers lay against her lips. "I mind."

"Okay." She gave up and sat down. "Thank you."

"What time is your appointment?"

"Ten."

"Will you be able to sleep tonight?"

"I hope so."

"Want to go out for some dinner?"

It would probably be a good idea. Although she wasn't hungry now, she'd be starving by the time she left the doctor's office otherwise. At least she could eat some soup. "Can we walk partway around the lake first? It's getting colder every night and pretty soon I won't even want to walk to the car. I spent enough time in California to be completely unprepared for a midwestern winter."

Ten minutes later, when they were walking the lit pathway, Luke asked, "Do you think of going back?"

She nodded. "Only when I think of Royce going back with her mother. Then I'd want to visit them there. I let my apartment go and put everything in storage. I need to decide what to sell and what to keep, but I have to admit the only thing I've missed a lot since we came here is my food processor. I like it better than Zoey's." A gust of wind made its way inside her coat, and she shivered. "And the weather. I think I'm going to miss it."

Something in his silence alerted her that there had been more to his question than casual conversation. She frowned. "Why? Do you think of leaving?"

Dry leaves skittered across the paved path, whispering their hurried escape. The water slapped against the shore. Restlessness filled the air. He walked on without answering her question. And then he did.

"Yeah, I do. Sometimes."

CHAPTER FIFTEEN

"DO YOU DREAD IT?" Luke looked over at Cass. She'd been quiet since he'd picked her up twenty minutes before for the two-hour drive to Kari's Indianapolis office. He'd reached for her hand and held it on the console between them in the confines of his car. She hadn't pulled away, but she hadn't turned her fingers to hold his, either.

She nodded. "The first time I had to go back for follow-up, three months after treatment, I was a basket case. It gets a little easier each time, and I hope after this I won't have to show up for a year. But I'm not intuitive at all. I never know what to expect."

He gave her a skeptical look. He'd have bet she was. "You sure intuited out the coffee shop, Sister Followed-Her-Instincts."

She laughed, although it sounded forced and didn't show up in her eyes. "Everyone gets lucky sometimes. But back when I had to go in after a mammogram showed something, I thought it was just a bad picture. I take terrible ones, after all. When they said I had cancer, I thought it was all a mistake because…well, because I should have known, right? But I didn't. And then I thought I'd get by with treatment or maybe a lumpectomy and didn't even worry about anything more invasive. I now have a mastectomy and reconstruction under my surgical belt. Following those instincts you just so rudely made fun of doesn't always work out well in the scheme of things." By the time she finished speaking, her voice was brittle, although her smile held firmly.

"Point taken. Just think about this, then, after you're done at the doctor's office—or offices, because you have to see the oncologist, too, right?—we'll stop for a lunch you don't have to either prepare *or* pay for. How's that?" He wanted to make her smile into a real one, but it wasn't working.

Ten minutes later, he remembered why it wasn't working. It wasn't the first time, either, although the memory had slipped away. "She did it for me."

Cass looked at him, a frown between her eyes. "Did what?"

"Oh, noth—" He stopped, swallowed and

went on. "I used to say ridiculous things to Jill when we were on the way to the doctor. Sing stupid parodies of songs. Tell horrible jokes. Anything to make her laugh. And she always did. Always." Pain angled sharply through him with the memory. "It just occurred to me—again—that she did it for me, to make *me* feel better. It cost me nothing to try to make her laugh—how much did it cost her to do the laughing?"

Cass hesitated. "I didn't know Jill, but I doubt if she laughed just to make you feel better. I don't believe you're that kind of needy." She grinned, turned toward him and pulled her knees onto the seat. Her fingers curled around his. "Matter of fact, if you look back really hard, wasn't there at least one time when she said, 'Hey, buddy, everything isn't about you,' and just ignored you?"

He raised an eyebrow, the last remnant of pain washing away in a tide of something else. Something warm and exciting and impossible. "Is that what you're saying to me?"

"Pretty much."

"Jill wouldn't have done that."

"Bet she would've."

"Yeah, you're right. She would've."

They laughed together, there in the cozy

warmth of the car, and Luke was pretty sure he heard a third voice in the laughter. He knew it was fanciful, but he wondered by the way she held her head if Cass had heard Jill laughing, too.

"Tell me about her. I've seen her picture at your house, but that doesn't really tell me what she sounded like or what music she liked or if she liked to read." Cass's voice gentled. "I'd like to be friends with her."

"She'd like that."

At first it was hard. He felt disloyal, but knew Jill would have been the first to snort at that very thought. Being loyal to a memory wasn't a concept she'd have appreciated. He thought of conversations with Mollie, which had given him such comfort after Jill's death when no one even seven-year-old Seth in his own profound grief—was willing to talk about her.

"Mollie said, after she died, that while she was an angel now, the Jill we knew hadn't been one at all. She was so funny." He thought for a minute, struggling with the memory, and went on. "When she was in the hospital the last time, she was worried about her hair because the last cut hadn't been a very good one. She told her doctor she couldn't die until her bangs grew out. He said of course she couldn't, but she could and she did. At the funeral home, he cried because he hadn't been able to keep his promise."

He knew that later that night Zoey would either call or text him and ask if Cass really was all right or if she was just saying so to keep her family from worrying about her. Luke would be as honest as he could without telling anything Cass might have asked him not to tell.

He wouldn't say aloud that talking to Cass about Jill was the closest he'd ever come to letting go of the woman he'd loved. He wouldn't admit that his clumsy attempt to make Cass feel better had ended with him realizing beyond all doubt that he wanted her to be a part of every day for the rest of his life.

However, he'd been there before and he couldn't go back. Even when he completed the process of letting go, he couldn't return to that place.

But he would think about that later, when Cass wasn't sitting beside him in his car. Her body was as aligned with his as if they were touching when they weren't really, other than her fingers tangled with his. When she laughed and leaned in his direction in tandem with the laughter, he could smell her hair and the scent of her skin that was both delicate and earthy at the same time.

He would think about it when he wasn't conscious of her leggings-clad knee so close to their hands that he finally moved their joined fingers to let them rest on the warm fabric. He could feel the smoothness of her skin through the soft knit, but he wasn't going to think about that yet. That would come later, too.

They parked at the medical building with ten minutes to spare. When they walked toward its doors, she reached for the hand that had held hers for the last hour. Her fingers were still warm from his touch, a little damp. They trembled within his, and his heart broke more than he thought he could bear. But he knew he had to put that new laceration away in a safe place or he wouldn't be at all what she needed today or ever. He would think about that later, too.

This was the point where Jill's courage would waver and he would power up his own.

He stopped, pulling Cass to a standstill beside him, and held her amazing turquoise gaze. "Don't be scared," he said, and it was as if he was hearing his voice say the same words a hundred times before. "I'll be right here."

For just a minute—no, less than that—Cass leaned into him, her fragrant hair soft and warm against his neck. She felt as frail as she had the first time he'd seen her, standing tall and arrow-straight in her too-big black dress and greeting mourners when her mother died.

She straightened, releasing his hand, and gave an assertive nod. "It'll be fine. *I'll* be fine."

Just as he had those hundred times before, he stretched his face into a smile and nodded, too. "You sure will. I can't manage that daggone coffee shop by myself. Come on, Sister Tall Woman, let's go."

"LET'S DO A BIOPSY." Kari Ross's voice was quiet and firm. The sympathy was in her eyes and the way they held Cass's gaze. "We're not going to panic or count our chickens before they hatch or any of that kind of thing. You know the percentages—it's probably a cyst. You've had them before."

"Or it could be cancer metastasized to my ovary."

"It could."

"Can we take care of this at home or do I need to come here?"

"We can do it at the hospital in Sawyer." Kari pointed at the screen. "Everything on every test looks good. Every single thing. But ovarian cysts are weird things, especially after breast cancer. We just have to be certain."

"I know." Cass took a deep breath. "I know."

"How's your arm doing?"

"It hurts sometimes."

"But no swelling?"

Cass thought about that and realized there wasn't, nor had there been for months. "None at all."

"Been doing the exercises?"

Her face must have been a giveaway, because Kari shook her head, grinning at her.

"Thought so. Do them. And don't work so hard. And don't be scared. When is your oncologist's appointment?"

"A half hour."

"We'll call over there with your appointment for the biopsy." The doctor's dark eyes held Cass's again. "I know you're going to worry. I'll make it as soon as I can. What color of balloons do you want?"

Cass frowned. "Balloons?"

"Yeah, for when it comes back benign. We tend to party a lot at the clinic on the lake." Kari squeezed her hand. "I know it seems like every step of this journey is uphill, and a ton of them are, but you're never alone while you're traveling. That's a promise from A Woman's Place."

She was still scared, Cass admitted to herself later, after hearing more encouraging words from the oncologist, but it was a different kind of fear than she'd felt before.

The restaurant Luke chose for their long-awaited lunch was crowded but quiet. They sat across from each other and drank their first coffee of the day, neither of them needing to talk about just how good it was. But Luke did anyway.

"It's better at the Round, so it's a basic requirement of our Keep Cold partnership for you to stay healthy."

"I'll give it my best shot." She finished the coffee. "And you're wrong—that was every bit as good as we make at the Round. I need more."

They talked about the coffee shop during lunch, still trying to decide on a definite closing time.

"There are evenings," he argued, "when there are only two people in there after six o'clock."

"And others when there are two dozen." A situation that was always unexpected and therefore the shop was understaffed, but she didn't want to mention that part.

"Why not just open it for events?" he suggested. "Meetings or parties. That's what Neely does with the tearoom. Libby did, too. That works."

"I know." But it wasn't what she wanted. She wanted accessibility for people who needed a place to go, whether it was to work or to be alone or even if they wanted to talk to someone. "But when I—" She stopped. She didn't intend to share her personal life, but this day had so much of it bubbling to the surface she didn't know what else to do with it.

"When you what?"

She looked down at her fingernails. They were short and neat and polished the purple Royce had festooned them with over the weekend. During chemo, Cass remembered, they'd become brittle and ragged and she'd spent hours on them, thinking they were at least one thing in her besieged life she could have control over. She'd been wrong, but she'd tried.

"When I was sick before, I still had computer work to do, but I couldn't concentrate at home for some reason. I think it was because instead of being alone, I'd be alone with cancer and, believe me, that's one nasty housemate." The words came out in a rush, and she met his eyes, asking him to withhold comment until she'd finished. "So I'd get up in the morning and take all my meds and then I'd go down to the coffee shop. It was only a block, but I had to drive or I'd be exhausted by the time I got there. After the first few days, they knew me—I was probably the only bald woman in the place most of the time—and my cup of medium grind with hazelnut syrup and half-and-half was ready for me before I ever got to the counter to order. They called me by name, and I knew all theirs. I always took the worst table in the place because I was a table hog, and pretty soon they took my coffee there so I wouldn't have to pick it up and struggle with it and my laptop and my purse. When my mother died, there was a bouquet of daisies and a card on the table."

Before she knew it was happening, tears

tumbled down her cheeks, and she looked away in embarrassment when the pretty server refilled their cups and gave her a glance that was both questioning and sympathetic.

Luke caught Cass's hand. "That's why," he said, "Ground in the Round is more than a coffee shop to you. It's a lifeline, isn't it? Not for you specifically, but for people who might need one."

She nodded. "Probably." She scrabbled in her purse for a tissue and turned away again to blow her nose. "I'm sorry. I didn't mean to go all drama queen on you. And I realize we don't have the coffee shop as a philanthropic entity, but—"

"We have the coffee shop for whatever reasons we choose, as long as they're legal and within our own moral and business values. I think what you're talking about fits those parameters just fine."

She picked up her cup, then set it down. "Are you really that nice of a guy?"

He straightened in his seat, scowling at her in phony outrage. "I am. Didn't my mother just tell you that at the festival? Were you not even listening?"

"No, she told me you'd never met a clothes

hamper you liked and that you hogged any device that even resembled a remote control. She didn't mention anything about a nice guy."

"I'm sure she meant to."

"She probably did." She met his eyes. He hadn't asked any questions after they'd left either doctor's office, other than, "Is there anywhere we need to go besides lunch?" She could see concern in his expression, but she knew he wouldn't ask unless she indicated she was willing to talk about the events of the morning.

She thought of Kari's promise and remembered the table in the Sacramento coffee shop. She'd felt alone then, she realized, but she hadn't been. Not really. And she was even less so now.

And she remembered that on the way here this morning, when her mind was on the sharper edge of crazy, he'd talked about Jill. He'd shared not only the joy of loving her but the pain of losing her. Sometimes his fingers had grasped hers so tightly it had hurt, but Cass would have allowed the grip to draw blood before she would have pulled away.

Neither of them wanted permanence in a relationship—that wasn't even in question.

Yet they had bonded over grief and laughter, two of life's great motivators. They had known, whether they said the words or not, that they'd ventured further into intimacy than they'd intended to go.

The tears threatened again, pushing at her eyes and making her find another tissue. She was afraid, and she wasn't alone.

She pushed away her plate and drew her cup closer. There was always comfort in a warm mug.

And she said, "I have to have a biopsy."

CHAPTER SIXTEEN

"JUST COME AND take a look," Dan Graham encouraged via Skype. "I'll even take you to check out a cider press while you're here if you're worried about wasting time away from your orchard. You can fly out one day and back the next."

Luke sat at his desk in the orchard's office. It was usually the most cluttered place in the apple barn, but the loss of a teenage employee's cell phone had necessitated a thorough cleaning. He had to admit it looked kind of nice this way. Professional, even. But he couldn't find a thing.

Dan looked tired, and Luke wanted to help him. The other man's mentorship had been priceless in those first years after college. It would be nice to repay some of that support.

"Monday?" he said. "The orchard barn is closed all week for Thanksgiving." A nice thing about having a rural business was that Black Friday shopping wasn't an issue. Cass had even agreed to close the coffee shop from Thursday through Sunday to give everyone a break.

"That would work. You want to get your flight and we'll reimburse? That way you can schedule at your convenience." Dan sounded pleased.

"Sure."

He hung up and gazed out the window over the desk at the neat rows of trees. He wouldn't have to tell anyone where he was going, although he'd probably tell Seth and their parents. But he didn't want Cass to know. Not yet. She had enough on her mind.

It was something he liked about their relationship, that they'd maintained a mostly strict hold on privacy, but it made him uncomfortable sometimes, too. He had a feeling she'd be upset if she knew he was considering leaving Miniagua, although she knew he'd intended to return to engineering someday. It was that "someday" that made the situation sticky—neither of them had ever given it a time frame.

Things had changed since the week before, when he'd taken her to the doctor in Indianapolis. They were closer in one way simply because of new things they'd learned about each other, but the revelations had made them both skittish—pulling away from each other for reasons he couldn't clearly define. He doubted if Cass could, either.

No, that was wrong. Not that he could explain Cass's motivations, but he understood his own quite well. He was falling in love with her. Three months of seeing each other nearly every day when there was an acknowledged attraction between them had led to a deeper attachment than he'd known in ten years. A whole lot deeper attachment than he wanted. Although he seemed to be developing an uncertainty as to exactly what he *did* want.

The next day was her biopsy at the hospital in Sawyer. When he'd offered to take her, she'd shaken her head. "Aunt Zoey will. Damaris has an appointment at nearly the same time just down the hall, so it will work out fine. She is so excited to get her cast off. Then she'll just be down to one boot for a few more weeks and using a quad cane instead of crutches."

On the surface, it was as if the conversations the day of Cass's doctors' appointments had never happened. Although they still saw each other, they were both busy virtually all the time.

Their longest and deepest dialogue had been during the weekly business meeting, when they'd argued once again about closing times. He wanted the coffee shop to close at six when the orchard store did, because it was safer. Although their exterior lighting was good, there was no getting around the fact that it was full dark on a country road and the working barista would be alone.

Cass wanted to close at nine. Even if the last few hours were slow, she argued, they could get the shop cleaned and ready for the next morning. They were on the sheriff's office patrol route and it wasn't as if Country Club Road was all that isolated anyway.

At the end of the meeting, nothing was resolved. The point was moot, anyway—the coffee shop was her baby just as the apple barn was his. He had to give her credit for never interfering with his judgment concerning apples, so common sense told him he should stay out of the coffee conversation altogether.

After locking the orchard store's doors, he walked to Ground in the Round. The only vehicle there was Cass's red one, parked off to the side. As usual, she was working long hours to make up for the time off she would need the following day. He admired her work ethic, but it made him angry all the same.

She brought out more feelings in him than he'd experienced in ten years. While it was exhausting, it was enlivening, too. Was it wrong to try to protect himself from the pain that was inevitable when the emotions were that engaged? He knew it wasn't, and he knew she was trying to protect herself in much the same way as he was. And yet he sensed it might not be working. That all their emotional armor was as ineffective as it was invisible.

When he stepped inside, she looked up from where she sat at her laptop. She looked beat, and he felt fear shudder through him. Was she sick again? "Hey." He made his voice cheerful, pushing a smile into it. "Harvest supper at St. Paul's. What do you say?"

He saw the refusal coming, but even as she shook her head no, she closed her computer and got to her feet. "Let's do it. I am so done with today that it can't end a minute too soon."

They drove to the little white church a few miles away and sat in wooden pews to wait until there was room for them at the dining tables in the basement. All throughout, and while they ate too much of a delicious meal, they talked nonstop.

They argued the merits of football versus volleyball in high school sports. Of the traditional schedule versus the year-round one. Of public versus private versus charter schools. They laughed because, being childless, they didn't have horses in that particular race, but having teenage siblings under their roofs gave them an added interest in the ongoing controversies concerning education.

They talked about apples; Cass was woefully uneducated and he was bound and determined she needed to learn all ninety-seven varieties the orchard produced.

"I only have ninety-two to go," she mourned to the woman sitting beside her, and everyone laughed.

They talked about the winter formal and how relieved they would be to have it over. Their sensible siblings had been proving themselves to be anything but, up to and including arguing about whose car they were going to borrow for the dance. Zoey had a vintage Mustang and Luke drove a five-year-old Camaro, both of which had been offered. It seemed neither of them was interested in Cass's SUV even though it was red and newer than either of the other cars.

"My money's on the Mustang," said Cass. "It's what I would have chosen. When Sam and I went to the winter dance, we had to go in his mom's minivan. It was traumatic."

He laughed. "I can imagine it was. So," he continued, gazing longingly at her pie, "you said you were 'so done with today.' What was that about?"

She rolled her eyes and gave him half the slice of sugar cream. "I talked to my dad this morning. I told him Tony and his wife had a little boy yesterday and Dad said he was sorry he'd never had a boy. Then he asked if the chemo and radiation I had meant I could never have children. It just—" She stopped, looking down at the pie. "I just didn't need that today, is all."

It occurred to him that in all their conversations, they'd never discussed children. It had been an easy decision for him—since he never intended to marry again, he didn't plan to have a family, either. But he didn't know how Cass felt. He didn't know the answer to the question her father had asked. Or how to ask it.

Cass wasn't finished. "Then I broke a coffee carafe. When it was full of coffee. Not your regular, run-of-the-coffee-mill blend but the pumpkin spice I'm trying to not run out of until people stop asking for it. A customer mentioned that I should get fired for that kind of clumsiness and when Penny Phillipy said I *was* the boss and I'd never fire anyone for something so trivial, he started cussing. I asked him to leave, and he did. Didn't pay his bill and stiffed the barista who had taken him coffee three different times because he had a complaint about every single cup."

"And then?"

"Then the woman who was going to work this afternoon called in sick. That was all right, really, because it wasn't that busy. But it's her third time to call in and she's only been working there for two weeks. I'm afraid I really *will* have to fire someone and I don't want to."

"A downside of being a boss." He hated it, too. He'd never managed to do it without losing sleep over it.

He leaned forward, capturing and holding her gaze. "How much of today actually has to do with tomorrow?"

She hesitated. "Probably everything."

"Do you want to talk about it?"

"No." Her answer was immediate and didn't invite argument. "But I'm glad you know."

"Me, too."

"We should go. I need to get to bed early."

He drove her back to her SUV, and they were as quiet as they had been talkative only minutes before. He parked and turned off the engine, looking up at the front of the round barn, and wondered where they were in their relationship and how they'd gotten to this place.

Because it seemed to be changing hour by hour. He didn't think he'd ever in his life been as comfortable with anyone as he was with her. Or as uncomfortable. As confident or as at a loss.

As lonely or as…no, that wasn't true. He was never lonely when he was with her, knowledge that added to his feelings of discomfort and uncertainty.

"I'll call you tomorrow night before I come over," he said. "Text me if you need me to do anything at all."

She nodded. "I will. I promise."

He got out of the car when she did, taking her into his arms before she could get into her SUV. They kissed for a long time, and did a little apple orchard waltzing around the gravel parking lot. He wondered as he held her if he was giving as much comfort as he was receiving.

After a prolonged kiss good-night, he opened her car door for her, but didn't let her get in. He held her hand against his chest and tipped her face so he could look into her eyes. "Tomorrow," he said, "remember I'm keeping you right there." He tapped her fingers against his heart. "I'm no superhero—I'd probably trip over my own cape—but I'm perfectly willing to sit and be scared with you."

She laughed, the sound husky and small at the same time. "Sounds heroic to me. I'll remember."

He kissed her again, closed the door when she'd gotten behind the steering wheel of her SUV and waited until she'd driven away, heading down the lane to Zoey's. He started to get into his car, then changed his mind, relocking it and taking off walking between the trees in the opposite direction of the farmhouse. He circled around, checking trees in a way that had become second nature, and ended at Cottonwood Creek.

He stood under the towering trees, watching the water. The creek ran uninterrupted behind the orchard, the golf course, the winery and Worth Farm as well as everywhere in between. It provided good fishing in a few places, good swimming in a few others and even boasted a waterfall that sounded glorious as it crashed against the limestone below.

The stream was placid at the back of the orchard, though. Slow-moving and welcoming. Back when he'd first bought into Keep Cold, Zoey said their portion of Cottonwood was a "Gentle on My Mind" kind of place. She'd said, with kindness in her dark blue eyes, that sometimes it was a good place to grieve.

And so he had. Often and always alone, for the life that had ended with Jill's death.

Tonight, sitting alone on a large flat rock and looking into the dark, quiet water, he grieved again. For Cass, because of her fear of cancer's recurrence. And for himself, because he had thought all along that it would be easier to walk away than to stay and face the possibility of losing another woman he loved.

He'd been wrong.

CASS ALMOST ALWAYS wrote on her computer, but occasionally she had to construct a scene in longhand simply because it wouldn't come together using the mind-to-keyboard-to-screen method.

Until a few years ago, she'd never kept a journal, either. Her father had given her a leather-bound book with blank, lined pages for her birthday once at some point after she'd given up on ever being able to please him. The book lay unused for years, and sometimes she thought her primary reason for not journaling was to frustrate him. Not a nice thing to admit about herself, but that was the way it went sometimes.

However, for some reason she still couldn't identify, she'd written on the first page of that book the day she got a mammogram because her gynecologist had told her it was time.

It's evidently some kind of baseline thing so they can identify changes later. My insurance pays for it and the doctor said I could do it now or wait until I'm forty and then have one every few years. Damaris, who has breast cancer in her family, urged me to go ahead. So we went to the hospital, got ourselves squeezed and went to lunch. It was a fun day.

More than two years later, she'd filled not only the journal from her father, but another one with lavender paper that Royce had given her for another birthday. Today's entry, written without the customary benefit of caffeine, was stark.

If I didn't have to fast, I could sleep. As it is, I'm awake long before daybreak, sitting here with Misty the kitten and watching the empty coffee pot. It's funny how that happens. Or should be. It's really not.

She didn't think it was going to be a fun day.

By the time everyone else got up, she was dressed and working. Surprisingly, the writing was going well. Lucy was close to finding answers, and Cass was almost certain she knew how the twisting plot was going to straighten out.

She remembered writing *The Case of Daisy's Ashes* during chemo, radiation and reconstruction surgery. She'd used information from the internet and from her own journal because her thought processes were so compromised by medication and pain that she could barely express a coherent thought. Damaris had earned herself a slot on the book's dedication page with her assistance.

Cass had turned the book in on the day it was due. It had required more editing than her previous ones, and she still couldn't bring herself to read it, but it had been successful. That, as much as anything else, had reassured her there was indeed life after cancer.

Remembering, she looked down at the words she'd written this morning. Hunger made her stomach rumble, but satisfaction overrode the sensation. She had survived before—she could do it again.

When she went into the kitchen to leave for the hospital in Sawyer, Luke and Seth were there. Zoey, Damaris and Royce were putting on their coats.

"What's going on?" Cass accepted the jacket Luke held out to her.

"I'm taking Royce to school in Luke's car." Seth smiled at her. "Zoey and Damaris are going in your car because it's easier for Damaris that way. You and Luke are going in Zoey's Mustang. Unless you want Royce and me to take it, that is."

"We talked about this." Cass lifted her chin and frowned at Luke.

"Yes, we did." He kissed her cheek. "But we didn't say enough. I'm going with you. Are you ready to go, or did you want to stand around and argue about it until you're late? You know you hate that."

He was right about that—she did hate tardiness, particularly her own. But—"I'm a big girl. You don't need to baby me."

"Right. And as soon as you and Damaris are off to have your respective procedures taken care of, Zoey and I are going to have breakfast and talk about you. Doesn't sound like babying to me."

"Unless he makes me buy breakfast." Zoey came to hug Cass. "You don't always have to be the strong one," she said, her voice very quiet. "I know you're good at it. I am, too. But occasionally it's just fine to lean."

Cass remembered the night before, when Luke had held her hand against his heart and promised to keep her there. That gesture, plus the toe-curling good-night kiss, had allowed her to fall asleep immediately when she'd crawled into bed. It was true it hadn't lasted that long, but she'd wakened with his touch and his promise still there in her senses.

Zoey was right. It was okay to lean. Just this once.

CHAPTER SEVENTEEN

"IF ANYTHING HAPPENS—because you know things can any time there's a medical procedure because that's one of the first things they tell you—Aunt Zoey knows where my will is. You need to know that everything I have or will have is to go to Royce. She can't have it now, except maybe for the car because that would save Damaris the expense of buying her one, but it's all hers. You'll be all right with that, won't you?" Cass was looking straight ahead. Her hands were together in her lap, her knuckles white.

It was a beautiful sunny morning, albeit colder than usual for late November. But Luke didn't think she was giving the weather any thought at all. They were having yet another serious conversation in a car and he was, frankly, unnerved by the statement she'd just made.

"With what?" Stopped behind a school bus, he stared at her. *Don't do this.*

"If anything happens," she repeated patiently, "Royce will inherit my half of the orchard. She's not an adult, so obviously she wouldn't step into managing it, but she would still be another Gentry sister you'd have to contend with."

"I'm not talking about this." He was surprised he got the words out, as hard as he was clamping his jaw. "You are having a biopsy, where they are going to clarify that you are fine, and then we're going home. You'll take a day or two off, whatever you need, during which time—" He stopped. She didn't need him getting all tense and living-in-the-past scared. She needed… "During those two days, I'll go into the coffee shop and rearrange everything to where you can't find it. I'll put up a huge, *huge* sign saying we close at six no matter what transpires." He held up a hand to add a little dramatic flair. "I'll put up another sign saying there will be no more pumpkin spice in Ground in the Round ever again."

Her cheek twitched and he knew she was trying not to laugh. When she looked at him, her eyes were sparkling. "You do realize that's something like saying there'll be no more Honeycrisp apples in the orchard ever again?"

He drove on when the bus did, wondering why he'd taken this road to Sawyer when he should have realized a school bus would stop at nearly every house on it. "That's un-American. I think there's probably a government agency that forbids it."

They laughed at their own silliness, but at the next stop, she said, "It is okay with you, isn't it? You'll watch over the property for Royce if something happens? Or buy it from her the way you wanted to from me?" She hesitated. "Just look after her."

You'll have to take care of Seth. I know your parents will, but he's so special, so much ours, that I need you to promise you'll take care of him the way we always have. Make sure he gets guitar lessons if he wants them, or you keep teaching him.

Jill's words echoed at the back of his mind, but that promise had cost nothing—Seth had always spent more time with his brother and sister-in-law than he had with his parents. After Jill's death, that hadn't changed. Having a small, noisy boy in their empty house when she wasn't there anymore had been a godsend.

Promising to take care of Royce was a different thing entirely. She was a sweet girl, but she wasn't family. Zoey and Damaris would take care of her anyway, so he didn't know why the thing Cass was asking was a big deal. But it was.

However, the anxiety in Cass's eyes was more than he could look away from. "Of course," he said, and lifted his foot from the brake when the bus moved forward. "You know I will." Because he would, whether he wanted to or not.

"Thank you." Her indrawn breath was tremulous. "I know her mother and Zoey will take care of her just fine if I'm not there, but she's become so special this fall, more than just a half sister I wasn't really attached to."

He thought of Seth. Their sisters always teased him about loving their little brother more than he did them. That wasn't it, though. It was that in addition to the love, he was responsible for Seth and always had been. That responsibility made a difference.

Responsibility *always* made a difference, and if he were honest about it, that was the real reason he didn't want to promise to look after Royce. Perhaps it was something he didn't want in any personal relationship. It went along with permanence and commitment and making a life with someone. He wasn't going there.

HAVING A PROCEDURE done in Sawyer's twenty-five-bed hospital differed greatly from Sacramento or Indianapolis if for no other reason than Cass knew several of the staff and she thought Luke knew all of them. A maintenance man even brought him coffee in the lobby and asked whether Seth was playing basketball now that Miniagua High School's football season had ended.

"How can you possibly know everyone here?" she demanded when she was sitting on a hospital bed in an oh-so-attractive gown and he was in the chair beside her. "And how can I possibly know half of them?"

"We have the best orchard and coffee shop around. What do you expect?" He grinned at Arlie when she came into the area wearing scrubs. "They'll all be wanting discounts, too. Right, Arlie?"

Arlie smacked him with the sheaf of papers she carried. "I'm here to deliver a baby, which makes me a rock star, so don't get smart with me, Rossiter." She leaned over to hug Cass. "It's gonna be fine," she said into her ear, "and if it's not, we're going to take care of it. Right? We are the Lakers, the mighty, mighty Lakers—"

"—everywhere we go, people want to know, who we are." Cass joined her in the high school chant until they were both laughing too hard to go on.

The nurse shoved aside the cubicle curtain. "Oh, good grief," she said, "you've got Sawyer's Comedy Central going on in here, don't you?" She made a shooing motion. "Tell them so long, because you're off to have a nice nap."

Cass was already drowsy, but she remembered the loneliness she'd felt when she'd had her mastectomy. Her mother hadn't come to the hospital even though she'd said she would; her father had been in Idaho and Damaris had been on duty. A pastor had prayed with her and held her hand on the way to the OR, but Cass hadn't even known his name.

Today, Luke and Arlie both walked beside the bed to the double doors, where Luke bent to kiss her gently. "See you soon," he promised, and kissed her again.

She smiled sleepily at him and raised her hand to wave at Arlie. "Thanks for coming."

That was all she knew until Kari Ross woke her.

From her angst-ridden adolescence on, Cass had always thought *love* was the most beautiful word in the English language. She still thought that, she reflected sleepily later that afternoon when she was resting in her room at the farmhouse, but *benign* was a close second. There would be more tests, Kari had warned, but it looked good. It looked very good.

LUKE HADN'T TOLD Cass why he was making the quick trip to Pennsylvania the Monday after her procedure, other than saying he was looking at a cider press and seeing his sisters and brothers-in-law. There was no point in talking about the interview unless he decided to take the job.

He met Dan in Hollidaysburg for lunch before touring the facility and talking to its personnel and project managers. He liked the people he talked to and was impressed with the projects the young company had already contracted. The salary and perquisites offer was even more interesting.

"Take your time deciding," Dan advised when he left. "I know you're not available full time until you get your brother graduated, but you can still do some telecommuting and some traveling if you decide to go with the company. I'd like working with you again." He extended his hand. "Sure I can't take you to dinner?"

The other man's handshake was as firm as it had always been, his gaze as level. Even if Luke wasn't eager to get back to engineering, he'd be glad to work with Dan Graham again. "No. I'm having it with my sisters and their families, and Jill's folks are coming over from Johnstown."

He loved Pennsylvania, although he seldom thought about how much he missed the mountains until he came back to them. He drove past the house on Jones Street where he'd grown up, slowing enough to note that it still looked as cozy and well kept as when his parents had owned it. He remembered how hard his mother had cried when she'd handed the keys, a houseplant and a manila folder full of appliance warranties to the new owners. It had been her dream home for the twenty years they'd lived in it. He thought it probably still was.

He drove around the block, stopping just down the street from the house to take a few pictures of it. The concrete drive where he'd taught the girls how to ride without training wheels. The big garage where he'd learned how to use tools and discovered both his interest in and talent for engineering. The window at the back of the house that had been his room. His father had replaced the window twice, but the wind had still whistled in at one of the corners. Luke wondered if it still did.

He'd had little sympathy for his mother when she'd had to leave the house she loved. She'd lived her dream for two decades—he'd known full well he and Jill would be lucky to get through one. He remembered saying that, too, speaking stiffly in anger and making his mother cry as she'd stood at the window of her strange new kitchen, looking out at a view she neither liked nor wanted.

On the way out to Collier and Leah's, he called Detroit. When she answered with, "Is that my biggest boy?" he laughed. And then he apologized. When he told her why, she cried again.

"Just remember, dreams change," she said, when he was pulling into the long lane of his sister and brother-in-law's farm. "Even when you lose them in hard ways, you had them.

It makes the journey very worthwhile." She hesitated, then went on. "Don't let remembering what you've lost close your eyes to new dreams."

He parked behind Collier's pickup and had to sit for a moment, waiting for the sudden moisture to clear from his eyes. People who'd been in the prom night wreck had made "let it go" their mostly unspoken mantra. They didn't ignore their grief, scars and guilt, but they didn't let the memories rule their lives, either. It was a lesson, Jack Llewellyn said, that was hard fought and nearly impossible to learn, but they'd fought it and learned it. Most of them had let go and started over.

He wasn't entirely sure that was true of Cass, and he knew—although he wasn't one of the survivors—that it wasn't really true of him, either.

The long table in Leah's big kitchen had every leaf in it and a card table added at the end and it was still crowded with her family, Rachel's family, Luke and Jill's parents. The food was plentiful and the conversation noisy. Luke was able to keep the attention away from himself until dessert was finished and his nieces and nephews had left the table to pretend to do their homework.

Collier went around the table filling coffee cups. "So," he said, "how did the interview go?"

Everyone fell silent, waiting for Luke's answer to a question he hadn't had the forethought to realize would be asked. He stirred his coffee, not sure what to say and thinking he probably should have told Cass about the interview. All of these people knew, Seth and their parents knew, but he'd purposefully not told the woman he was seeing.

It felt wrong. Probably because it was.

"It went well," he said finally. "They solidified the offer, which was substantial. They're giving me time to consider it." The words sounded stiff in his own ears. They made him *feel* stiff, as if he was talking about someone else, someone he didn't actually know.

"It would be great if you came back here," said Leah. "I'm sure Mom and Dad will when they retire. If we could talk Seth into it, the whole family would be in the same place again."

"What about Cass?" Rachel asked. "What does she think of the idea?"

His mother-in-law spoke into the silence that fell, her soft voice retaining some of the

Pennsylvania Dutch she'd grown up speaking. "You are seeing someone, Luke?"

"It is about time." His father-in-law answered before Luke could. "And not our business, Anna."

"Of course it is our business." Anna's eyes were so much like Jill's it was hard to look into them, but she held Luke's gaze. "You are as much our son as if you'd been born to us. We want you to be happy. Like Dad says, it's about time."

Luke nodded his head. "We are seeing each other. She is my business partner and a nice woman besides. You would like her, Anna."

Jill would have liked Cass, too, although she'd have envied her certain things. Her business acumen. The travel she acknowledged but never talked about—no amount of Dramamine had made any kind of travel anything other than misery to his wife. The number of books on the shelves in the room Cass had made into her office. Even, he thought with a half smile, her height.

"Well?" said Rachel.

"I don't know," he said. "I don't know about the job and I haven't discussed it with Cass."

No one gasped, but he was almost certain his sisters wanted to.

"If you ask me—" Rachel began.

"—which he did not," Abe finished with a nod in his wife's direction. "Leah, is there more pie?"

"There is." Leah got up, waving for Collier to sit back down. "Come on, Luke. You can help me serve it—it will get you off Rachel's inquisition list."

"For the moment," Rachel muttered. When she glowered at Abe, everyone laughed. Finally, she did, too. "I like her, though. I hope you don't hold that against her."

"She likes you, too." Luke brought two plates back to the table and set them at his in-laws' places. "I don't even hold *that* against her."

He spent the night at a bed-and-breakfast in Hollidaysburg, texting Cass when he woke.

How are you feeling?

Good. I may go to work.

Well, this was an easy conversation.

Don't. See you tonight.

After a daybreak meeting with Dan and the other managers of the firm, he stopped on his way out of town to gaze up at where Chimney Rocks stood guard on the mountain with a panoramic view of the town. He and Jill had spent a lot of time up there.

He drove slowly through Duncansville and parked for a long moment in front of the little brick rambler where he'd lived with Jill. It was such a plain house that she'd painted the trim blue and yellow. The colors were still there, right down to the mailbox on the front stoop.

What a happy place it had been. Spying two tricycles at the side of the house, Luke hoped it still was.

And then he went to the cemetery beside the church he and Jill had attended all the years they'd known each other.

She'd chosen her own resting place, taking Seth with her and explaining to him that she would have to leave him soon but that he was always in her heart. The two of them had chosen a shady spot near the back of the small churchyard, and when Luke had wanted to pay for two plots, she'd been adamant that she was flying solo.

"You're not even thirty, doofus. What are

you going to do? Sit around and mourn forever?"

Ten years later, he laughed out loud, looking down at the small marker Seth had picked because it was *little like Jill and me*. He put the coppery chrysanthemums he'd brought into the vases on the concrete base. "You had it right all along, didn't you, Mrs. Rossiter?"

Because the time had come. He didn't think he was anywhere near to wanting either marriage or a family, but he realized it wasn't realistic to live the rest of his life with memories as its only viable content. No matter how good they were, they were no longer enough.

The wind rustled through the leaves on the ground, and he realized a tear was trickling down his cheek. "Oh, Jilly." He traced the letters of her name on the granite. "I'll always love you."

He knew he was being fanciful, but the breeze that dried the dampness on his face felt like a kiss. Fanciful or not, he recognized it as a kiss goodbye.

Driving away from the old cemetery, he felt lighter, as he had when he'd finally broken down and taken the last of Jill's clothing to the church's thrift shop.

When he saw Cass that night, he would tell her his family had asked about her. He'd talk about Hollidaysburg and how good it had been to grow up nestled there in the Alleghenies. He'd show her the pictures of the house on Jones Street and Chimney Rocks.

He'd tell her about the job interview, too. He was sure she would be excited for him, although maybe not so thrilled he hadn't mentioned it in the first place. They'd talked about how much he sometimes missed working in his field—keeping the cider press and the sorting table operational wasn't always fulfilling—so she wouldn't be surprised.

In the airport bookstore, he bought a mystery by Cassandra G. Porter. He'd read some of her books, but not all. The copyright date on *The Case of Daisy's Ashes* was the year before, so it was evidently one he'd missed. He always liked the settings of Lucy Garten's dilemmas, placed as they were right in the Wabash Valley where Miniagua was. Some of the places and people in the stories sounded uncannily like ones he knew.

The flight from Pittsburgh to Indianapolis stopped in Chicago long enough for him to eat lunch, drink two cups of coffee and read a fourth of the book. At that point, he went back to read Chapter Two again. Because the familiarity of certain parts of the story was progressing beyond uncanny to something downright weird.

It wasn't surprising that he saw characters in the book as people he'd seen on TV or in the movies—he figured everyone did that. Tall, slender Lucy Garten, as a matter of fact, appeared in his mind's eye as a thirty-something Sandra Bullock. However, Lucy's mother, who lived in a farmhouse and helped with her daughter's sleuthing shenanigans, looked like Zoey Durand. Her appearance included Zoey's elegant sweep of silver hair, dark blue eyes and the floaty tops she loved to wear. She even sounded like Zoey, and she had a special name for her daughter. She called Lucy Cassiopeia.

Back in the air, Luke read further, getting halfway through the book by the time the plane landed in Indianapolis. He closed the book, dropped it and picked it up again, pausing to stare at the photograph of the author on the inside of the back cover. It was sepia-toned and undoubtedly a terrible picture because there were no distinguishing features to be seen.

Except one. Cassandra G. Porter's slim

right hand almost totally obscured the lower part of her face, but she wore a narrow band on her thumb. A thumb that was just slightly crooked from when Cass had broken it playing volleyball the week before the prom.

CHAPTER EIGHTEEN

NOT WORKING WAS exhausting. By noon on Tuesday, Cass had dusted everything she could think of to dust and hauled an unconscionable number of totes labeled "Christmas decorations" down from the attic. While she was at it, she put her summer wardrobe away in the attic storage room—an act which woke her to the realization that she didn't really *have* a winter wardrobe. She'd written twenty-seven words in the last chapter of her book-in-progress. When that stalled, she started to knit a baby blanket for the woman who cut her hair, only to turn the yellow yarn into a misshapen dishcloth after the first hour.

She was a little sore from the biopsy, but not enough to induce her to take a pain pill or remember instructions to take it easy. When she tried to get Misty to play, the cat leaped onto the windowsill and turned around three times before falling asleep with her back to the room. After watching two episodes of Zoey's favorite television drama, Cass no longer cared what happened to its protagonists.

Zoey and Damaris went out to dinner and were going on to the book club at the library. Royce went to the lake clubhouse with a group of friends to help decorate for the winter formal. Cass, who often enjoyed being alone, wasn't enjoying it at all. At eight o'clock, when Luke texted that he would be there in five minutes, she brushed her teeth and her hair and was waiting on the porch when he pulled up.

"How was your trip?" she called as he walked toward her. "How's your family?"

"It was fine. They're fine. They said to tell you hello and that you should come along next time." When she came down to him, he bent his head to kiss her, pulling her close with an arm around her waist. "How's your recuperation coming?"

"I'm all done with that. I don't have time." She drew back, searching his face for whatever was wrong. Because something was. She could feel it as certainly as she could November's threatening temperature drop.

He was smiling, but the expression stopped

before it reached his eyes. This was what Tony had looked like in the last weeks they'd lived together, when they'd both been giving the marriage its last chance. If she was honest about it, this is what she'd seen in the mirror then, too.

She wasn't ready to see it again. She'd known from the first that she and Luke weren't a forever couple. She'd not only known it; she'd reminded herself of it on a daily basis. But she wasn't ready for it to end, for the interest to fade away the way interest always did. She wasn't ready for the blank expression in his eyes.

When she'd gotten sick during the long winding-down days of her marriage, Tony had offered to stay, to give it another try even if it was only for the duration of her surgery and treatment. She'd turned him down, not wanting to be anyone's responsibility. Life with her parents had taught her she was better on her own than with someone who didn't really want her.

But she didn't want to be on her own now. Later, maybe, especially if the word *benign* became wishful thinking instead of fact. She'd be stronger then because she'd have to be. She would have time to remind herself often enough that falling in love was foolish for someone like her. Someone who did better on her own.

Because she did. At the end of the day she always did.

"You know," she said, "you were right about me not going back to work today. I'm not sure I'll be ready tomorrow, either." She rested her loosely fisted hand on her left breast, where the tactile sensations were still different than they used to be. Sometimes in the deep of the night when sleep eluded her, she wondered if that was just one more thing she'd lost forever.

But she couldn't think about that now. There was raw new pain working its way to the surface that she was going to have to deal with. She squeezed her fingers, tightening the fist until her nails bit into her palm.

"I think I probably need some more sleep. I'm sorry—"

He caught her hand in his, turning Nana's old wedding band around on her crooked thumb. "Volleyball?" he said.

She frowned, bewildered. Hadn't she told him that? "Yes. Right before prom. It was swollen up like a sausage. Everyone kept looking at it, or at least I thought they did.

You're pretty full of yourself when you're seventeen." She smiled, willing him to return it, with the expression lighting his eyes, too. Maybe his withdrawal was in her imagination. Maybe he— "We both have walking, talking and complaining evidence of that living with us every day."

"We do." But he didn't smile.

She shivered, regretting she'd come outside without a jacket on over her flannel shirt. "Do you want to come in?" She forgot she'd told him she was tired and needed more sleep. All she knew was that she was cold and that she didn't want him to leave. Not with that look in his eyes.

Without waiting to see if he followed, she pulled her hand from his and went back up on the porch. Not until she opened the door did she look back.

He still stood at the bottom of the porch steps and he still wasn't smiling.

"Luke?" She opened the door, then turned back, half in and half out of the kitchen. "You have to tell me what's wrong." She firmed her mouth so that it wouldn't tremble, and straightened away from where she'd leaned against the doorjamb. She wasn't going to beg. He could tell her or not. "Whatever you decide to do, I'm going in the house. It's cold out here. You're welcome to come inside or you're welcome to leave. Your choice."

In answer, he took something out of the pocket of his coat and held it up. "Does this look familiar to you?"

Of course it looked familiar to her. She hated the picture with the pot of daisies in color and the black-and-white urn in the background. Lucy Garten's stories weren't grim, yet the cover of *The Case of Daisy's Ashes* was bleak and hopeless. She'd felt that way herself then so she hadn't complained, but neither had she promoted the book whole-heartedly.

She hadn't had to—it was her bestselling one to date. Her editor told her the mail all leaned toward readers liking the cover and loving that Lucy's personal life had gained so much space in the story.

It was the book Cass had written when she hadn't had the energy to maintain her Cassandra persona. She had been almost disappointed that it was such a reader favorite when she considered it so flawed. Even when she'd admitted to Holly that she was indeed Cassandra G. Porter and during the conversations since, she'd never talked about *Daisy's Ashes*.

Now here it was in Luke's hand. And he was waiting for an answer.

"Yes," she said, "it's familiar."

"Are you—"

"Yes." She felt as emotionless as the word itself. "I'm Cassandra G. Porter."

She shivered, standing there, and he came up the steps. When she stepped back into the house, he followed and closed the door behind him.

"Can you explain to me why that particular subject never came up?" He sounded more hurt than angry.

Across the kitchen, she poured coffee for them both, wondering if that should be her response to the world coming to an end—*Wait a minute on that bomb, will you? The coffee's almost done.*

They sat at the table in the chairs they always chose, their cups in front of them, the paperback lying between them on top of the spread pages of her next contract—how ironic was that? The cracked spine indicated the book had been read. She wondered if he'd read enough to recognize Zoey in the characters. Or Cottonwood Creek in the setting. Or Linda's shouted laughter in the departed Daisy.

But, no, he hadn't known Linda.

Cass looked down into her cup, not wanting to meet the cold gaze that made her want to flinch even when she couldn't see it. "When I first started writing, I used a pen name because it was easier than dealing with my father and my husband. I also used the pseudonym because when I left Miniagua, I cut off all connection to it except for Zoey and my grandparents. Even when I came back for Nana and Grandpa's funerals, I only stayed long enough for the services and I didn't talk to anyone. It was like a scene out of a movie you wish you hadn't paid to see."

"Why did you cut off that connection? I still don't understand that."

"Guilt. I was alive and Linda wasn't. I had no scars and virtually everyone else did. My grandparents, who were ill when I came to stay that year, got sicker so fast it made my head spin. I still think they probably would have lived longer if they hadn't had me to worry about." Cass shrugged. "But we all have guilt over one thing or another. Coming back here, being around the rest of the survivors and my family and…and you— that's given me a kind of confidence I've never had before. It's put the guilt wherever it is we keep it, because I don't think it ever goes away."

"Not completely, probably." He tapped the front of the book. "Does everyone know this is you?"

"My family does. Holly figured it out. I think most of the survivors do, by now. I stopped keeping it a secret, but I haven't gone out of my way to tell anyone, either." Cass picked up her cup, then set it down. She had to stifle the tremor of her lips again, biting down hard on the bottom one. "I don't know how to explain to you what I don't fully understand myself. I think I was waiting for the right time and it never came. And I suppose I'm afraid of commitment—there's that, too. Letting you see who I really am would be getting too close."

"What I don't like is being the last to know." He hesitated. "Although I have to admit the two-people concept is a little disconcerting. Which one do I know, or do I know either of you? It feels like a lie by omission, Cass. A big one."

"I understand that." She did understand it. She should have told him. She should have told him everything.

But then he'd have known the real Cass, and she'd been so happy the way things were. Happier, she realized now that she wasn't, than she'd ever been. Because of Royce, Zoey, Damaris and the old farmhouse.

For so many reasons.

Because of the friendships she'd renewed and others she'd made since coming back to this magical place. Because even with fear of cancer's return creating a huge cold place inside, she felt neither alone nor lonely, and being scared was a lot easier when you could share it.

And because of Luke. Because for the first time in her life, she felt for herself what she'd seen and envied in other people she'd known. She understood Grandpa and Nana sitting in their recliners in front of the TV and laughing together at things no one but they considered funny. She'd wished the best for her friends who were couples and felt as if it might really happen—for them *and* for her.

But now, before she'd even given voice to the joy of the developing relationship between Luke and herself, she was going to lose it just as surely as the cold November sun would slide up over the apple trees in the morning.

She thought, for no particular reason, of the Robert Frost poem that had given the orchard its name; she'd seen the verse so often that she had it mostly memorized. Its first line said, "This saying good-bye on the edge of the dark…"

It was full dark, but she was almost sure about the "saying good-bye." Her heart ached.

"I don't use Cassandra's name, but I've tried to make myself into her. She's the one you know, I hope. I like her better than I like Cass."

"Why is that?"

"I don't know how to say it without sounding like a world-class whiner." She met his eyes, then looked away. The chocolate brown that was always so meltingly warm was anything but.

Another line from the poem slipped into her mind: "Its heart sinks lower under the sod."

Frost had been talking about an orchard, not a woman who'd made a mess of her life, but the sentiment resonated. Her heart, feeling as leaden as the knot of fear she'd been carrying around for too many days, sank still lower.

"Just say it." He leaned forward in his chair, meeting and holding her gaze.

She had to look away before she could answer, "It's pretty simple. My life as Cass has been a series of losses and bad choices and underachieving. When I first sold a book as Cassandra, I was able to be someone else, someone with curves instead of angles. When I got cancer and had to have a mastectomy… I don't care that it is the twenty-first century—I felt disfigured and scared and as if I'd failed not only my parents but myself because it was just one more thing wrong with me."

"That's crazy." His voice was flat. A frown made a sharp vertical line between his brows.

"It is, I agree." She turned the book over, hiding its cover, then lifted her eyes. "Did you feel like a failure when Jill died?"

The flinch was no more than the tiny jerk of a jaw muscle, but she saw it. He nodded. "Sometimes."

"That's crazy," she said.

"I know it is, but it's not something I hide behind a pseudonym, either." He picked up the book, holding it up. "Is that the real reason your picture is unrecognizable, so that no one will know you carry the same kind of scars everyone else in the world does?"

She started to answer, then stopped. Was he right? Was she so filled with her own importance that she wanted to be better than anyone else? The thought horrified her into silence, then she shook her head.

"No."

"Then you're going to have to explain it to me."

"It's pretty simple, really. I didn't like the person I was, the one I thought was a complete disappointment and failure to everyone, who let her best friend die in her place, so I wanted to be someone else." She stopped for a moment, her throat closing. Tears trickled hot and fast from the corners of her eyes "Cassandra, on the other hand, is fine. She's a good sister, a good niece, a good writer, a good business partner. She's the one you know, the one I want to be. Is that so unreasonable?"

He took her hand, stroking a finger over the worn wedding band, and lifted it to his lips to kiss the crooked knuckle. "I think it is. All those things you just mentioned *are* Cass, because we're all what our lives have made us into." He released her fingers and got to his feet. "Cassandra's just a name on the front of a book. It's Cass I want to know."

CHAPTER NINETEEN

"Seriously?" Seth put the basketball between his feet so it wouldn't roll away and straightened to stare at Luke. "You're really thinking of leaving the lake?"

"Not until spring. You'll be able to stay with me until you graduate. Even after that, I'll keep the house. It'll be available for the family when it's not rented out. I'll probably retire here."

"In about a hundred years, about the same time you get the bathroom finished." Seth picked up the ball again, dropping a shot cleanly from three-point range. "I thought you loved it here."

"I do love it here. I also love Pennsylvania and engineering." Luke caught the ball and dribbled it to the side of the concrete court that was part of the lake's playground adjacent to the clubhouse. "You knew I'd go back there someday."

"No, I didn't. I mean, I did, but not really.

It's been years and you haven't missed engineering since you came here. Why now all of a sudden? The orchard's going great and you'll even have the new cider press next year to make life easier. You'll be able to sit around the Ground in the Round and drink half caff breakfast blend all day long."

Luke hadn't been in the coffee shop since the week before. It was unbelievable how much he missed it.

"I haven't decided yet. I just wanted you to know I was seriously considering the job." He shot, frowning when Seth snatched the ball before it tipped into the rim. "I'm aging, you know. You need to give me a break now and then."

"What does Cass say?" Seth gave him the ball with a hard bounce pass.

Luke ignored him and went in for a layup. He hadn't talked to Cass in the three days since Tuesday night. She was avoiding him as studiously as he avoided her. Neither Zoey nor Royce had mentioned her to him. He assumed they hadn't talked to Cass about him, either, although he saw the worry in Zoey's eyes and the questions in Royce's on Wednesday when he stopped by the farmhouse to drop off one of the fresh turkeys he'd picked up at the Detwiler farm.

Seth rebounded, then tossed him the ball. "Luke?"

"Let it go, Seth." Luke shot again, from the free throw line, and tried to ignore the stab of pain brought on by saying the words *let it go*.

"What are we doing on Christmas?"

The change of subject was so sudden, Luke had to give his mind a moment to catch up. They'd spent Wednesday night and Thanksgiving Day with their parents, then driven back to the lake to get Seth home in time for basketball practice on Friday morning. Luke had worked in the house all day, putting finishing touches on window trim. He'd cut some tiles for the bathroom shower and given up when he couldn't concentrate on the pattern.

"I don't know," he said, when his mind wouldn't cooperate fully with the question—focus really was becoming a problem. "Mom would like everyone to come to Michigan. The girls would like to gather in Pennsylvania. What would you like to do?" Luke didn't care about the holidays—he hadn't since Jill's death—but Seth was still a kid. They mattered to him.

"Stay here."

Luke started to protest, to remind him that their parents were already giving up a lot by allowing their youngest to spend his last year in high school away from home. But Detroit had never been Seth's home. He had no friends there, no family ties beyond Mom and Dad.

"I'll ask." He shook his head when Seth offered him the basketball. "Maybe everyone would like to come to the lake for Christmas. What do you think?"

Seth laughed. "I think your house is nowhere near big enough."

"If they'll come, maybe we can rustle up a rental that will hold everyone. There are always cancellations, plus central Indiana doesn't exactly scream tourism during the winter months."

"Do you think? Will you ask them?"

"No, you can ask them. If you get good answers, I'll start nosing around for a place big enough to house a bunch of Rossiters and Friesens."

"Can we invite Royce and Cass and Zoey and Damaris to have Christmas with us, too? They're like family. I can just hear it if Zoey and Mom were both in the kitchen, can't you?"

"Let's not get the cart before the horse. Talk to the family first, and we'll go from there."

They walked home in the brisk air, jogging sometimes to stay warm and bounce-passing the basketball back and forth across the narrow gravel road. The lake was smooth and gray and Luke regretted having already put the boat in winter storage—a ride would have felt good tonight.

He needed something to feel good.

"I'm going over to the orchard for a little bit," he told Seth when they got back to the house. "We're behind on some things after the season rush. I need to start catching up."

Seth's head appeared through the neck of the hoodie he was taking off. "Want me to go with you?"

Luke ruffled the boy's hair, shorter and neater than his own. "I need some quiet time, and I'm sure not going to get that with you around." He stepped back toward the door. "If you get into that food Mom sent home with us, don't eat it all. I'm still the favorite son."

"Nope. You're old and worn out, so she

likes me best now." Seth's eyes, mirrors of Luke's own, were troubled despite his teasing rejoinder. "Hey."

Luke sighed, but waited with his hand on the doorknob. "Hey what?"

"This thing with Cass… I don't know how you screwed it up. But you've always been the fixer. For me, for Jill, for Zoey. You need to do it for yourself now, too."

Anger and hurt and frustration twisted inside him, and Luke wanted to yell at his brother. *When does someone do the fixing for me? I've been broken for ten years.* But the knowledge that the kid standing there in a sweaty T-shirt would go to the ends of the earth to do exactly that stopped him.

"Sometimes," Luke said instead, "I just can't."

"You mean you can't even stay until after the dance?" A wobble in Royce's voice at the end of her question betrayed her upset. "You're barely off crutches, Mom. Surely the army doesn't need you right this very minute."

Damaris looked past her daughter to meet Cass's eyes. *Help me out here.*

But Cass shrugged and shook her head slightly. She was on Royce's side in this one.

She might not *tell* her sister she was, but she was.

"Honey, I don't know how to make you understand that what I do is important. When they tell me I'm needed by Wednesday at 0800 hours, they don't mean Saturday after my daughter's dance. You're an army brat—you both are—so you know I don't have a choice." Tears slipped from the corners of Damaris's eyes as she sank into a kitchen chair, making her look not only tired but distraught. "Believe me, if I did, I would choose to be here. I want to take pictures of you in your dress and tell Seth not to keep you out too late and to drive carefully. I'd like to sit in the living room with Zoey and watch old movies on TV until you get home and then go to bed really fast, so you wouldn't know I was waiting up."

"You could have retired when you got hurt, Mom." Royce hadn't reached the point of being resigned to the inevitable yet—her voice was still all hurt child. "You've given the army twenty-five years. When is it time for you? For your family?" *For me?* She wouldn't say the words, but Cass knew they were there at the tip of her tongue. She'd thought them herself a hundred times about her own father by the time she was Royce's age.

Damaris knew it, too. "I'm sorry, baby. I wish it were different."

"Me, too. Happy Day-After-Thanksgiving to us." Royce turned away, going to the back stairway without looking at either her mother or her sister. "I'm going to bed."

When she was out of earshot, Cass spoke quietly. "Three more days, Damaris? Really?"

Her stepmother, always militarily straight even when she'd been in a wheelchair, slumped. She looked older than the forty-seven Cass knew her to be. "Yes, really. I tried, Cass. You have to know that."

She did know that. Cass relented, stepping over to hug the woman sitting at the table. "I know. I wish I'd had you long before I did. But it's going to be hard for her. I understand that it's hard for you, too, but it's not going to seem that way to her." She shook her head. "Actually, unless she's a lot different than I was, she won't *care* if it's hard for you. Sixteen and selfish tend to be synonymous."

Cass didn't say things like "She'll come around," because she knew Royce wouldn't. At least, not quickly enough to make her mother's leave-taking an easy one. "I'll take care of her," was all she could think of to make Damaris feel better.

"I will, too." Zoey came into the kitchen in her robe and slippers, and went to the window over the sink, looking out into the darkness. "She'll be fine."

Cass looked at the clock. "I'm going for a walk, and then I'm going to come back and work for a while."

Zoey frowned at her. "Do you think walking at ten o'clock at night is a good idea? It's supposed to snow tonight, too."

"This is the orchard, Aunt Zoey, remember? And I've been waiting for snow ever since I left here when I was seventeen." Cass pulled on the quilted jacket she'd broken down and bought for herself. "I have my can of stuff that's supposed to repel all perpetrators in one pocket and my phone in the other."

"Just be safe." Damaris's smile was weak, but it was there. "Royce is already mad at one of us. If you get hurt, she's going to be all the madder." She came over, scarcely limping, and put her arms around Cass. "I know it's a hard time for you, too, with waiting for test results and…and whatever's happened between you and Luke. I hate adding to it."

Cass hugged her back. "We'll survive, Stepmom. We've all had worse."

Once outside, she looked around, acknowledging silently that it might not be such a good time for a walk. It was a cloudy, starless night. The flashlight Zoey had urged her to carry had been a good idea. The thermometer that hung on the wall of the back porch had assured her it was indeed cold enough to snow. She hesitated, then stepped off the porch. She needed the air.

She wanted to be excited about snow. About Christmas coming. About finishing her book in the last hour of the last day before deadline. About the other book that would be released in just a few days. In *The Corpse in the Cornfield*, Lucy Garten's hair grew back, and Cass had been as eager writing about it as she'd been when her own scalp had been covered again.

But she couldn't seem to call up any excitement now. As she walked through the rows of trees, she saw the light on in the office in the apple barn and knew Luke was there. She wondered if he was as miserable as she was.

She hoped he was. She hoped he missed

her and that he would eventually make at least some effort to understand why she hadn't told him about Cassandra or the books. Or much at all about who she'd been.

At the Ground in the Round, she let herself in, turning on just enough light to get around, and made a pot of coffee. She wouldn't drink it all, but she could leave it in a thermos until the next morning. The coffee shop was closed for the weekend, but she knew she'd be in anyway. It had become her safe place. She squirted pumpkin syrup into the fresh brew, added a shot of cream and sat at the table she always shared with Luke.

Loneliness was much worse after having experienced a few months of almost constant companionship. She'd shared more affection with Luke since August than she'd known in the last couple of years of her marriage, more intentional time together than she and Tony had spent in longer than she could recall.

The coffee was so good that if she closed her eyes and breathed in its aroma, she could almost pretend the chair on the other side of the table wasn't empty. In her mind's eye, she could see Luke sitting there with his own cup—the one Royce had painted with the words *Cool Hand* over his first name. He was wearing flannel shirts every day these days, ones that started out with creases in their sleeves and neatly tucked into jeans that fit the way the denim gods intended. By mid-morning, the sleeves were always rolled up and his shirttails hanging out. He wore a hat all the time outside, but took it off whenever he went indoors, so his hair was always as rumpled as his shirt.

The word rumpled *had probably been invented for him,* Cass thought, *because he undoubtedly wore it better than anyone else ever had.*

She had thought waiting for the final results of scans and biopsies made for the longest weeks in the world. When you added in the loneliness factor, the days grew longer.

The back door she'd locked behind her opened as she sat there, and she knew without looking that it was Luke. She recognized the sound of his footsteps on the plank floors and his soft half humming, half singing that she'd learned to ignore after asking, "Did you say something?" ten times or so.

No wonder he'd felt so close when she sat down with her coffee—he'd *been* nearly that close. She hadn't even started when the door opened.

"Cass?" His voice was near, but he didn't come into her line of vision. "You all right?"

No. Are you? But she couldn't say that. "Fine." She made the word crisp. "I brewed some coffee if you want a cup."

"Thanks." She could hear him as he found his cup and poured the coffee.

"It's not half caff," she warned.

"Doesn't matter. I think my brain's decided sleeping is optional anyway."

He sat across from her, and the room felt warmer than the sixty degrees that was the nighttime setting in the shop. "How've you been?" she asked, because she couldn't stop herself and because he looked exhausted.

He shrugged. "Not so good." He met her eyes. "I don't like how we left things."

Her heart leaped in her chest, and she started to apologize again, then stopped herself. She'd already done that and it hadn't helped. "I don't, either."

She didn't know where to go from there, and sensed he didn't, either. Was this it? Had they become so close only to have their budding relationship sundered by their first emotional dispute? She'd thought disagreeing about virtually everything to do with business had prepared them for this. But it hadn't. It hadn't at all.

Cass swallowed some coffee and rushed into the silence. "Damaris has to report to the Pentagon on Wednesday morning. Royce is really upset."

Luke whistled. "I don't blame her. That's tough."

"I don't blame her, either, but Damaris tried to put it off and Royce knows it. It's disappointing, but it's not something that could be helped."

"Mom and Dad can't come down, either. Thank goodness for Skype. Dad made Mom promise not to cry when she sees her baby all decked out for the dance."

Cass chuckled. "One thing about living in a house full of women is that, while none of us are big-time weepers, there are situations that will set one or all of us off. You just never know what it's going to be."

She could almost see the question in his eyes. *Have you cried over us?*

Yes, she had.

"I may be leaving Miniagua at the end of the school year." His voice was sharp and clear in the otherwise silent room. It was as if his words were stones, falling on to an empty plate.

"Leaving?"

"I've been offered a job in Pennsylvania, working with a guy I've worked with before. He was my mentor, although he's not all that much older than I am. The money's good. The position is challenging in a different way from being an orchardist."

"What about the orchard?" *What about all of us? Mary and Isaac and Lovena and all the others? I thought we were a family.*

"We'll be able to hire a manager. Or you can run it. You're probably better at the business end of things than I am."

"Do you want to sell your half?" She didn't want to buy it, but she could if she had to. She was home, and she wasn't leaving again. If becoming sole owner was what it would take to keep the orchard family together, that's what she'd do.

"No. At least, not now. I'm not even sure yet that I'm going."

Something was missing from the conversation, but she wasn't sure what it was. He didn't look any happier than she felt, and there hadn't been even a hint of excitement in his voice when he'd mentioned the new job.

He'd always said he'd probably go back to engineering someday, but she hadn't expected it now, nor had she expected him to leave the area. She knew jobs in his field weren't ones that showed up often in small towns or rural areas, but she'd thought he'd hold out for something closer than Pennsylvania.

Pennsylvania. Where he'd gone last Monday. Had he known then?

"Was that why you took that trip last week?" she asked. "To see about a job?"

He nodded. "Mostly."

Anger came so thick and fast it made an echoing sound in her ears. She set down her cup. Picked it up. Then set it down again to keep from throwing it. "You didn't think of mentioning it? I mean, not that I would have a vote in your decision, but you didn't think telling me might be a good idea?"

He hesitated. "I did think that, and Rachel let me know in so many words she did, too. I can't say for sure why I didn't tell you, other than I really wasn't interested in the job. I went because Dan was so insistent." He met her eyes again, and she didn't look away, just held his gaze and hoped she didn't start to cry. That could definitely wait until later.

He'd told his family, but he hadn't told her. That made sense—his lifelong relationship with them certainly held more weight than the three-month one he and Cass had shared. But it still hurt.

So did something else. "Maybe," she said carefully, "you can make clear to me why my not telling you about things important in my life was an unpardonable relationship sin, yet it's perfectly all right that you didn't even mention a job interview that would affect not only our personal lives but our business partnership as well." She got up from her chair, not waiting for his answer, and went behind the counter to pour the rest of the pot of coffee into a thermos. She was taking it home with her; she thought she might be needing it.

"I was wrong. I know that."

"You certainly were." She was proud of how crisp her voice was—she didn't feel the least bit crisp. "I believe that's called betrayal, isn't it? Or is it just sexist? You know, okay for the big, strong man to lie by omission but not for the little woman."

"You know me better than that."

"No, I don't. I thought I did, but I was wrong, wasn't I? Again. I do just make the most wonderful choices. I should probably give a class on it." Crispness gave way to bitterness. She rinsed out the coffee carafe, her hands shaking.

He followed her, waiting until she finished what she was doing. "I should have told you, but my reasons for not doing it weren't sexist. Stupid maybe, in retrospect, but... I didn't want to hurt you, Cass."

"Whoa." She raised an eyebrow at him. "Tell me if I'm overthinking it, but I'm almost certain you went about that the wrong way."

"You're not overthinking it," he admitted. "It was wrong from start to finish." He rinsed his cup and dried it before putting it back in its accustomed place. "I never hid the fact that I didn't want our relationship to become serious, did I? We knew we weren't forever."

"No. Neither of us wanted that." At least, she hadn't thought she had. It wasn't his fault she'd changed her mind in the middle, that she'd come to think *forever* wasn't the fairy tale word she'd so long believed it to be.

She met his gaze in the dusky light of the coffee shop and realized he was as scared as she was of the future. What she couldn't see in the regret his features revealed was how he felt about her now that they'd betrayed each other's trust for the first time.

The other part of that was she wasn't sure how she felt about him, either. Anger had a way of twisting the emotions until they were snaky, hurtful things that created abrasions so deep they should have bled.

She turned away, picking up the thermos and moving toward the back door. "I guess we got what we wanted, then, didn't we?" Her throat hurt, and she knew if she didn't leave, there'd be no holding back the tears. "Remember to lock the door when you leave."

It had begun to snow while she'd been in the coffee shop. The flakes were thick and soft and silent, covering the ground quickly. She wished she could appreciate the beauty of the snow after all the years she'd waited to see it again. Had it really only been an hour ago she'd left the house?

She'd never fallen out of love with Tony for the simple reason that she hadn't been in love with him in the first place. The affection they'd shared in the early years had given way to friendship and, finally, to disinterest. Her anguish over the dissolution of their marriage had had more to do with feeling like a failure—Ken Gentry's daughter hadn't been raised to fail, for heaven's sake!—than with the actual ending of the relationship.

She'd only gone about twenty feet when Luke fell into step beside her. "You left your flashlight," he said, extending it to her. "I'll walk you to the house."

"You don't have to," she said stiffly, shoving the torch into her coat pocket. "I know the way."

He didn't answer, just accompanied her to the porch of the farmhouse. Once there, he stayed at the bottom of the steps until she got to the door where, in spite of herself, she turned to look at him.

"We both thought we knew the way," she said quietly, "but I have to admit I'm as lost now as I ever was."

He nodded. "Who's lost? Cass or Cassandra?"

"Both." She tilted her chin. "Who's moving to Pennsylvania? You or the guy I thought I knew?"

He didn't answer. Unshed tears made her eyes feel swollen and hot even in the cold night air. She turned away and went inside. She reached to turn off the porch light, then let her hand drop.

She might be closing the door on their relationship, but she wasn't ready for the symbolic lock the darkness would put on it.

CHAPTER TWENTY

"She could have gotten out of it."

Exasperated, Cass put the silver slipper back into its box and closed the lid. "I swear, one more spoiled-brat remark and you can wear last year's flip-flops to the dance. It won't bother me the least little bit."

It had probably been a mistake, bringing Royce to the mall after going to the airport, but it's what Damaris had asked her to do. Three shoe stores and at least twenty try-ons later, Cass was nearly to a screaming point. "Let's get lunch," she said instead.

"I'm not hungry."

"That's too bad, because I am." With an apologetic smile at the associate who'd brought out the last five pairs of shoes Royce had hated, Cass walked away, leaving her sister to follow. Or not. Although leaving her in a mall in Indianapolis probably wouldn't fly with either Damaris or Zoey.

In the restaurant, Cass stared across the

table at Royce until the girl met her eyes. "What?" The unaccustomed defiance was almost comical, but Cass thought it was preferable to the silence that had accompanied them across the country in August.

"I'm going to talk a minute, Little Sister Princess, and you're going to listen. I'm not taking a vote here or saying 'poor baby' or any of that. You're a good kid and I'm proud of you, but you're being a pain in the... You're being a pain and it needs to stop here."

"You don't know how it feels."

"The heck I don't. I was an army brat, too, remember?"

"You didn't have both parents in the army. Your mom was a normal mom. She kept fruit on the table in the same green bowl everywhere you moved to. When Dad had an assignment where you couldn't go, they didn't ship you off to the lake with Aunt Zoey every time."

Cass frowned. She hadn't realized sixteen-year-old memories were that convenient. "Of course they did. You know that. And thank goodness they did. We lived on some okay army posts, but none of them were home. Same with my mother and the stepfather du jour." She leaned forward, clasping Royce's fingers in her own. "Even when I wasn't here for however many years it was, it was the one place I knew I could come back to. The one place I *did* come back to."

"And look how that turned out." Royce didn't wear sarcasm well, but the words were effective nonetheless. "You and Luke barely speak to each other. It's like you and Tony all over again except that you're hurt more this time, and Luke is, too. You can see it in his face every time he looks at you. Is that what *home* means?"

Cass had to catch her breath, and Royce's face fell.

"I'm sorry. I didn't mean it. Really, I didn't, Cass."

"Honey, it's okay to be mad—even at me. Especially at me—after all, I'm Sister Perfect, right? In a way, I guess it *is* what *home* means. Luke and I are mad at each other and we're probably breaking up and you're right, it hurts like—what is it Lovena says?—the dickens. That's it. It hurts like the very dickens. But I have you. I have Zoey. I have your mom texting me back no matter where she is. And I have Miniagua. I'll never again have to be as alone as I was before I came back here."

"When you were in California, it was

home." Royce said sulkily. "Your mother was there. Mom and I were. It was home."

"In a way, I guess it was. It was the longest I ever lived in one spot. You, too, for that matter. Even with Tony, we flipped houses and businesses often enough I never felt at home, and I never settled into California. Remember, I never even hung pictures on the walls in my apartment. I went to a different church every couple of weeks. I never called the mail carrier by his first name or gave bottles of water to the UPS guy when he delivered a box of books. When your mom let me bring you here, she wanted you to have what I had at the lake when I was your age. What I have there now."

"I really do love the lake," said Royce, her young face wistful enough to break her sister's heart. "But I want her to be there, too."

"I know, but do you remember wishing Dad was like other fathers? He used to shake hands with us when he came back from a tour, for heaven's sake. We wished for what everyone else seemed to have, but it didn't happen and we're okay, aren't we?"

"We have a broken family."

Cass waved an impatient hand. "Everyone has a broken family. Look at this." She took the miniature photograph album she always carried out of her purse and opened it to a picture of a girl in a tiara. "Do you know who this is?"

Royce frowned. "No, but you've always carried it."

"Her name's Linda. We were best friends that year I lived at the lake and she died in the accident—sitting where I should have been. Her family was irretrievably broken that night. Arlie and Holly's dad died—their family was broken, too. Jack and Tucker's dad caused the accident and then died—that was a double hit for them. Remember the green bowl?"

"We just talked about it. Of course I remember."

"If you look at it, you'll see that it's been broken right across the middle and put back together. My mom threw it at me once. She missed, but the bowl broke when it hit the floor. It was symbolic, I suppose, of the brokenness we're talking about, but it was also something we kept and put back together. Because that's what you do when things are broken—you put them back together and live with the scars and work at making them as smooth as possible."

Royce smiled, with just the slightest lift of one side of her pretty mouth. "Are you admitting I'm scarred by Mom leaving before the dance?"

Cass gave her hair a tug. "I'm admitting nothing, but you need to give some deep thought to how many scars your mom has because the main purpose of her profession is to keep us all safe. Both physical and emotional."

"I need to call her, don't I?"

"Yes, you do."

"I'll text her now and apologize and then call her when I can send pictures of those silver shoes I just tried on." The smile slipped into a grin. "Thanks, Sister Wise One."

Cass grinned back at her, relief that they were back on happier footing making her as hungry as she'd said she was a half hour before. "Is Seth getting you flowers?"

"I don't even know if they do that here. A lot of the guys didn't at my other school because they thought it was lame."

"Do you think it's lame?"

"No."

"Well, then, if he does, that'll be a cool thing." Should she call Luke to make sure Seth brought a corsage when he showed up

Saturday night in the Camaro they'd decided on taking to the dance? The last thing Royce needed was more angst.

No, probably the *last* thing she needed was Sister Overbearing interfering any more than she already had.

They went home with silver shoes for Royce and manicures and pedicures for them both. They picked up pizza for supper with Zoey.

The house felt empty without Damaris. When a friend asked Royce to go to a movie, Cass allowed it even though it was a school night. Zoey built a fire and made hot chocolate, and they sat and watched the flames and talked. In the interest of avoiding some subjects, they opened others.

"Are you sorry you never married?" Cass had always wondered but had never asked, afraid of hurting her aunt's feelings.

"Not really." Zoey looked thoughtful. "I've liked my life." She smiled at Cass. "But you're not me, sweetheart."

Cass snorted. "I failed at marriage from the very beginning. Doing it again, especially with the cancer recurrence thing hanging over my head? I don't think so."

"Are you afraid?"

"A little. If everything's fine and just a cyst, it will have still been a good reminder that Luke and I need to back away from each other. He lost his wife. The last thing he needs is to become serious about someone whose percentages are a little more worrisome than most."

It was Zoey's turn to snort. "I may have never married, but if I wanted to, I wouldn't let that kind of worry stop me. I don't think Luke would, either. At least, I'd be very disappointed in him if it did. In you, too."

"If it had been meant to be, we wouldn't have given up at the first rough spot, and we did. We both did." The words were painful and she stared into the fire until she could regain her composure.

"Will you still stay here?" Zoey asked softly. "If Luke leaves and Royce goes back to California, will you go, too? You can, if that's what you want. The orchard isn't one of those businesses that's been in the family for a gazillion years. Your grandfather got it because the previous owner had a gambling problem and he lost it—Dad bought the debt. I couldn't keep it up. That was why I sold to Luke."

"I'm not leaving and I'm not selling my

half. Ground in the Round is like writing books. It's a dream I never expected to come true. It's up to Luke what he does." She thought about the coffee shop and realized that it had been the dream of the Cass side of her. It was every bit as imperfect as she was, but words failed when she tried to explain—even to herself—how happy it made her. Even without Luke.

In lieu of the business meeting, he had sent a printout with Zoey and a scribbled response to a note Cass had written earlier and left on his desk. He'd stopped coming by the house for coffee before work. His texts were purely business.

When she woke at night, sometimes she cried. But she'd survived worse than this. Been lonelier and sadder. She'd be fine. One day at a time.

"MAKE SURE HE takes her flowers. Real ones, if he can get them, but they don't have to be." Rachel was as bossy as ever. Luke was surprised she hadn't shown up to make sure Seth's shirt was ironed.

"He's got them ordered already. One of us will pick them up tomorrow morning. He's washed my car three times in the past week.

He has plenty of money to take Royce out to dinner before the dance and there's an umbrella in back in case it snows. Which it's supposed to, by the way, and there's absolutely nothing I can do about that." Luke kept his voice patient. He'd already had this conversation with his mother.

"When Mom calls, pretend the Skype thingy isn't working. She's going to cry and Seth will get upset. He's more sensitive than the rest of us."

Good point. "Jill's influence," he said, surprised at how easy that had been to say.

"Yes. Too bad it didn't rub off on you, too. I know she tried."

Luke laughed. "She did, at that." He forgot sometimes how close Jill and Rachel had been. All the years his sister had badgered him to make a new life for himself, she was probably just doing what Jill would have wanted her to do. "Hey, I gotta go. The orchard's still a busy place."

"Okay. You dumb brothers take care, okay?"

"You dumb sisters, too. Hey, Rach?"

"What?"

"Thanks for everything."

He knew she understood. They may have

spent their lives as affectionate adversaries, but they knew each other very well. "Don't let it pass you by, Luke," she said softly, and disconnected.

The orchard *was* a busy place, but nowhere near as much as it had been before Halloween. He was able to let everyone go home early and man the store by himself until closing time.

He walked over to Ground in the Round, the snow crunching under his feet. The parking lot was crowded, and when he stepped inside, the coffee shop was full, too. And noisy. Three guitarists and a woman with a violin were in the corner. They were playing a vintage Charlie Daniels song, and they had the crowd in their pocket. Cass was behind the counter, building lattes and mochas with Libby and Holly and laughing.

The sound of her laughter and the light in her eyes seemed to grow the ache of how much he'd missed her in recent days. It made him wonder if she'd missed him at all, and he flinched from the realization that maybe she hadn't.

But then their eyes met across that crowded room someone had written a song about once, and he knew she had missed him. Knew she still did.

"Hey, Luke," called one of the guitarists. "Come and join us for a few."

Luke held up his hands. "No guitar."

Cass's voice rose over the hubbub of a full house. "Seth keeps one here if you'd like to play. It's in the office."

He met her eyes. "You don't mind?" It wouldn't fix everything, but music always made him feel better.

She shook her head and looked away.

He got the guitar, feeling like a trespasser when he was in her office, and took a seat with the other musicians, all people he'd jammed with on other occasions. He took the cup of coffee Cass brought, feeling a familiar spark when his fingers touched hers. How long would that last?

Maybe forever.

He nodded his thanks and smiled at her. She smiled back, and he thought maybe they could do this thing after all. The truth of the matter was that they were probably better off not trying to combine romance and business. They didn't even have to be friends to be professional partners, although it would help to at least stay amicable. Her smile promised that.

The touch of her hand, warm against his when she handed him the cup, was something else again. Something more. But they could deal with it, at least until he accepted the job and prepared to move to Pennsylvania.

He enjoyed playing, liking the camaraderie with the other players, although the music sounded a little hollow sometimes. As he drove home later, he reflected that it didn't sound any hollower than he felt.

The house was dark except for the light over the sink in the kitchen, which meant Seth was not only home but in bed. Luke changed and went for a run, thinking of a pair of turquoise eyes that had an ache around them and warm fingers that he had once wanted to take and hold. Forever.

CHAPTER TWENTY-ONE

CASS RECORDED A video of Luke's black Camaro as it drove down the farmhouse's driveway. "We now have more footage and still shots of one high school dance of Royce's than we have of her entire life before this, going all the way back to the DVD I filmed in the delivery room because Dad was in Iraq or somewhere when she was born."

Zoey laughed. "I think yours was on VHS, wasn't it? I forget where he was then, too."

"Probably. It didn't survive its last move, thank goodness."

Zoey squinted, scrolling through the pictures on her telephone. "They're so beautiful. He got her exactly the right flowers. The shoes were perfect. Did she have money and her phone with her?"

"Yes." Cass put down the camera and hugged herself against the chill that had slipped in unnoticed.

Zoey looked over at her, concern darkening her eyes. "Cass? Something wrong?"

"Just some déjà vu going on, I think." She looked out the door again. Shivered again. "It was dark like this the night of the prom." There was no moon and we couldn't even see the stars. Venus was always Libby's guardian planet, and I remember her saying later that she couldn't see it that night."

"You've changed so much since then. I think your fear of not being good enough stems from guilt over what happened. But you've taken care of a lot of that since you came back to the lake. Don't let whatever's happened between you and Luke get you started back down the same path." Zoey checked her makeup in the mirror inside the mudroom door, something a houseful of women found extremely handy. She ran a critical finger over the smooth curve of her hair and got a coat from the row of hooks.

Cass raised an eyebrow. "A date?"

"Yes." Zoey smiled mysteriously. "Kari Ross's father is spending a few weeks at Kari's lake house while he's in the process of downsizing. I met him at the festival and he called today to ask me to have dinner with him. We're both single and I'm old enough to think last-minute is more charming than thoughtless, so I'm going to meet him at the Grill."

"Have a good time. Stay safe."

"Don't wait up."

When Zoey had left, Cass exchanged texts with her stepmother, reassuring her that Royce looked even more beautiful than her pictures, then carried Misty into her office. It was time to start a new book. It wouldn't do for Lucy to have too much time off.

Cass never listened to music when she wrote. Lyrics got in her way and even instrumental pieces affected the lay of the story. But something made her start the CD they'd made of Luke and Seth's performance at the festival. Luke's baritone, so quiet it didn't seem as if it would carry but it did…it did… washed over her like the waterfall in Cottonwood Creek. The song was "Try to Remember," a ballad that had made Zoey and Gianna and Luke's mother sway and sing along with tears in their eyes.

Cass typed as she listened, the words to the song carrying her into the first chapter. The story would take place in December and Lucy would be visiting her cousin in an apple orchard near a lake. Her heart would be newly broken.

Life was supposed to imitate art, not the other way around. The thought made Cass smile a little. When the songs ended, she ejected the CD from her laptop and kept on writing. His voice stayed with her. His laughter between songs. His *Whoa, little brother,* when Seth hit a very bad note. His *Hey, Cass, what do you think of this?* when he played the opening riff of "Layla."

She was writing, she realized, as Cass. Cassandra had become, as she should have been all along, merely a pseudonym. Perhaps at some point…some later point…both her heart and Lucy's would be unbroken.

THE DAYS WITHOUT her in them were far too long, and when Seth was gone in the evening, that time was long, too. Luke played guitar for hours on end, wearing his fingernails down because he didn't use a pick, and had the bathroom almost finished enough to please even Rachel. But the rest of his life seemed to be kind of a…well, a gap. It didn't just *have* an open, empty place in it, it *was* an open, empty place.

Dan had called shortly after Seth left for

the dance, wondering if Luke had decided on the job. He offered to bring him back out to Hollidaysburg to spend more time with the staff and get a better look at the projects. Before he'd hung up, he'd said, "Sometimes the best things really aren't. You know that. I don't mean to sound like your mother, because you have a fine one of those already, but it's perfectly all right if you're a good engineer who doesn't really want to be one."

Luke thought about the words later, as he sat on his couch with a guitar. He was a pretty good player for a banger, but he'd never be good enough to make it his life's work. He was a good orchardist, too, for one who'd gotten his training walking between the trees and making notes on napkins and fixing that godforsaken cider press.

He strummed, playing part of "Classical Gas." It was a favorite song, especially when Seth was there to play it with him. Luke loved the guitar. And the orchard. Even though he'd never be as good at either of them as he'd been as an engineer, he loved them.

Across the room, Jill smiled at him from the photograph of her that sat on the mantel. "What do you think, Jilly?" he asked softly. "You'd have forgiven me, wouldn't you?"

Of course she would have. They'd forgiven each other many things in their time together. That's what people who loved each other did.

He hadn't been sleeping well, so he was surprised that he fell asleep on the sofa. When the sound of his phone woke him, it took him a minute to get oriented. The number on the screen was unfamiliar. Why would a robocaller dial at this time of night? Irritation gave way to foreboding in the space of a heartbeat, and he swept the telephone's screen. "What?"

Five minutes later, he was in the truck and on the road. He spoke into his phone. "Are you already on your way or do you want me to pick you up?"

"On my way."

Sawyer's hospital was small, set well off the street in a parklike setting. There were walking paths all around it. The wrought iron fence that had surrounded the old building had been moved to this new location and now surrounded the visitors' parking lot. Luke didn't go there, though, nor did he notice the bucolic setting or the two-story Christmas tree that sat in the lobby. He parked beside

Cass's SUV, the truck's tires slipping on the ice, and knew a moment's wondering.

Had the Camaro slipped on the ice?

But he wasn't going to think about that now. Only about the boy and girl who'd been in it. Who'd been injured, but that was all the disembodied caller would say. "You need to come if you can, sir."

"Please," he said aloud on the way to the emergency room doors. "Please." Father Doherty stood at the door, waiting, and Luke slowed his step, his tennis shoes skidding in the slush. "Please no. No."

The priest shook his head and put an arm over his shoulders when Luke stepped abreast of him. "Come on in, son. I just came out to wait for you."

"He's not…they're not…"

"We don't know anything yet."

"How did it happen?"

"That's part of what we don't know."

"How many…" Luke's voice faded away. He couldn't bear to think of that yet.

Father Doherty didn't accompany him inside, and Luke looked back to see him standing where he'd been before. Waiting.

Cass was alone in the visitors' lounge, her face colorless above the neckline of her gray-

and-white-striped sweatshirt. He wondered if she'd already been in bed when she'd gotten the call, but of course she had been. It was long after midnight and he was sure she'd been up early—she always was. Her hair was flat on one side, a detail that was heartbreaking although he wasn't sure why.

She stood at the window that looked out on the parking lot, as taut as the proverbial piano string. He thought if she moved, she'd break. He was afraid if he touched her, she'd break anyway.

"Zoey?" he said instead, surprised her aunt had allowed her to come to the hospital alone.

"She went to get Mary's and Isaac's parents."

"Oh." He prayed again, silent and fervent and apologetic. *I know I'm not good about praying, but I'll do anything. I'll never ask for anything again.*

He'd promised that before, sitting in a different hospital with Jill. Offering his life in exchange for hers if only she could be spared one more time. It hadn't worked. It never worked. But he offered again. *They're just kids, and I swear I'll never ask for anything again.*

"Did you call Father Doherty?"

Cass shook her head. "He was here. He was here—" She drew a shuddering breath and then another, and Luke put his arm around her. If she *did* break, she wasn't going to do it standing alone. "On prom night, when the first ambulance got here, he was waiting for it. I don't know how he knows."

Luke shook his head. He didn't understand it, either.

The next time the automatic doors opened, Zoey came in with Mary's and Isaac's parents. A few minutes later, the doors swished again and a couple Luke didn't know entered. The man was shouting and shaking his fist. When he looked over at where Luke and Cass stood, he aimed the fist in their direction. "It was your two that caused this. And you'll pay. You'll pay."

"Sit down, Gavin." The woman with him sounded weary. "We don't know what happened. Father Doherty already told you that."

Luke recognized the name then. Gavin Granger was Chris's older brother. He lived in the family mansion at the end of the lake and had a son in Seth's class. The younger Granger played on the basketball team, but Seth never said much about him.

"Just don't get too comfortable with owning that orchard." The man's fist was still waving, and Luke felt an unusual urge to end his angry rant with a well-placed fist of his own. "I'll sue you for every nickel you ever thought you'd have."

Luke ignored him and pulled Cass close. In this, at least, they were together. They started to walk away, as in step as they had ever been. When Gavin spoke again, Luke turned to face him. "Later," he said as quietly as he could manage. "Whatever you have to say, I will listen to later. For now, just shut up and sit down."

The other man sat. His wife, if that's who she was, looked apologetic, but remained quiet.

A volunteer came into the room, wearing a coat over her pink smock, to tell them all someone would share information as soon as they could. She didn't offer coffee, but a short while later returned with a pump thermos and a stack of cups.

A faint but distinct thwapping sound came from overhead. A siren sounded.

They waited.

IT FELT LIKE it had that night half her lifetime ago. Cass hadn't known what to do then, either, when she wasn't hurt and everyone else was. She'd walked around in the blue satin dress she'd worn to the prom that had a wide streak of blood down its front. Even now she couldn't bear to speculate on whose blood it was.

The trauma department of Sawyer's hospital had been remodeled since then, leaving the area virtually unrecognizable. But Father Doherty had been there that night, too. She remembered volunteers coming in, buttoning their smocks and distributing coffee and whispered reassurances.

Most of the people in the waiting area had looked shell-shocked, just as they did now. Mary's and Isaac's parents sat silent. As their relatives joined them, they spoke quietly among themselves. Cass knew being Amish didn't actually guarantee peace of mind and heart, but it had always seemed to her they had it.

The doors to outside swished open and closed every ten minutes or so. Before she even realized what was happening, all the survivors from the prom night accident were in the room. Offering blood if it was needed. Hugging her. Talking to her one at a time.

"How did you know?" she asked Arlie, who had gotten there first.

"Kari was here with a patient when the call came in and she let me know. She's back there now, helping. I texted Holly and Libby and Mama, and it went on from there. It's amazing we're all here. Nate's almost always in North Carolina this late in the year, but he and Mandy are still here after spending Thanksgiving with his mother."

Cass was so grateful; she had no words. She looked over at where Luke stood talking to Chris Granger and couldn't remember why she'd been so angry. Or why he had.

They'd made mistakes with each other. Ones they shouldn't have made. Did those really matter that much?

"Cass." It was Sam, handsome as ever. He stood in front of her, his arm around his wife. "Penny and I were talking about how you and I broke up. She wanted to thank you."

It was such a relief, there in that room full of fear and grief, to share an eye-roll and a grin with Penny, to accept the tight, quick hug from Sam, to turn slightly and find Luke there beside her again.

The waiting was so hard. She hadn't contacted her father and stepmother. She had nothing to tell them.

The doors whispered open and the county sheriff came in, accompanied by a deputy. The room went completely and eerily silent.

Although both county and state law enforcement frequented the coffee shop, Cass hadn't talked to them very much. But when the sheriff took off his hat, she remembered him from prom night. He'd been a deputy then. Young and scared and hating what he had to do.

She watched, her heart thumping so hard she felt light-headed, as he looked around at the group. "I hate this," he said quietly. "I hate it for all of you."

"Can you tell us what happened?" Gavin's voice was snappish, but nowhere near as confrontational as it had been when he got there.

"Gav, stop looking for someone to blame," said Chris. "Especially before we know anything."

"I know my son is in there. Your nephew. Maybe alive and maybe not. What else do I need to know?"

"There were three cars and a horse and buggy involved," said the sheriff. "It was at the bend out by the country club."

He waited, then, as they absorbed the knowledge that lightning sometimes did indeed strike twice in the same spot. The road had been widened, signage improved upon, but that particular curve was still there. The carved crosses that provided a perpetual memorial were still in the same place. The lazy S curve was far from the tightest one on the serpentine road, yet it had changed the lives of nearly everyone in the room.

"We've pieced together what happened. Two cars, one in front and one behind, were providing the buggy escort." The sheriff sat down, exhaustion darkening every line on his face. "As you all know, it's darker than inside sin's billy goat out there. The Camaro was behind the buggy and a white Ford in front of it. The Ford had just reached the top of the S when a Mercedes came around on the outside of the curve—only he was in the middle of the road and traveling at an excessive speed."

"That's hearsay and you'd be better off not telling it, Sheriff." Panic laced Gavin's voice.

"Shut up, Gavin," said Chris. He nodded at the sheriff. "Go on, please, Matt."

The officer looked at where Mary's and

Isaac's parents sat with relatives. "This will be hard to hear."

He explained what had happened. That the speeding car had pushed the white Ford into the ditch at the side of the road, going on to hit the buggy broadside before crashing head on with the Camaro. When they asked him about injuries, he refused to speculate.

"Thank you for letting us know." Luke's voice was husky. He leaned back on the institutional settee he shared with Cass, his arm warm and tight as he held her close to his side.

And still they waited.

CHAPTER TWENTY-TWO

AFTERWARD, CASS REALIZED it wasn't really all that long. It was still dark when some of the survivors took the Amish families back to their homes. Zoey drove Mary's mother to the Indianapolis hospital she'd been transported to for surgery, so that when the girl woke she wouldn't be afraid. Kari's father rode along, and Cass was relieved that her aunt wouldn't have to make the trip home by herself. Eighty-seven miles could be a long way when you were alone.

Isaac went home, bandaged and sore and worried. He wanted to go with Zoey, to be there for Mary himself, but the doctor had joined ranks with his family and hers. "You'll do her no good if you collapse."

The family of the driver of the white Ford left when the helicopter carrying their son to yet another hospital lifted off. "He'll be all right," the ER doctor had said, "but he needs more orthopedic care than we can give him here."

His date had been released to her parents' care.

Gavin Granger and his apologetic wife had left as soon as their son's facial cuts were stitched. They walked out with him between them, none of them speaking to anyone. Chris had watched his brother leave, his expression thoughtful, then sat back down to wait.

Father Doherty moved between them, as much a prom-night-accident survivor as if he'd been in one of the cars.

Cass stirred restively. "How can it feel as if it's been all night when it's only been a couple of hours?"

"Because it's been eighteen years," said Holly, and the others nodded.

"Let's take a walk," Luke suggested. "We can pretend we're walking through the orchard."

They walked up and down the corridors of the hospital's first floor. Fifty feet one way, fewer the other direction. It was nothing like the orchard, but there was a level of peace to be found in moving.

"Have you called your folks?" Cass asked, nodding at the phone in Luke's hand.

"Yes. They wanted to get on the road, but I talked them into waiting until I call back. They've got snow knee-deep up there. You?"

She shook her head. "I will when I have something to tell them."

"It's funny how different our families are, isn't it?"

"Are they so different?"

"You're right. Jill and I raised Seth as much as Mom and Dad did. You and Zoey and even your mom have looked after Royce with no questions asked. It's loving and taking care of each other and being there at the end of the day."

She thought for a minute, walking in silence, about what a non-guy thing that had been to say. At least, compared to her father and Tony. The major had taken care of his family the only way he'd known how, but whatever affection he'd felt had gone unvoiced. Tony was just Tony. He was funny and—usually—kind, but he would never have talked about love or family dynamics. If he'd been with her tonight when the police called, he would have patted her shoulder and told her to let him know if she needed anything. Then he'd have gone back to sleep, because in his family, waiting and worrying were woman things.

"Are you afraid?" asked Luke, catching her hand and holding it.

"Are you?"

"Yes."

They moved closer, so that their upper arms touched when they walked. They fell into the step that had been so natural to them. He'd loved her long stride. She'd loved that he didn't shorten his to accommodate her.

"My mother was as tall as I am," she said suddenly, "but she tried so hard not to be that she ended up stoop-shouldered. Elegantly so, but stooped nonetheless. It's important to me that I always stand straight and that Royce does, too. That's a Cassandra thing."

Luke stopped when they reached the end of the hall, and she turned to meet his eyes. He put his hands on her shoulders. "You need to know something. I meant what I said about Cassandra being a name on the front of the book. You are Cass, who stands straight," he said quietly, "who walks as fast as I do and climbs trees that scare the bejabbers out of me. Who writes books about crazy mysteries on the Wabash and about empowerment of people who need it. You may use a pen name, but the writing comes from you. From Cass. And that's who I'm in love with."

"Mr. Rossiter? Ms. Gentry?" The voice was tentative from several feet away, coming at the same time as Luke's phone chimed and Cass's vibrated in her pocket. "I'm so sorry to interrupt," said the lady in the pink smock, "but the doctor would like to see you both."

LUKE REMEMBERED TELLING Jill's mother that the long struggle was over for the young woman they'd both loved. He recalled walking down the hall of the hospital in Altoona. The scent of Jill's hair was still in his nose, the touch of her soft skin against his lips. He could still feel the palm of her hand against his fingers.

It had been the longest, hardest walk of his life. Anna had wilted before his eyes, but by the time he'd reached her, she'd stiffened again. She'd taken him into his arms and held him as he wept. It had been the most loving of gestures.

Luke thought he couldn't bear to lose Seth; he *knew* he couldn't bear to tell their mother. He thought of Royce, and his hand tightened on Cass's. *Please. Please.*

And then he heard the voice.

"You don't understand. My brother loved that car. I think maybe you should put me back to sleep or he's going to want to do it for himself."

And, from the next cubicle, behind the curtain came another voice. Sounding very much like a frightened little girl. "Seth, are you okay?"

Cass sagged against his arm, and Luke caught her before she could fall, holding her until Kari appeared from behind the curtain. "Cass?" She gestured. "Come on in. Someone needs to see you." She smiled over at Luke. "Right in there, Luke. The doctor's still with Seth."

Luke knew as soon as he stepped up next to the bed that his brother's senior year basketball season was over. "The knee's a mess," said the young ER physician, "but a good orthopedic surgeon can take care of it. It might look like a Jenga game in X-rays, but I'll lay you dollars to doughnuts he won't even limp." He grinned at the boy on the bed. "Stitches in his left arm and a couple of ribs that are going to cause some major discomfort for a few days. He says he plays the guitar and I'm to tell you that of course he can keep playing it, but that he absolutely cannot shovel snow. Take what you will from that."

"He'll be able to earn enough money to pay me back for a totaled Camaro?" Luke stroked a hand through Seth's hair and let his hand rest on his shoulder. He couldn't help himself. *He'll be okay, Jilly. He'll be okay.*

The doctor's grin became a laugh. "Eventually. For a day or two, though, we want to keep him here. He's going to sleep a lot, and he's already given you a bad night, so I suggest you call your folks so they can hear his voice and then go home. You can see him tomorrow."

Luke met the plea in his brother's eyes. "Royce?"

Seth nodded. "Will you check?"

"I will." Luke tapped in his parents' number and handed Seth the phone. "Talk to Mom and Dad. I'll be back."

In the cubicle next door, Royce was being prepared for a ride upstairs. "Spending the night for observation purposes," Cass explained. "But she'll be fine."

She had stitches, a broken collarbone and a black eye. "Mary?" she said. "Tell me about Mary."

"Aunt Zoey just texted," said Cass, releasing Kari from worrying about sharing confidential information. "It's her spleen, but she'll be okay." She closed her eyes, tears leaking from under the lids. "You'll all be okay."

In the lobby, Luke and Cass shared the good news with the group gathered there, then got into the orchard pickup and drove toward the farmhouse because Zoey had Cass's SUV. They rode in silence, delivered from grief yet unable to address the emotion that filled the cab of the truck. When he parked, Luke didn't turn off the engine. He just got out and walked around to open the door for Cass.

"I can't—" she began, when they reached the door.

He laid gentle fingers against her lips, their softness nearly his undoing. "Not now. We'll talk, but not now."

He waited while she unlocked the door, then started down the steps. At the bottom, he turned and went back up to take her in his arms. "But we will do this." He kissed her. Long and leisurely and warm, pouring everything into it he felt and wanted and needed and drawing the same back from her.

"Tomorrow," he said. "Tomorrow, we'll talk."

It wasn't a surprise that he woke Dan when he called him before sunrise. Well," said his friend, "this either means you can't wait to get here or you're not coming at all. Which is it?"

Luke lifted his guitar into his lap and felt peace seep in to all the places that had felt open and wounded before this long and frightening night. "I'm not coming. I'm a good-enough orchard guy and I play an all right guitar and my life is here."

"There's a young lady there, too, isn't there?"

"There is. I'm anxious for you to meet her."

"I'll be out to visit soon."

"Good." He told him about the accident then, about his fear for his brother and the memory of losing Jill. "It makes me realize that if I'd lost Seth, I'd still have Rachel and Leah. Every day you love someone, you risk losing them. So, would I give up my sisters rather than take a chance on losing one of them? Loving someone after Jill is that risky, too, every single day, but I'm not going to give it up rather than get hurt again."

"Good thinking, my friend."

Luke hung up and sat and played his guitar until the sun crept up over the lake. He was waiting. After this long and—in the end— blessed night, he was still waiting.

THEY'D AGREED NOT to open the coffee shop on Sundays, but Cass wanted the comfort of it. The peace of it. The knowledge that this was her safe place.

What if he hadn't meant what he'd said?

What if there were other secrets he'd kept?

What if he never forgave her for not telling him who she was?

What if he went to Pennsylvania?

Without her.

She made coffee and, while she was at it, made decaf as well. She'd learned that if the shop opened, coffee drinkers would come. She called her father and stepmother, telling them about the accident and assuring them that Royce would be fine.

Just as she knew Seth's parents would be there before the day was over, she knew Royce's would not. But that was okay, because Sister Coffee Shop would be there for her forever if that was what she needed.

She poured her coffee and, while she was at it, a cup of half caff in the mug emblazoned with *Cool Hand Luke*. If she poured it, she thought, maybe—like the other coffee drinkers—he would come.

And he did.

He walked in, took her in his arms and kissed her as he had a few hours before.

"Seth made me promise to ask you first thing if your family would have Christmas with ours."

She blinked. "Where?"

"Probably your house. It's bigger."

"Well, then, yes. Zoey will be thrilled." She leaned into his embrace for a long moment before leaning back and looking into his eyes.

"I'm sorry," she said. "Sorry I didn't tell you."

"I'm sorry, too." He kissed her again. "But the truth is, I'll probably do more than one stupid thing over the next fifty or sixty years. Are you up for forgiving me?"

"I'll probably slip back and forth between Cass and Cassandra enough to drive you crazy over the next fifty or sixty years. Can you deal with that?"

"I can." He stroked a hand through her hair, and she leaned into his touch. "Cassandra's in your head," he said, "and I guess you sometimes need her there." He took her hand and laid it on the chest of his flannel shirt. "But you…Cass…you're in my heart."

"I love you, Luke." She reached for his cup, then watched as he tapped something into his phone. "Everything okay?"

He grinned at her, taking the cup from her and leading the way to the table they always shared, sitting across from where her laptop sat open. "I was texting Royce," he said. "I told her Sister What's-Her-Name said yes."

* * * * *

*If you couldn't get enough of
Luke and Cass, be sure not to miss a single
Lake Miniagua story from*
USA Today *bestselling author
Liz Flaherty.*

Back to McGuffey's
Every Time We Say Goodbye
The Happiness Pact

*Available now from
Harlequin Heartwarming!*

Get 4 FREE REWARDS!

We'll send you 2 FREE Books plus 2 FREE Mystery Gifts.

Love Inspired® books feature contemporary inspirational romances with Christian characters facing the challenges of life and love.

FREE
Value Over
$20

Get 4 FREE REWARDS!

We'll send you 2 FREE Books plus <u>2 FREE Mystery Gifts.</u>

Love Inspired® Suspense books feature Christian characters facing challenges to their faith... and lives.

FREE
Value Over
$20

HOME on the RANCH

YES! Please send me the **Home on the Ranch Collection** in Larger Print. This collection begins with 3 FREE books and 2 FREE gifts in the first shipment. Along with my 3 free books, I'll also get the next 4 books from the Home on the Ranch Collection, in LARGER PRINT, which I may either return and owe nothing, or keep for the low price of $5.24 U.S./ $5.89 CDN each plus $2.99 for shipping and handling per shipment*. If I decide to continue, about once a month for 8 months I will get 6 or 7 more books, but will only need to pay for 4. That means 2 or 3 books in every shipment will be FREE! If I decide to keep the entire collection, I'll have paid for only 32 books because 19 books are FREE! I understand that accepting the 3 free books and gifts places me under no obligation to buy anything. I can always return a shipment and cancel at any time. My free books and gifts are mine to keep no matter what I decide.

268 HCN 3760 468 HCN 3760

Name _____ (PLEASE PRINT)

Address _____ Apt. #

City _____ State/Prov. _____ Zip/Postal Code

Signature (if under 18, a parent or guardian must sign)

Mail to the **Reader Service**:

IN U.S.A.: P.O. Box 1341, Buffalo, New York 14240-8531
IN CANADA: P.O. Box 603, Fort Erie, Ontario L2A 5X3

* Terms and prices subject to change without notice. Prices do not include applicable taxes. Sales tax applicable in NY. Canadian residents will be charged applicable taxes. This offer is limited to one order per household. All orders subject to approval. Credit or debit balances in a customer's account(s) may be offset by any other outstanding balance owed by or to the customer. Please allow 3 to 4 weeks for delivery. Offer available while quantities last. Offer not available to Quebec residents.

HRCBPA18R

Get 4 FREE REWARDS!

We'll send you 2 FREE Books plus 2 FREE Mystery Gifts.

Harlequin® Special Edition books feature heroines finding the balance between their work life and personal life on the way to finding true love.

FREE Value Over $20

YES! Please send me 2 FREE Harlequin® Special Edition novels and my 2 FREE gifts (gifts are worth about $10 retail). After receiving them, if I don't wish to receive any more books, I can return the shipping statement marked "cancel." If I don't cancel, I will receive 6 brand-new novels every month and be billed just $4.99 per book in the U.S. or $5.74 per book in Canada. That's a savings of at least 12% off the cover price! It's quite a bargain! Shipping and handling is just 50¢ per book in the U.S. and 75¢ per book in Canada*. I understand that accepting the 2 free books and gifts places me under no obligation to buy anything. I can always return a shipment and cancel at any time. The free books and gifts are mine to keep no matter what I decide.

235/335 HDN GMY2

Name (please print)

Address   Apt. #

City   State/Province   Zip/Postal Code

Mail to the **Reader Service:**
IN U.S.A.: P.O. Box 1341, Buffalo, NY 14240-8531
IN CANADA: P.O. Box 603, Fort Erie, Ontario L2A 5X3

Want to try two free books from another series? Call 1-800-873-8635 or visit www.ReaderService.com.

*Terms and prices subject to change without notice. Prices do not include applicable taxes. Sales tax applicable in N.Y. Canadian residents will be charged applicable taxes. Offer not valid in Quebec. This offer is limited to one order per household. Books received may not be as shown. Not valid for current subscribers to Harlequin® Special Edition books. All orders subject to approval. Credit or debit balances in a customer's account(s) may be offset by any other outstanding balance owed by or to the customer. Please allow 4 to 6 weeks for delivery. Offer available while quantities last.

Your Privacy—The Reader Service is committed to protecting your privacy. Our Privacy Policy is available online at www.ReaderService.com or upon request from the Reader Service. We make a portion of our mailing list available to reputable third parties that offer products we believe may interest you. If you prefer that we not exchange your name with third parties, or if you wish to clarify or modify your communication preferences, please visit us at www.ReaderService.com/consumerchoice or write to us at Reader Service Preference Service, P.O. Box 9062, Buffalo, NY 14240-9062. Include your complete name and address.

HSE18

Get 4 FREE REWARDS!

We'll send you 2 FREE Books plus 2 FREE Mystery Gifts.

Harlequin® Romance Larger-Print books feature uplifting escapes that will warm your heart with the ultimate feel-good tales.

FREE Value Over $20